WHILE THE SAVAGE SLEEPS

WHILE THE SAVAGE SLEEPS

ANDREW E. KAUFMAN

47NORTH

The characters and events portrayed in this book are fictitious. Any similarity to real persons, living or dead, is coincidental and not intended by the author.

Published by 47North

PO Box 400818
Las Vegas, NV 89140

ISBN-13: 9781611099782
ISBN-10: 1611099781
Library of Congress Control Number: 2012955306

Dedication

To the memory of my mother, who gifted me with her love for the written word.

Prologue

Far beyond the rough-hewn mountaintops, beyond the pathless desert flowing with cacti, yucca, and sagebrush, two stony peaks rise through the air like massive, chiseled arms reaching for the heavens.

At first glance, they can almost pass for mirror images of each other; but as you steady your gaze and narrow your focus, the illusion begins to fade—so, too, do the similarities, and it is there you find that the two are nothing alike.

High River Peak is green, picturesque, and well-traveled, its swift-moving rapids a sure bet for those seeking recreation as well as reprieve from New Mexico's searing summer heat.

Sentry Peak is its antithesis.

Vacuous, dismal, and barren, it's a no-man's-land. The only sign of life is an old and abandoned six-story building resting along the easternmost bluff—although *rest* would hardly describe what it does. It *looms*, much like a hungry vulture eyeing its prey: imposing, hostile, imminent.

There is one thing the two peaks have in common, and that is Faith.

Tucked away like a well-kept secret, Faith, New Mexico, lies nestled directly between them. It's the kind of place where, if you didn't know better, you'd almost swear time stands still. No fast-food chains here, no superstores, no multiplex movie theaters—everything is still mom-and-pop operated. Residents dwell in cozy pastoral farmhouses passed down through generations, white sheets sway on clotheslines—wiggling and puffing to the commands of a fitful wind—and people get their milk not at the corner convenience store but from cows grazing just a few hundred feet from their front doors.

Highway 10, the region's time-honored thoroughfare, edges its way along the town's outskirts. It captures the classic image Madison Avenue has for years tried to duplicate in both TV and print ads: terrain dominated by flat, dusty stretches of sun-beaten blacktop, along with nostalgic-looking filling stations and greasy-spoon diners, each decked out in luminous, wandering neon. You can almost hear the scratchy old vinyl forty-fives spinning in the background as an unforgiving sun bakes the midday air, forcing temperatures to teeter just a few degrees beyond livable. It's not Route 66, but it's close, and Faith is about as apple pie as any town can get without tasting too saccharine.

The much-celebrated annual fair and rodeo begins on the Fourth of July, an unofficial induction to the dog days. Arcade games bang and clang, organ music swells, and auctioneers prattle. Through the causeway, the smell of fried grease and cotton candy locks horns with the moist, earthy tang of livestock, while amusement park rides dance in the distance against a moonlit sky. The whole scene is noisy, chaotic, and in its own sort of way, enchanting—a rhythm of life, effortlessly weaving together into one pleasing rhapsody. This is Faith at its best: a picture-perfect snapshot of good old Americana.

Not for a second could anyone imagine that the picture had another side. Nobody knew that beneath the broad smiles, the beaming faces, and the stirring moments—beneath the surface—lay something else.

Chapter One

Saddleback Ranch
Faith, New Mexico

The clock struck midnight.

Something in the air seemed to change. Something sudden, mysterious, and filled with bad intent. Wind-driven clouds gained momentum, swirling into the path of a fiery moon.

What once was settled began to stir. Where there had been order, there was unrest, and from the gathering darkness, new life emerged.

The sort born of pure evil.

Deputy Bradley Witherspoon felt an odd chill run through his body but didn't know why. He'd parked along a shadowy frontage road running parallel to the Saddleback Ranch, one of Faith's oldest and more established cattle producers. The old dirt path was barely drivable and punished by years of neglect. Deputies referred to it as The Refueling Station. Translation: the perfect spot to stay beneath the radar and catch up on much-needed sleep. For those working swing shift, it seemed a good place to find a refuge and restore sanity—or at least meet up with it for a brief visit.

On a scale of slim to none, chances wavered near zero that anyone would bother making the trip to check on the deputies' whereabouts. One needed only travel a few feet down the pitted path to understand why: a vigilant pack of cattle dogs kept close watch over the property. More than capable of making themselves heard, they remained on the lookout for the first sign of unwelcome company. This gave the deputies enough warning to wake up and look sharp in the unlikely event someone *did* arrive to check on them. With all those safeguards, you might think it would be difficult to catch a deputy dozing off.

You would be wrong.

Witherspoon caught himself nodding off several times before drifting toward a more restful state of sleep that didn't last long. He woke to the sound of stirring behind his seat, a rustling noise like plastic bags rubbing together. Before he could turn around and investigate, he took a swift blow to the head from something cold and heavy, something metal. Right away, he felt a warm liquid trail from his ear. Blood trickled alongside his neck, then into his lap, where it began to pool.

He tried getting his bearings, but another piece of thick metal slammed into him, this time just below his Adam's apple; it coiled around his neck, pulling him straight back, jerking him hard against the headrest.

Panic struck. Witherspoon reached up instinctively with both hands, choking for air, trying frantically to pry the hook loose. But before he could free himself, the other hook came swooping down, landing inside his mouth, piercing skin, and driving a hole through the side of his cheek. Like a catfish snagged on a line, he felt his jaw jerk wide open, far beyond its normal limits. The skin on his neck and face tightened as both hooks worked in unison, ratcheting into flesh, stretching it in directions it was never supposed to move.

Bradley Witherspoon understood his life was about to end. He knew each shallow breath could be his last. Tears rolled down his cheeks as he thought about his wife, his kids, about never seeing them again. Then he prayed for death to come quickly and end his pain and suffering.

No such luck.

The deputy felt a sharp tug, followed by an intense rush of pain as his captor yanked him between the two front seats and toward the back. The assailant pulled him out the rear door—hook still lodged inside his cheek—and launched forward, leading the deputy by the mouth. Witherspoon let out a shrill, childlike scream. His attacker answered back by jerking the hook harder, continuing to drag him.

In a haphazard, clumsy manner, Witherspoon scrambled across the ground on all fours in a desperate attempt to keep pace. The slower he moved, the more intense the pain became as the forward movement tugged at his flesh. He wanted to look up at his assailant but could not. The hook inside his cheek assured it. Turning his head would have driven the hook deeper into his skin.

Witherspoon could not keep up any longer. His body was just too weak. He stumbled, lurched forward, and felt his skin split and separate as the hook sliced across his cheek, shifting position and penetrating deep into the roof of his mouth. From there, it moved higher into his sinus canal. Blood began draining into the back of his throat. He choked as it spilled out from his mouth and down the front of his chin.

Their journey ended at the foot of an old feed shed topped off with a rusty metal roof. The assailant grabbed Witherspoon by the shoulders, pushed his heel into the small of Witherspoon's back, then shoved him forward several feet, where he slammed into the ground, face-first.

Witherspoon tried to get up, but the attacker leaped on top of him. Grabbing a lock of hair, he yanked the deputy's head close to his lips and in a breathy voice whispered, "Just curious: How's it feel to know you're about to die?"

Witherspoon recognized the voice. He felt his gut tighten, then a warm, wet sensation slowly crawl between his legs.

Chapter Two

Saddleback Ranch
Faith, New Mexico

When Assistant Sheriff Cameron Dawson arrived on scene, he barely recognized the dark, obscure object hanging stiffly in the distance; it looked like an old blanket left out to dry. But as he drew closer, he began to see what—or *who*—it was. As soon as he made the connection, he felt the bile rise up, burning through his throat.

The scent of death hung heavy in the air, a coppery, metallic odor—blood, and far too much of it. The corpse dangled upside-down from the roof of the shed, suspended by a hook lodged into its scrotum.

Cameron gazed at the two deputies standing guard, their expressions somber, then returned his attention to the victim. The weapon of choice: a pair of hay hooks—thick, curved metal fashioned into crooks with spear-like tips, and at the other end, heavy wooden grips resembling shovel handles with leather cuffs draped around them for better grabbing power. Ranchers use the implements to move large bales of hay weighing more than seventy-five pounds, thrusting the sharp, honed hooks into each end to lift them.

The killer had stripped the body nude, exhibiting it in a manner so peculiar, so hideous it barely looked human. Bent in two at the waist, it gave the illusion of being half its normal size. As Cameron moved his gaze downward, he noticed the ankles and wrists were sliced vertically, then hogtied. This caused the spine to bow and the body to bleed out, while giving it a grotesque, humpbacked appearance. The hook lodged into the groin came straight up between the legs, past the buttocks, with a rope tied to the handle. The other hook stuck out of the corpse's mouth, which hung wide open, leaving the eerie impression of an eternal, silent scream.

Cameron moved closer. On the back of one arm, a dried ribbon of blood ran down past the wrist to a drooping hand and then alongside the index finger. From there, it had broken away, where it joined a large pool on the ground.

The killer had created a crude hoisting device to lift the body, tying one end of the rope to the steel push-bars on Witherspoon's squad car. The other went toward the shed, where it looped over a steel-beamed roof support, then straight down to the hook's handle. The perp only needed to back the vehicle up, hoisting the body, where it remained suspended in midair.

This was not the Bradley Witherspoon Cameron remembered, athletic, vibrant, good looking. This *object*—this tangled mass of flesh hanging before him like a side of beef—bore no resemblance to the man with whom he'd worked.

Cameron's horror turned to disgust, which quickly erupted into rage. He looked up at the deputies, almost as if demanding an explanation for what had happened. They answered back with blank, hesitant expressions, breaking eye contact, looking off to the side—anywhere but across the path of his glare. Realizing he'd unnerved them, he looked away.

Cameron moved behind the body, and something instantly caught his attention. He tilted his head, knelt, then focused on a spot just below the right rear shoulder blade.

"Sir?" offered Deputy Jim Avello, wondering what his boss had seen.

Cameron didn't respond. He just stared, eyes narrow, head jutted forward, gaze immovable.

"Sir?" Avello repeated.

"Jim," Cameron finally said, his attention fixed on the body. "Go and get the metal briefcase from my car."

Avello hurried toward the vehicle, pulled out the briefcase, then came back.

"Tweezers," Cameron ordered, holding out his palm, eyes still focused on the one spot.

Avello flipped open the briefcase, found the tweezers and placed them in Cameron's hand.

With great care, the sheriff moved the implement toward the victim, mindful not to disturb the dried blood, debris, or scratch marks on the skin. He pinched something, then held it up to the light.

Resting between the tweezers was what appeared to be a tiny gemstone fragment, black, and no bigger than the tip of a ballpoint pen. Cameron wiped it clean on his pant leg, then tilted it back and forth, watching it twinkle in the reflected morning sunlight.

"Evidence bag," he said loudly to no one in particular.

Avello reached inside the briefcase, producing a clear plastic bag. He handed it to Cameron, who lowered the chip inside, then sealed it.

Avello glanced up at him.

Cameron said, "Looks like our killer left us a little surprise."

Chapter Three

City Morgue
Faith, New Mexico

A chill cut through Cameron's body, making goose bumps swell along his arm. He shivered and rubbed a palm against his skin, wondering if his reaction was from the room's coldness or because he was standing over Bradley Witherspoon's remains.

Cameron's boss, Sheriff Frank Donato, did not appear cold at all—he'd come dressed appropriately, wrapped in a cloak of despair. As Cameron's shock began to fade, Frank's had just begun. He looked up from the body toward Cameron, trying to gauge his reaction, then let out a heavy sigh, one that seemed to express what he could not say. The sheriff's department was a family, and a close one. They'd just lost a brother in the most violent, brutal way imaginable…and that wasn't all.

Also gone was the sense of security they'd once enjoyed while protecting and serving their community. There had never been much reason to worry about their safety before—not in a town as small as Faith; it just wasn't a concern. The deputies knew they faced potential dangers on the job, but that possibility seemed remote. Now Bradley Witherspoon's murder had changed that.

As for the locals, the word *homicide* might as well have been part of some foreign dialect. The only murders any of them had ever witnessed were the kind they watched on television. Things like this happened in other places. Not in Faith. Theirs was a peaceful, close-knit community, the kind where everybody seemed to know one another, if not on a first-name basis, then certainly by sight, where a trip to the local diner felt more like a social event than a meal. The victim being a sheriff's deputy made matters even worse. After all, if the person who was supposed to protect them wasn't safe, where did that leave *them*?

Earlier that morning, Frank had to perform a duty he'd hoped he'd never have to do: tell a family member her loved one was killed on the job. As soon as Bradley's wife opened the door and saw Frank's expression, she knew something horrible had happened. He watched her cheeks go from rosy red to lily white within seconds, her expression turn blank. She collapsed into his arms, burying her face in his shoulder and letting out an agonizing wail.

For Frank, it all brought back memories of Bradley as a rookie—so young, so green; but Frank had watched him develop into a man, one of the most competent, dependable deputies the department ever had. Not only did he see him grow as a deputy, he also saw Bradley mature in his personal life too, as a husband, and then a father to two great children.

So much to live for, Frank thought. *All of it gone. Just like that.*

The most tragic irony of all: Witherspoon was murdered during the last few hours of his shift—one he wasn't even supposed to be working. Another deputy had called in sick at the last minute that evening, and Witherspoon had offered to take up the slack. That was typical. He was always trying to help out wherever he could. Sadly, the reward he'd gotten for his generosity, at least in this case, was death.

The corpse lay on a flimsy stretcher covered by a thin, white sheet. Frank stared at the shapeless form for several minutes, preparing to view what was just beneath it. He grabbed the cloth; it felt cold against his clammy palm, as thick and heavy as a wet blanket. Then he pulled the sheet back, revealing the head and upper torso. He cringed.

Witherspoon's face looked so disfigured that Frank barely recognized it. The upper lip was busted open, a gash running vertically toward the nose, much like one sees in photos of children with cleft palates. But that wasn't the worst of it. His left cheek was torn as well, leaving a large flap of skin hanging beneath it. As a result, the entire inside of his mouth was visible from the side, leaving, in effect, half his face missing—just teeth and jaw exposed.

Frank yanked the sheet back over the body and looked away toward the opposite wall.

Cameron didn't say anything. He knew what Frank was feeling. He'd experienced the same thing earlier that morning when he first saw Witherspoon hanging from that shed, a strange combination of sadness and revulsion twisting inside him. The two emotions had not mixed well for Cameron, and judging by the look on Frank's face, they were not sitting well with him, either. This murder was so disturbing, so senseless, but most of all, so infuriating.

"What's the timeline?" It wasn't a question as much as a demand.

"Last time anyone heard from him was just before midnight," Cameron replied. "They started looking for him around five when he didn't answer his radio...found him around five forty-five. That's all we have."

Frank pursed his lips and nodded, expression stoic, eyes fixed back on the body. The way he folded his arms looked awkward, as if he didn't know where to put them. "Got any theories?"

Cameron looked at his boss, then up toward the ceiling. His eyes appeared wet, and Frank couldn't tell if it was from sorrow or exhaustion. He decided it was probably both. "I just don't know, Frank. This goes so far beyond anything we've ever seen…" He paused, started to speak again, then shook his head in frustration.

Frank nodded toward the body. "There's some kind of pathology at work here, you know."

"The way he was put on display," Cameron agreed, the last word sounding as if he'd tasted something bitter. "Like the killer was proud of himself, showing off. Strung him up like some kind of prized catch."

Frank looked up at Cameron. "The thrill of the hunt. A textbook case of sociopathic showmanship."

"Yeah, but something else."

"What's that?"

"The weapon."

"The hooks?"

"It shows he improvised, grabbed whatever was handy," Cameron said.

"A disorganized kill."

"Has all the earmarks."

Frank lowered his gaze at Cameron, then furrowed a brow. "I see where you're heading, and I don't like it."

"I'm not saying we could have the start of serial killer, but I will say one thing—there's something about this that bothers me, Frank, really bothers me."

"Well, yeah, judging by the way he was left—"

"More than that, even. It's the killer's motivation."

"Motivation?"

"I'm willing to bet this wasn't just about murder."

Frank looked back down at Witherspoon's body, then up at Cameron. "What else is there?"

Cameron paused for a moment. "I think he was sending out a message…and loving every minute of it."

Chapter Four

Filbert Train Station
Faith, New Mexico

The old brown pickup sat parked along the tracks near the intersection of Quincy and Baseline Roads. That's where it was most Friday evenings around this time, and that's where you could find Jet Stevens—planted right behind the wheel.

He liked to watch the trains go by, had been doing it for as long as anyone could remember. Said it helped him wind down. As for those who knew him, most would have agreed: if he were any more relaxed, he'd probably be fast asleep.

Jet and his family were as firmly rooted in Faith's historic landscape as the trees that stretched across its dusty plains. His great-grandfather, Samuel Stevens, was one of the original settlers. After the war in 1846, railroad companies began laying tracks across the state, and the cattle industry boomed. Sam Stevens got in on the ground floor and cashed in big, becoming one of New Mexico's wealthiest cattle barons. The family had owned the Saddleback Ranch ever since, and ever since, the money had been flowing.

But you wouldn't know that by looking at Jet—he'd been driving the same beat-up Dodge for as long as anyone could remember, still wore the same tattered cowboy hat that looked as if the truck itself had backed over it a few times.

Six feet tall and about 165 pounds, Jet had rough-and-tumble good looks combined with dark skin, dark eyes, and even darker hair. Rumor had it he was part Apache, but nobody dared approach the subject with him; it was dangerous territory, strictly off-limits. Jet's dad, it seemed, had trouble in the sexual discretion department—he was presently working on his fifth marriage—and his escapades in and around Faith were legendary. It was suspected by some, common knowledge to others, that Jet himself was the product of one of those romps. Many figured it was also the reason he and his father did not get along.

Cameron pulled alongside the truck, got out of his car, then slid up into the passenger seat. Once inside, he stared out through the windshield. Jet didn't bother looking at Cameron; he was too busy watching the tracks, his only visible movement a toothpick shifting from side to side in his mouth.

The sound of clanking glass finally broke the silence as Jet reached into his cooler and produced two frosty bottles of beer. Gazing off into the distance, he dangled them in the air, toothpick still sliding back and forth.

Cameron grabbed one. He screwed his face into a tight grimace, struggling to keep the bottle from slipping in one hand while twisting off the top with the other. Once removed, he held the cap up, turning it around, studying it, and said, "Figured you'd be here."

Jet was still watching the tracks. He reached for the toothpick, gave it a few turns, then extracted the mangled end from between his lips and replied, "If my name is Jet and it's Friday night—then you know I'm here."

Cameron acknowledged the comment with the slightest grin, then looked down at his bottle and started peeling the label.

Jet said, "Keepin' busy these days, I see."

"Busy…" Cameron replied, shaking his head, staring at the floorboard. "Busy doesn't begin to describe what I am. Crazy—now that's more like it."

Jet brought the bottle to his mouth but instead of taking a sip, produced a combination nod and shrug, as if confirming his own thought. "Got a murdered deputy…people runnin' around, lookin' as nervous as bastards at a family reunion. That'll make you crazy."

"So to speak," Cameron said.

"Weird, though, huh?"

"What's that?"

"The whole thing…what happened."

"Weirder than weird," Cameron said, watching a car drive past. The reflected sunlight cast an orange glow across his face. "And right there on your ranch."

Jet was mid-gulp when he stopped, squeezed his eyes tight, then shook his head, looking as if he'd just swallowed vinegar. "Mmm. Not my ranch—my daddy's ranch. Ain't mine."

Cameron studied Jet for a few seconds, thinking before speaking. "Didn't happen to see anything that night there, did you?"

"Anything like what?"

"You know, anything unusual…out of the ordinary. See anyone walking around? Anyone who shouldn't've been there?"

Jet looked at Cameron briefly, then out his side window, slowly shaking his head. "Naw. Ain't nobody goes up that road, 'cept for the deputies. No need to. Doesn't go nowhere. Everybody knows that."

A train finally rolled past, just a few freight cars and a flatbed heading out of town. Jet watched with mild interest, following them until they moved out of sight, then tossed his empty bottle into the backseat, where it clanked against a number of others.

"Well, somebody found reason to be there that night," Cameron said, "and that reason was to kill Witherspoon."

"Uh-huh. That's for damn sure...figure someone had a score to settle...wanted to even things up."

Cameron was about to take a sip but stopped, eyeing Jet with interest. "Why you say that?"

"Nothin' special," Jet said, attempting a casual shrug. "Just guessing, is all."

Cameron relaxed slightly: Jet didn't have any concrete information. He put his bottle in the cup holder, spinning it around a few times, staring at it. "Jet, I know you said you didn't actually see anyone hanging around there that night, but did you see *anything*...anything *at all*?"

"Anything at all..." Jet said, repeating Cameron's words, as if it would somehow give them more meaning.

"Maybe see something unusual later on that seemed out of place, like it didn't fit...didn't belong? Something like that?"

"Naw, not really."

"Not *really*, or *not at all*? Think hard, Jet. It's important."

Jet was now moving his eyes back and forth along the dashboard as if following a thought, then stopped like he'd found it. He looked at Cameron. "Well, there was...but *naw*. That wouldn't be nothin'."

"What? Tell me. What is it?"

Jet pushed the brim of his hat back an inch or two, scratched the part of his head now exposed, deliberating on a thought before speaking. "Found something on the ground later that day. Figured one of the deputies tossed it. But now that you mention it..."

"What was it?" Cameron asked.

"Slip of paper."

"What was on it?" Getting information here was like pulling teeth.

"Your department's name...and a phone number."

"Do you have it?" asked Cameron, anxiety in his voice despite his best efforts to conceal it. "Did you keep it?"

Jet thought for a moment. "No, but I think I know where it might be."

"Where?"

Jet gave Cameron a lingering look, his mouth pulled tighter on one side. Opening his door, he shoved a leg through, then stepped out of the truck. As he walked toward the back, Cameron jumped out on his side as well, following quickly.

Both stared into the bed. There were more empty bottles, some ropes, an old saddle.

But no note.

Still gazing into the bed, Jet shrugged, cupped his palm over the crown of his hat, tilting it back some. "I threw it back here. Guess it blew out."

Cameron folded his arms and rested them on the bed railing, releasing a long sigh. "Do you remember the numbers, Jet, *any* of them?"

Jet looked at the ground, kicked some dirt. "The first three numbers were five-seven-one…don't remember the rest."

"Five-seven-one," Cameron repeated, knowing it meant very little. There were only two exchanges in Faith—that and five-six-two. Without the rest, connecting them to something significant would be next to impossible. "And you're *sure* you don't remember the others?"

"Naw," Jet replied, then threw his hands up. "Wish I did."

Me, too, Jet, Cameron thought. *Me, too.*

CHAPTER FIVE

7543 Sunshine Way
Faith, New Mexico

Cameron checked with each of the deputies on the scene after Witherspoon's murder. None of them knew anything about a slip of department stationery bearing those numbers; that meant it could very well have belonged to Witherspoon, maybe even have fallen from his pocket while he was murdered.

A potentially valuable piece of evidence lost. Just the thought of it made Cameron's gut tighten into a fist-sized knot.

Whether or not the paper was relevant to the crime was anyone's guess, since finding it would be next to impossible, and a number with the five-seven-one exchange would only narrow things down to about half the town.

Turning his focus toward new evidence, Cameron thought about his next step, probably the hardest one of all: to speak to Witherspoon's wife.

Bradley's house was a modest-looking ranch-style home located only a mile or so from the sheriff's station.

Cameron arrived just as another visitor was leaving. Witherspoon's wife, Shelby, stood in the darkened doorway, saying good-bye to another woman; she looked over her guest's shoulder and caught Cameron's gaze. The other woman swung around, saw him, then turned back and continued talking. They embraced, then the guest turned to leave, and she passed Cameron as she headed toward her car.

Shelby's eyes were rimmed in red, her nose a deep shade of pink. Cameron reached for her hands, gave her a somber, sympathetic smile, then instinctively wrapped his arms around her. She hugged him back, and he could hear her soft sobs against his shoulder. He continued holding on to her for a long time, as if doing so could somehow help drain away her sorrow.

Finally, she pulled away. Grief-stricken eyes peered directly into his.

Cameron shook his head, fighting back his own tears. "I don't know what to say, Shelby, I just..."

"I know..." she said, looking down at her feet, nodding, her voice shallow and weak. "I know."

A few moments of awkward silence stretched between them. Then, softly, Shelby said, "Why don't you come inside?"

Cameron nodded and followed her through the doorway.

The dining room table was awash in a sea of baskets, cellophane wrapping paper, bows, and flowers: all tokens of sympathy, of love, for the wife of a slain deputy. Shelby moved past them all as if they didn't even exist, then went into the kitchen. She reached for the refrigerator handle, opened the door and stared inside for a long time, her back to Cameron, almost as if she'd forgotten why she'd gone there in the first place. Finally, she let out a deep, helpless sigh, her shoulders falling an inch or two. "Can I get you anything? Something to drink?"

Cameron stood in the doorway watching her. Having something to drink was the last thing on his mind. "No. Thank you."

She turned around to face him and shook her head. "I don't know what I'm doing. My mind…it's just—"

"Sit down, Shelby," Cameron said softly. "You don't have to do anything."

Shelby closed her eyes and nodded. She walked slowly past him into the living room, sat down tentatively on the couch, dropped her face in her hands and began crying.

Cameron took a seat beside her, placed a hand on her shoulder, and kept it there, silently.

When Shelby finally lifted her head, Cameron reached for a box of tissues—nearly empty—on the end table and handed it to her. She took one, wiped her nose.

A long, labored silence filled the air again. Cameron glanced around the room as if searching for words. "So where are the boys?"

"My mother took them to her place for the afternoon. Guess she figured I needed a break…" she said, her voice trailing off, "although the quiet seems worse."

Cameron shifted his weight nervously. "I have to do this, Shelby. I don't want to—you know I don't—and I'd do anything not to have to put you through this right now, but—"

"I know," she said, her voice changing, becoming steadier now. Shelby had been a cop's wife long enough to realize what was coming next.

"I'll try to make this as quick as possible," Cameron assured.

"I know it's hard for you, too—all this—I know it is. Brad thought the world of you."

"Thought the world of him, too," Cameron said, looking down at his hands, nodding, remembering. "I really did."

"I want to help you find whoever killed…" She stopped, closed her eyes. "Whoever did this to him."

"I need to know if you saw or heard something—*anything*—suspicious in the last few days."

She looked away and stared absently across the room, shaking her head slowly. "No. There was nothing."

"Are you positive?"

"I would have known if something was wrong." Shelby turned back toward Cameron. She shrugged. "There just wasn't."

"What about someone else? Anyone you can think of who'd have reason to want to hurt him? Hurt you?"

"You knew Brad. He didn't have a single enemy. Not one."

It was true. Bradley was probably the best-liked deputy at the station. Cameron couldn't think of anyone who'd want to do him harm. He thought some more, then spoke. "There was a slip of paper found at the scene later with department letterhead and a phone number written on it."

She tilted her head. "Let me see it."

"I can't. It got tossed. Accidentally. I don't even know if it was Brad's or not. All I have to go on are the first three digits of a telephone number."

Shelby just stared at him, vacantly.

Cameron knew what she was going through—really knew—and yet he felt helpless. His own sadness and loss seemed to be coming to the surface once more, as though the grief had been waiting for just that moment to own him. "What can I do for you right now, Shelby? How can I help?"

"Find him, Cameron," she said, her voice becoming firm and harsh, her expression unforgiving. A single tear rolled down her cheek. "Find whoever took him from me."

Cameron nodded. It was all he could do.

"Find the bastard, then make him pay. Make sure he never sees the light of day again. *Never.*"

Chapter Six

Eisenhower Middle School
Faith, New Mexico

Thirteen-year-old Ryan Churchill sat behind his computer, pounding the keyboard as he worked on his research paper. Alma Gutierrez smiled, pleased to see him looking so inspired, so motivated. She'd been tutoring him for several months, and he'd improved in ways even he never imagined he could.

Ryan had started out as a below-average student, barely making Cs and Ds. Now, however, he'd been bringing home As and Bs, thanks to Alma's help and careful guidance.

A quiet kid, and a bit on the awkward side, he had a plump, round body, flushed, full cheeks, and a smile that could light up a room…when his shyness permitted. Before Alma, Ryan had been an underachiever, and no one could figure out why. Certainly it wasn't for a lack of intelligence, as all his test scores showed otherwise.

That was why they'd sent him to see Alma. She soon discovered why he'd been doing so poorly in school: Ryan Churchill was dyslexic. He saw the world differently than everyone else did, a mirror image of itself, everything backward. All these years he'd suffered a limiting disability that kept him from reaching his potential.

But not anymore. Alma worked with Ryan, teaching him how to overcome his problem, and he'd been improving rapidly ever since.

Alma enjoyed the work. There was sweetness about the boy that made it hard not to like him. While it took some time to gain Ryan's trust, once they'd forged a relationship, he'd begun to excel.

After the dyslexia was discovered and addressed, there was no stopping Ryan. As it turned out, not only was he bright, he actually belonged in the gifted category. Finding that out, and realizing he had a diagnosable disability—that he was not *stupid* or *lazy* as people had often told him—made all the difference in the world to the boy. Before long, Ryan began to feel like he had value and purpose in life. Most of all, he was grateful to Alma for freeing him from the stronghold the disorder had placed on him.

Ryan started picking up his typing speed, and Alma looked up from her work and smiled. "You're doing so well, Ryan. I'm very pleased."

Ryan flashed his bashful smile, the one Alma had become used to seeing, the one that would win her over every time.

She often wondered how the boy did around the other children. Kids like Ryan in general faced one of two reactions: they either went unnoticed or suffered the opposite effect, becoming the target of ridicule and cruel jokes. It would break Alma's heart if she found out he'd suffered the latter. She'd never broached the subject with him, though she thought perhaps someday she might.

Ryan had been laboring away on his research paper for almost twenty-five minutes now, with a fervor Alma had never before seen in him, almost as if he couldn't type fast enough to keep up with his thoughts.

"You must really be on to something, Ryan," she said with a grin. "I've never seen you type so fast."

"I have a great idea!" he replied, enthusiasm evident.

"Good, good! That's wonderful! I can't wait to read it."

"Neither can I," said Ryan. "I really want you to see it."

She was pleased. "Keep up the good work, kiddo. You're doing great!"

Bashful smile again.

Alma reached down into her drawer for a pen, fishing around for a moment in vain. "Shoot," she said, looking up at Ryan. "I have to go to the supply room. Will you be okay while I'm gone for a few minutes?"

Ryan kept typing and did not look up. "Sure. I'm fine."

When Alma's office door clicked shut, Ryan froze instantly, almost as if on cue. He pushed his chair back and locked his fingers behind his head, taking a good long look at his work, admiring his accomplishment.

He smiled, but this was different—nothing bashful or endearing about it.

On the screen, sentence after sentence, paragraph after paragraph, page after page, the same passage repeated over and over:

He hunts his prey, a troubled soul.
Murderous thoughts as dark as coal.
The need to kill, it rules his mind.
With bloodstained hands, a heart maligned.

Ryan pulled the hunting knife from the sheath inside his boot. He gazed with admiration at the seven-inch blade with its razor-sharp serrated edges glistening and its tip pointed. He felt a rush of adrenaline shoot through him. It made his spine tingle, was invigorating. A wicked smile widened across his face.

It would feel so good driving his knife through that bitch's heart.

The door opened, and Alma entered the room. She noticed he was no longer typing.

Ryan dropped the knife down to his side and away from her line of sight.

She turned her back to him and closed the door. "Done so fast? Ready to give it to me?"

Chapter Seven

Eisenhower Middle School
Faith, New Mexico

"Get ready. It's ugly in there. Real ugly," Deputy Shawn Callahan said to Cameron. Authorities had sent the students home early and put the school on lockdown. Alma Gutierrez's office was now a crime scene and a gruesome one at that.

The door was open just a tiny crack. Cameron nodded to the deputy standing guard outside. He stopped for a few seconds, trying to gather his thoughts, then pushed it open with a gloved hand.

What he saw first was a woman's shoe, lying on its side, in a corner, and covered in blood; it looked as if it had been thrown across the room. But what he saw next was even worse.

It was Alma—or what the killer had left of her. Cameron moved very slowly, very cautiously, toward the body; as he did, his jaw tightened and his temples hollowed. The similarities to the Witherspoon murder were impossible to ignore.

Alma Gutierrez was suspended upside down, nude, with her legs spread apart and a broomstick lodged deep into the tendons just above her ankles. A bloody strand of rope wound around her feet, securing it all in place.

Cameron moved around the corpse, studying it closely. Images of Bradley Witherspoon flashed through his mind. *Another murder victim left hanging upside down*, he thought: *a pattern.*

"It's called field dressing," said Callahan, a note of disgust in his voice. "What hunters do to age venison before eating it. Hung her by her feet like some damned animal. Used the broomstick as a gambrel…cleaned her out, too."

"Did what?" Cameron asked, turning quickly toward Callahan.

"Sliced her right down the middle from breastbone to pelvis," he said, pointing at the long incision on Alma's naked body, "like a cool melon on a hot summer day."

Cameron looked at Callahan, almost as if making sure he'd heard him correctly, then stepped forward to examine the gaping hole in Alma's body. He turned back toward Callahan again, shaking his head slowly.

Callahan continued. "Took out all her organs. She's hollowed out…empty as air."

Cameron glanced around the room. "So where are they?"

Callahan walked behind Alma's desk, pulled open the top drawer. The killer had organized Alma's internal organs, neatly, from small to large.

"The heart, spleen, and kidneys are in this one." Callahan closed the drawer and opened the next two, one at a time. "The stomach, intestines, lungs, and the rest are all in here. I'll give 'em one thing: this killer knew what he was doing. The organs seem to have been removed with surgical precision."

It was true. Alma's body had been prepared in a meticulous, almost clinical manner. The procedure seemed to follow the most stringent of guidelines employed for field dressing an animal carcass. The killer had even severed the jugular to drain the blood. Alma's corpse was nothing more than a hollowed-out shell stripped of its organs, stripped of its dignity.

Cameron placed his hands on his hips and looked down at the floor, studying it. There were blood smears everywhere, but not a footprint to be found: the suspect had covered his tracks, albeit sloppily.

But the message seemed clear: Alma was his prey, stalked, killed, and then processed for transport and eventual consumption; only the perp had done neither, instead leaving her violated body behind and on display so everyone could witness his vulgar accomplishment firsthand.

Again. Just like Witherspoon, Cameron thought, then felt the hairs on the back of his neck rise. He drew air into his lungs and exhaled. It felt like the first time he'd breathed since arriving there. "What about a suspect?"

"A couple of ideas, nothing concrete. The last person to see her was her two o'clock appointment." He tilted his pad up and glanced at it. "Ryan Churchill. Next appointment was at three thirty. Luckily, a teacher came in and found her before the kid did." He hesitated. "It was Laura Hightower. She stopped by to pick up some student assessment reports. Not too lucky for her, though. Pretty shook up. They had to take her to the emergency room. Damned near had a nervous breakdown."

"Understandable," Cameron said. "Anyone talk to the kid?"

"Nope. Nobody can find him. We're looking."

"Let's make that our number one priority, then…and check his locker for clues as well."

"For sure, boss."

Cameron couldn't help but feel like he was singing the same old song, only in a different key. He sat on the edge of a student desk just across from Alma's, thinking. As he did, the movement caused the computer monitor to light up, going from power-save mode to illuminated. The flash caught his attention, and he glanced down at it for a moment, then away, then back down at it again. He jerked, almost falling off the desk.

"Shawn?" Cameron said, now crouching down, face level with the screen.

Callahan had been taking notes. He stopped and looked up. "Yeah, boss?"

"You won't believe what I'm seeing here."

The deputy walked around and stood behind Cameron, looking at the monitor.

"Make sure this computer's been dusted for prints," Cameron said. "I think we have a confession."

CHAPTER EIGHT

Sheriff's Station
Faith, New Mexico

With the poem as evidence, Ryan Churchill was now the number-one suspect in Alma Gutierrez's murder.

Now all they had to do was find him.

But that was going to be a challenge. Nobody had seen or heard from him since Alma was killed. Like a shadow before the setting sun, the boy seemed to have faded into the scenery, no sign of him anywhere.

Cameron walked into Frank's office with an old, tattered book in his hand, which he dropped onto the desk as he passed by, then settled into the chair opposite him, arms folded, waiting for his boss's response.

Frank picked it up, opened it to the bookmark, then gave it a fleeting once-over. He looked up at Cameron. 'The Hunted Soul'?"

"It's a poem by Virgil Morrison."

"Never figured you for a poetry buff."

"I'm not. Look closer."

Frank glanced over the words, then quickly up at Cameron. "It's what Ryan had on the computer."

Cameron nodded with something half resembling a smile. "Word for word."

Frank looked down at the book again. "It's about somebody huntin' a deer."

"And Alma was field-dressed," Cameron said, "just like a deer."

Frank rubbed his cheek with his hand as if someone had just slapped it. "What's going on around here?"

"I'll tell you what's going on," Cameron said. "The kid 'fessed up."

"Not exactly a confession," Frank corrected, "but a start."

"Frank, it went on for pages—over and over—the same damned passage. You don't think it's a confession?"

"No. 'I killed Alma Gutierrez'... *That* would be a confession. This is just evidence." He slammed the book shut. "By itself, it wouldn't hold up in a courtroom."

"Confession or not," Cameron said, "nobody's getting any sleep at night knowing Ryan's on the loose."

"Can't say I blame 'em."

"Similarities and differences," Cameron suddenly said, thinking aloud.

"Huh?"

"The two murders: different weapons, different methods, but they still look a lot alike. Both bodies raised in the air, both hung upside down, both mutilated."

"But that's where the similarities end," Frank pointed out.

"True, but it's enough to make you wonder."

"Wonder *what*? We're not going back to a serial killer theory again, are we? 'Cause if that's the case, then we've got about the youngest one *I've* ever heard of."

Cameron shuddered. "I'd hate to think so, but it sure would explain things."

"Look, I can see the kid overpowering the teacher—she was tiny—but a deputy? One that's six foot two?"

Cameron stood up and began pacing. He stared down at the floor, nervously running his fingers through his hair as he spoke. "I've been thinking about that. Theoretically, he could have pulled it off, *if* he did it right."

"And how would that work?"

Cameron stopped and looked directly at Frank. "Bradley went for gas before he was killed. Sam Parkins over at the gas station confirmed it."

"Okay," said Frank, gesturing for Cameron to continue.

"The evidence shows Bradley was probably attacked from behind with the hooks, right?" He didn't wait for Frank to respond. "So say the Churchill kid sneaks into the car at the gas station and hides in the backseat while Bradley goes to take a leak, or leaves the car for...whatever."

"Go on..."

"It's no secret the road next to Saddleback is where the deputies go to take their naps. Heck, they've been doing *that* for years. And we know Witherspoon was pulling a double. He probably went there after the gas station to catch a few winks."

"So the kid attacks him while he's sleeping," Frank said, slowly nodding.

"Yep. Never got to put up a fight. Never even had the chance."

"But here's where you lose me. How'd the perp manage to nail him from the back of a squad car? How'd he get past the barrier cage between them?"

"Didn't have one," Cameron replied. "His vehicle broke down while he was working the earlier shift. He took the new car. The cage hadn't been installed yet—they were still waiting on parts."

"Not the safest move...or the smartest," Frank said.

Cameron shrugged. "Had no choice. There were no other vehicles around."

Frank reflected for a moment. "Think someone knew that? Maybe even planned it?"

Cameron shook his head. "Doubtful. Witherspoon's car had a rusted cylinder. Normal wear and tear. Not much time or opportunity to plan a killing."

Frank groaned. "Just his luck. But again, if it *was* Churchill, how the hell does a boy his size manage to move a body the size of Witherspoon's around?"

"That's a little tricky, but he could've dragged him. Wouldn't be easy or quick for him, but it could be done."

"This kid have any history of mental problems?"

"Already checked. Nothing."

Frank put his thumb and index finger on each corner of his mouth, tapping them alternately as he processed a thought. "You know, there's still one other possibility."

"What's that?"

"You think maybe Witherspoon was banging somebody's wife?"

Cameron looked up at him quickly. "Bradley?"

Frank tilted his head and threw up his hands. "I'm not saying…I'm just saying. A good-lookin' guy like that? A hook through the nuts sends a pretty clear message. Can't ignore it."

"If it'd been anyone else, I'd have to agree with you…but Bradley? If he'd been having an affair, I'd've heard about it. In fact, in a town this size, somebody else would have, too. Besides, that just wasn't him. You knew him. I knew him too. His family was his world."

"Yeah," Frank said, scratching his head, "suppose you got a point there—still, stranger things could happen."

"Stranger things have *already* happened, but not that. I'm just not seeing it."

"What about with Alma—what's going on with her? Any word from the ME?"

"Just got off the phone with him. Not much work left to do—the killer did most of it for him. Since the organs were already removed, only thing he had to do was inspect and weigh them."

"Thoughtful," Frank said with a sarcastic smile. "What else?"

"Suspect drove the knife directly into her heart."

"We can be thankful for one thing, then."

"What's that?" Cameron asked.

"At least she wasn't alive while he performed his spur-of-the-moment autopsy."

Cameron looked down at his feet, then up at Frank. "Yeah, about that..."

"What?"

He stared at him for a moment. "According to the ME, the heart was still pumping when the organs started coming out."

Chapter Nine

Sheriff's Station
Faith, New Mexico

Cameron sat in his office trying to think his way through all the recent events.

On the floor beside his desk was Bentley, his chocolate Lab, who couldn't have looked more relaxed. The canine let out a lion-sized yawn, smacked his dangling chops and then dropped his head to the floor, falling asleep instantly.

"Yeah, easy for you to say," Cameron remarked.

Bentley's one ear perked, then an eye opened. He let out an exhaustive harrumph and again drifted peaceably, back toward sleep.

Cameron couldn't help but envy the dog; he had not a care in the world, his only concerns when to wake up and what was for supper. *Not a bad life*, he thought. *Not bad at all.*

In his own life, things were far from easy. For a town like Faith, where traffic tickets and an occasional domestic dispute were about as bad as law enforcement got, it was a rude awakening to be thrown into not just one but two homicides. Even worse was that they'd occurred only a few days apart.

Still hounding Cameron were the similarities between the two cases—there were just too many of them. Like Bradley Witherspoon, Alma Gutierrez had suffered a merciless round of torture before succumbing to death, and like Witherspoon, was hanged upside down and put on display in a most disturbing way.

For now, the main focus of his investigation centered on two victims but only one possible suspect: Ryan Churchill. From all accounts, he was a quiet, well-mannered kid. In fact, no matter whom Cameron spoke with, it always seemed to be the same old story, that Ryan adored Alma. But if that were the case, why would he not only turn against her but do so with such vengeance? It just didn't add up.

Of course, Ryan killing Witherspoon made even less sense. Other than probably seeing each other around town, the two hadn't really known each other. Why would the boy want to go after him? Although plausible, there wasn't nearly enough evidence to support the theory.

Cameron did learn that Ryan's family background hadn't been a stellar one. His father disappeared soon after he was born, and his mother dropped out of the picture several years later. After that, Ryan's grandmother had raised him.

Broken homes often create broken children, Cameron thought. Speaking with the grandmother might be the first step in finding out where Ryan went wrong, and why.

~

4087 Falcon Street
Faith, New Mexico

Bobbi Kimmons rented a one-bedroom apartment near the center of town. The place was actually nothing more than a garage converted to a granny flat off the main house. Whoever changed it into living quarters hadn't done much to hide that. The structure itself was flat and boxy, with a nondescript window hanging off to one side. Nothing fancy, for sure, not even a driveway to park a car. In fact, it looked as though she kept hers in an alley butting up against the neighboring hardware store.

Much like the apartment, Bobbi's '86 Camaro also seemed less than adequate. On one side, the rear bumper hung loosely, and on the other, a tattered strand of rope held it in place. The oxidation process had taken its toll on the body, robbing it not only of its original color but of its smooth finish, giving the texture and appearance of sandpaper.

Cameron parked behind her, then crossed a front yard teeming with crabgrass, along with an assortment of other weeds in various stages of bloom. At the front of the house, rusted hinges dangled off the frame where a screen door had once hung, and the main door itself seemed in need of a refurbish. It appeared someone had made a feeble attempt to paint over the warped, cracked wood, but that was already starting to peel away. *Not the best place to raise a kid*, Cameron thought, *but at least the boy stayed with family.*

He rang the doorbell, then knocked when he didn't get a response. A few seconds later, the door opened to a narrow crack, revealing a ruby-tinged, twitching nose.

"Assistant Sheriff Cameron Dawson," he said to the nose.

The door moved open some more, exposing the face that went with it, which did not welcome, nor did it speak.

"I need to talk to you about your grandson, Ryan."

"One minute." Bobbi said, in a husky voice that sounded like too many cigarettes. She pushed the door closed, and Cameron heard the security chain disengaging. When it opened again, an odor of stale cigarette smoke emerged almost instantly, as did the hollow-cheeked woman herself.

"Well, don't just stand there," she snarled, her thick voice tempered with a combative undertone. "Come in!"

Ignoring the less-than-warm welcome, Cameron followed her inside.

"I figured you'd be coming," she said, ambling toward the kitchen. "I made tea."

Cameron heard glasses clanging together, combined with the faint sound of sniffling.

Bobbi emerged from the kitchen holding two glasses filled with iced tea, placed one on a TV stand by the couch and then motioned for Cameron to sit there. She took the other glass to a threadbare recliner. After lowering herself into it, she reached for a pack of nonfiltered Pall Malls and pulled one out, almost as if having one were as much a part of her responsibility as speaking to him. Holding the cigarette to her lips with two fingers, she lit up, took one long drag and inhaled every bit of it deep into her lungs. Two thick jets of gray smoke escaped through her nostrils, becoming thinner with each passing second. Looking much more relaxed after a calming dose of nicotine, she looked up at Cameron. "So what can I do ya for?"

"Tell me," Cameron said, deciding to delve right in. "What happened with Ryan's parents?"

"My daughter?" she said, then snorted. "Haven't seen hide nor hair of her in years. Heard she's living somewhere in Arizona. As for the father, well, we never figured out who *he* even was."

"Why did your daughter leave?"

"She didn't leave—not really. County took Ryan away." Bobbi pulled another drag from her cigarette, rolled her eyes, then forced the smoke out through her mouth. Her tone was singsong. "It's a long story. If ya got a few hours, I'll tell ya 'bout it. Otherwise, I'll just give you the short version and say she wasn't fit to raise a canary, let alone a child."

"Drugs?"

"Ha!" she said with a deep cackle that morphed into a wet cough. "Drugs, drinking, gambling, men, you name it, she had her hands full of it. A real winner, my daughter."

"How old was Ryan?"

Bobbi looked toward the ceiling and moved her lips as if counting. "I wanna say…yeah, when Ryan was ten. She tried to make a go at parenting. Failed miserably, of course."

"What happened?"

"Went out to get stoned one night—or whatever she was into at the time—and left Ryan at home all by himself." She took another quick drag, then spoke, exhaling simultaneously. "Used to do it all the time. Well, *that* time it was one too many. Ryan got into some kinda trouble—can't remember what—and a neighbor called the cops. When she finally came home, the boy was gone, and there was a nice little letter from the county stuck to her front door."

"And then you got him?" Cameron asked.

"Not right away. There were hearings in front of the judge. Don't think she even showed up. Pathetic. I was there, of course, just like always. It was the least I could do. Poor kid. Wasn't *his* fault his mother was such a screwup. Anyway, surprise, surprise, they deemed her an unfit mother. And guess who they awarded custody to?"

Cameron mindlessly watched the end of her cigarette; it was becoming long, the ash about to fall off. He nodded toward it. She looked down, flicked, sucked twice and then put it out in a plate that looked like it had once accommodated something with mustard. A thick, creamy puff of smoke jumped from her mouth, then two thinner jets rushed from her nostrils.

"You didn't want to take the boy?" he asked.

"Well, not at first. I hadn't raised a kid in years." She looked at him with a deadpan expression. "I wasn't exactly up for Mother of the Year after my first tour of duty. I sure as hell wasn't thrilled about having to do it all over again."

Cameron attempted a sympathetic smile.

She reflected for a few seconds, eyeing the pack of cigarettes as if contemplating another. "But Ryan, he was different. Kid'll grow on ya if ya let him. Cute, too. Real sweet. And smart? Oh, you shoulda seen him. Don't know where *that* came from. Sure didn't get it from this side of the family."

"Did his learning disability cause him much trouble?"

"Oh, I knew it hadda be somethin'. He was too smart to be pullin' the kind of shitty"—she stopped, smiled, then corrected herself—"*bad* marks he was gettin'. I figgered either he was goofin' off too much, or there was somethin' else wrong."

"The dyslexia," Cameron suggested.

She moved her index finger around in circles beside her head. "Head problems. They finally figgered it out…the *geniuses*."

"And that's how he met Alma Gutierrez."

Bobbi grew quiet all of a sudden, and her eyes began to glisten. She reached for another cigarette, lit it fast—something to comfort herself. "Yeah, that's when everything went all wrong. He liked her. Talked about her all the time. I just don't understand how he could—"

"He never displayed any sort of violent behavior?"

"Ryan?" She looked at him as if the question were absurd. "Never. He was a pussycat. Wouldn't think of hurting a soul."

A pussycat who sliced his teacher in half, pulling her organs out of her body as if it was some kind of carnival grab-bag.

"I know what you're thinking!" she snapped. "But that's not Ryan." She looked away, then, "That's not my grandbaby."

"What do you think happened, then?"

She looked down at her cigarette as if she'd forgotten it was there, tapped the ash off onto her plate, then took one long, final drag before snuffing it out. "I don't know, but as sure as I'm sittin' here—that boy ain't the violent kind. He'd never hurt anyone, especially not Alma. He loved that woman."

"There's a history of substance abuse in the family. Any signs Ryan might've been using?" Cameron suggested.

She looked back at him, appalled, almost as if he'd just asked her to take off her clothes. "You *must* be joking. Ryan hated that stuff. He saw what it did to his momma. Wouldn't have no part of it."

Cameron shifted gears. "Did Ryan ever go hunting?"

"Hmmm. The *deer* thing." She said the word as if it smelled like rotten egg. "Heard about that. Kinda figgered *that* was coming. Yeah, Ryan used to go with his grandfather, my husband."

"He still around?"

"No. *My Henry* passed on several years ago." Bobbi paused to think, as if taking a trip back in time, then shuttled back to the present. Her tone suddenly grew quiet. "Cancer."

"I'm sorry," Cameron said. "How long ago?"

She let out a sigh with sound. "Seven years. It's been seven years now."

"They hunted together? He and Ryan?"

"Yeah. Before my daughter lost custody. Henry used to take him out during buck season. He was about five or six. Quality time. You know?"

Cameron nodded.

"Gives a young man a sense of accomplishment. Teaches him responsibility," she said, almost as if defending her deceased husband. "Henry was good with Ryan."

"So the boy knows how to prepare the animal once it's killed?"

"If you're talking about the field dressing, then yes," she said, "Henry taught him that. Ryan was too young to actually shoot. Used to go along and help, but I'll tell you what: my husband's probably turning in his grave right now. He'd kick that boy's ass from here till next Tuesday if he knew..." She stopped, shaking her head in disgust.

Cameron glanced around the room. "Did Ryan sleep in the bedroom?"

"No, I do...figger, why not? I pay the rent, I get the bennies, right?" She pointed at the couch where Cameron was sitting. "He slept right there. Folds open to a bed."

Cameron looked down at the couch, then back up at her. "Where did he keep his personal belongings?"

"Boy didn't have a heck of a lot. I could barely afford to keep clothes on his back—thank you Jesus for SSI—so he lived pretty simple, but not by choice. Didn't seem to mind it much, though." She nodded toward a corner of the room. "Kept his clothes in that dresser over there."

"Mind if I take a look?"

"Be my guest. Take you all of about…what…like, two seconds? Like I said, kid didn't have much."

Cameron walked over to the dresser, pulled open each drawer and looked inside but found nothing other than a few polo shirts, underwear, and socks. After closing the final drawer, he thought for a moment, then looked at her. "Any idea where he might be right now?"

She threw her hands up. "Damned if I know."

Cameron nodded, deliberating for a moment. "One last thing. Did Ryan have access to a hunting knife of any sort?"

Bobbi eyed him suspiciously. "Hunting knife?"

"Yeah. Alma was killed with one," he said, a reminder, even though he knew she needed none.

Bobbi's eyes widened, and her voice got defensive. "If he did, he sure as shit didn't get it from me."

"I wasn't suggesting that, ma'am, just wanted to know if he had access to any. If you ever saw him with one."

She drew a ragged breath and thought—or at least that's what she appeared to be doing—then said, "My husband had one, but that was a long time ago."

"Any idea where it is now?"

"Haven't got a clue." Bobbi shrugged. "Wouldn't even know where ta start lookin'."

"Think harder, Ms. Kimmons." Cameron took a step closer toward her.

Bobbi stepped back, shot him a look, then reflected. A moment later, she pointed toward the bedroom. "The trunk under my bed—that's where I saw it last."

"Can we check?"

She sighed, then gestured toward her bedroom.

Cameron went through. He knelt down by the bed, pulled out the trunk and opened it.

No knife. Not anywhere.

Cameron looked up at Bobbi.

She said nothing; she didn't have to, but her eyes revealed plenty: a combination of surprise edged by uncertainty. Bobbi shifted her weight nervously from side to side.

Cameron closed the trunk.

"Sheriff," she said, shaking her head. "I got a strange feeling this is gonna end up bad… *Real* bad."

Cameron had the same feeling.

Chapter Ten

Old Route 15
Faith, New Mexico

Eleven-year-old Ben Foley sat straight up in bed. His pores flared open. His breathing accelerated. His heart began to pound.

Then thoughts began flooding his mind, violent ones that grew more volatile, more deadly with each passing second.

A feverish rage—or something like it—burned deep within his gut. The sensation began to rise and swell; it coursed through his veins, gathering intensity, spreading like wildfire. The feeling was now feeding upon itself, wheeling toward the desire to kill.

His energy was changing; he knew it. He felt different now: cool, enormously powerful, and dangerously bent on causing harm. The effect was wild and intoxicating. Eyes cold and vapid, movements robotic, he barely looked human.

He ran out into the hallway and snatched the rifle from a storage closet.

Staring vacantly ahead, the boy moved through the shadows and toward the other bedrooms, each step becoming more determined, more urgent. He dragged the gun behind him, its rusted barrel scraping against the hardwood and producing a high-pitched squeal; it sounded eerie, menacing.

Ben Foley went calmly from bedroom to bedroom. Each time he got to one, he stood in the doorway, raised the rifle and took aim, gazing with indifference into the pleading eyes of those who loved him. Then, with the pinpoint accuracy of an expert marksman, he fired, extinguishing each life as if it meant nothing.

Nothing at all.

Earsplitting shots slapped at the air and traveled swiftly through the house, bouncing off walls, then moving outside, where they evaporated into the evening air.

In a matter of just a few minutes, Ben had done the unthinkable, wiping out his entire family, the ones who had nurtured and loved him all his young life.

Effortlessly.

When he was done, he walked back down the hallway toward his bedroom, calm, detached, as if nothing had ever happened. Then, almost dutifully, he stepped into his closet, closed the door and sat against the rear wall. Inserting the rigid metal barrel up into the roof of his mouth, he used his toe to engage the trigger. A muffled bang sounded off from inside the closet. And then there was silence.

Complete silence.

Unnatural stillness lingered afterward. The house, once filled with life, joy, and vitality, had been transformed into something different—a place of violence, of death.

There was blood—lots of it—spattered in all directions and in every corner; it covered the walls like chaotic graffiti. Bodies lay on the floor in freakish and unnatural positions, as if posed.

But that wasn't all that was left behind. Along with the carnage, the mess, the utter disarray, was also a question: *Why?*

Why would an eleven-year-old boy gun down his whole family, then kill himself?

Only one person knew.

Unfortunately, Ben Foley took that answer with him to his grave.

Chapter Eleven

Old Route 15
Faith, New Mexico

The neighborhood, once calm and quiet, became a storm of restless activity.

Blinding halogen lights bathed everything in a strange, icy glow, creating an almost theatrical presence. A twisting labyrinth of yellow crime tape wove in and out of trees and bushes, clinging precariously to anything that could hold it in place, encircling the perimeter like a giant tangle of snarled yarn.

News vans dotted both sides of the road. Before long, crews were set up, camped out and ready to go, in time for the early-morning newscasts.

The Foley murders were big news, not just for Faith but also for the state of New Mexico, and the media delighted in covering them. In industry jargon, this was a "sexy" story, one with every element to quench the public's insatiable thirst for the proverbial sex, drugs, and rock 'n' roll—something the stations eagerly sold, charging by the hour, dishing it out like soft-serve ice cream on a hot July day.

Suddenly, the neighborhood felt like a different place, the confusion driving the intensity to newer and higher levels. The accompanying sounds only added to the effect. A car door creaked open, then slammed. Radio chatter jammed the airwaves. A child cried.

All of it seemed surreal.

Closer to the house, a strange, haunting silence lingered thick in the air. The front door hung wide open, so far back on its hinges that it looked almost broken, a yellowy, incandescent light spilling out, bleeding into darkness. Beyond that were the locals—a crowd of them—gathered behind the tape, anxiously waiting and watching, their fearful eyes like mirrors reflecting tragedy.

~

6623 Hunter's Run
Faith, New Mexico

Three-seventeen a.m.

Cameron was wrestling his way through a fitful sleep when the phone rang.

Bentley reacted automatically with a single, sharp bark.

"Dawson," he said with a groan, his voice gritty and tight. Calls at this hour spelled trouble. He'd had his share of that for the past few days. He didn't need any more.

"Avello here," said the deputy.

"Yeah, Jim."

"We got problems, boss, big ones, over on Old Route 15, at the Foley house."

Cameron could now hear commotion in the background.

"The *Foleys*?"

"Yes, sir," Avello replied.

Cameron ran his palm over his face, then up toward his forehead, where he held it for a moment, still trying to get his bearings. "What's up at the Foleys'?"

"More like what went *down* at the Foleys'. Homicide, sheriff, times three."

"You've *got* to be kidding—"

"No joke, boss. It's bad…worst I've ever seen."

"Good Lord," Cameron said. "What the hell's going on around here?"

"Dunno, but you'll wanna come down here," Avello said, "and quick. Place is a madhouse. Crawling with news media…damned near all of 'em, looks like."

Cameron slammed the phone into its cradle and within minutes was fully dressed, out the door and on his way.

Chapter Twelve

Old Route 15
Faith, New Mexico

When Cameron arrived at the house, things were already in full swing and moving quickly toward unqualified chaos.

An on-scene deputy waved him through so he could enter the area. As he pulled up, a few overzealous news crews tried to catch up with him, running alongside the car, shouting and aiming their cameras directly into his windshield. Cameron had to shield his eyes to see where he was driving.

Deputy Chip Harkins met the sheriff as he stepped from his car.

"It's a massacre," he said, looking at Cameron, then at the house, then back at Cameron again. "Bodies everywhere. And blood…lots of blood."

Harkins was twenty-four years old and every bit as green as he appeared. A tight crew cut accentuated his boyish appearance, along with high cheekbones, awash in a flush of red—a good-looking kid by most anyone's standards, in a high-school-football-star-turned-local-cop sort of way. He'd joined the department less than a year before and seemed anxious to prove his worth.

"We know how all this started…or why?" Cameron asked as they reached the front of the house, stopping at the top of the steps.

Chip shook his head with more enthusiasm than the situation warranted. He was out of breath.

Cameron studied his eager expression, then poked his head through the doorway, peering down the foyer. He looked over the doorframe, following the weather stripping from one end to the other, searching for signs of a break-in, then leaned in closer, inspecting the locking mechanisms, careful not to touch them with his hands. "How 'bout a suspect?"

"Got one," said Chip, sticking a pen in his mouth and frantically flipping through the pages on his clipboard. "It's the son, Ben."

Cameron stopped what he was doing and felt the blood drain from his face. He looked up at Chip. "*Ben*? You're telling me *Ben Foley* is the cause of all this?"

"Hell, yeah…I mean…well, sure looks that way," Chip replied. He frowned. "You know the kid?"

"Ben, yeah, I knew him," Cameron said, sighing, nodding. "Coached his Little League team last summer."

"*Wow*," the junior deputy said, shaking his head.

Cameron stared at Chip again, then gazed up at the second floor as if it were harboring some kind of secret. Memories of the previous summer flashed through his mind: a balmy evening in a dusty parking lot at the Dairy Queen. Kids in soiled uniforms perched on tailgates, feet dangling as they celebrated victory. Laughing. Hurrying to finish ice cream cones that were quickly melting in their small hands. Ben was there, too.

Chip had been talking, but Cameron barely heard a word of it. He was pretty sure he hadn't missed much, catching only the tail end of a sentence. "You okay, boss?"

"Is he in custody? Ben?" Cameron finally said after returning to the present. He surveyed the area, then rubbed the back of his neck. "I'm gonna need to speak to him."

"He's dead, boss..."

Cameron flinched.

"Killed himself. He's still in there. Hey, you gonna be okay?" Chip asked, cocking his head and trying to make eye contact with his boss.

Cameron nodded but didn't look back at Chip. Instead, he stared into the front entryway, wondering how the boy he'd taught to catch a fly ball could turn cold-blooded murderer.

Ben Foley a killer? Not even close.

Chapter Thirteen

Old Route 15
Faith, New Mexico

Cameron passed through the front door, careful not to touch or disturb anything while trying to absorb his surroundings.

He stopped at the bottom of the staircase and took a deep, steady breath.

Climbing the steps, he looked down and scrutinized every inch he traveled, knowing even the smallest bit of evidence could turn out to be a big break. But when he reached the top, he got far more than he'd expected: stamped across the floor were small, bloody footprints that went past him, then vanished down the dimly lit hall. A *child's footprints*, he thought, knowing they probably belonged to Ben. A sudden wave of nausea began to arc through him while thinking about the eleven-year-old boy, walking through the house, tracking his slain family's blood on his feet.

Entering the parents' room was like stepping out of one nightmare and into another. The scene was a bloody battlefield—bodies lying tossed about like rag dolls, walls perforated with bullet holes, the mattress a giant sponge for all the blood.

No matter how hard he tried, Cameron still had trouble envisioning Ben Foley—the unassuming kid with a big heart and even bigger smile—as the one responsible for the massacre before him.

"Looks like the dad took the first shot," said Deputy Jim Avello from behind, surprising Cameron. "Probably never even knew what was coming. His head never left the pillow."

Cameron turned around, studied the deputy's face for a moment, then gazed back toward the victims. "I suppose that's for the best."

"Doesn't appear the mom was so lucky. I'm guessing she woke up when she heard the gunfire. See how she's lying across her husband's lower legs?" Avello asked, running a pointed finger back and forth to illustrate direction. "Threw herself over him out of pure instinct…tried to protect him."

"It would make sense," Cameron agreed, kneeling down by the bed to take a closer look at the gunshot wounds, "since the bullets look like they entered through the right side of her body."

"Not much of a payoff—they both ended up dying."

Cameron shook his head. "I don't think she was looking for a payoff."

"I mean in terms of saving her husband's life."

"What about a make on a weapon? Got one yet?"

Avello walked over and stood beside him, staring at the bodies. "A 30/30 lever action of some sort, looks like. Gun's in the closet with the boy, but you can tell just by the number of shots fired. With a bolt action, it would have taken too long to chamber the rounds."

"And required more strength than Ben probably had, considering his build," Cameron added. "He wouldn't have been able to operate it quickly enough to deliver that kind of power in such a short period of time."

"You can get all the specifics—make and model—once you check the boy. I didn't get close enough to look." Avello frowned. "Left the honors for you."

Cameron caught his gaze and nodded but said nothing.

"The picture's not much better down the hall," Avello added. "You have a little girl in the first bedroom. Then farther down is the boy's room."

As soon as Cameron crossed the threshold into the girl's bedroom, he stopped abruptly and stared, dazed. The child was sprawled on the floor, facedown, arms splayed out in front of her. To him it seemed suggestive of fear, panic, or both. A puddle of blood converged around her head and drenched her hair, with the nightgown she wore sopping up the rest.

It appeared that Ben's sister had been awake just before he gunned her down. Cameron theorized she'd woken up to the sound of gunfire coming from her parents' bedroom, then, before she could do anything, saw her brother standing in the doorway aiming the rifle at her. From there, she probably jumped off the bed and tried to get away. Cameron wondered what went through the poor child's mind when she saw her brother's face at the end of that long metal barrel.

Her bedroom had all the requisite heartbreaking little-girl things one might expect. A collection of dolls. Posters of the boy-band flavor of the week. A series of award ribbons for scholastic achievement.

Cameron took a few steps toward her desk, just a couple of feet from the bed. A picture frame sat on top, decorated with a colorful array of circus clowns and balloons. He pulled a pair of latex gloves from his pocket, snapped them onto his wrists, then held the picture in his hands. *A beautiful child*, he thought—milky white complexion, eyes bright and cheerful, and head tilted sideways. Big smile for the camera, almost to the point of silliness. Cameron realized she looked nothing like her brother. He had brown hair and darker skin—she, blonde with fair features, appearing to be around five or six.

The same age his own son had been.

He dismissed the thought, leaving the girl's room and moving to the end of the hall, toward Ben's bedroom, farther down on the opposite side.

Once inside, Cameron paused and stared at the closet door. He stepped up to it, then placed his hand around the thinnest outer edges of the knob so as not to disturb any prints on the front or back sides. Giving the door a gentle tug, he pulled it open.

Ben Foley lay in the corner, crumpled up like a pile of dirty laundry. The sight wasn't just tragic, it was revolting. Blood saturated the carpet beneath him, turning it a deep shade of red. Right beside him was the gun, a Winchester Rifleman, and—just as Avello had called it—a .30/30 caliber.

The impact from the blast had probably slammed Ben against the rear wall. From there, he likely plummeted forward, chin tucked against his chest as he flipped sideways, leaving the body strangely contorted on the floor.

For Cameron, no matter how many times he'd seen death, smelled it and touched it, each time, it seemed just as familiar, just as vivid, and worst of all, just as unsettling as the last. As much as he wished it would, the ugliness never faded.

Cameron stepped away from the closet and turned his attention to the rest of Ben's room. All around were signs of a burgeoning adolescence beginning to take shape. It seemed a contradiction of sorts, a typical representation of a boy passing from childhood into his early teens—still a lot of little-boy things, but also signs of approaching pubescence. The baseball memorabilia was falling away, becoming upstaged now by his new heroes, the ones holding electric guitars instead of baseball bats. It seemed Ben had bypassed the rap scene in favor of heavy metal. Posters hung along the walls featuring his favorite groups: Mary's Stepchild, Revenge, and Daily Spawn. Typical kid stuff, he figured, a boy struggling to find his way in the world, searching for something to which he could relate.

Cameron walked over to Ben's dresser and began pulling out drawers. After removing the clothing, he looked inside, searching for false bottoms, then he held them up and looked underneath; these are common places kids often use to conceal contraband, but there was none. He walked over to the stereo speakers positioned on the floor and removed the cloth grills, shining a flashlight through to the hollow spaces inside, but again, nothing was there.

~

The sun was beginning to rise as Cameron headed out the front door. It imbued the air with warm, orange-hued rays of light, almost as if washing away the lingering negative energy surrounding the place.

Almost, but not quite.

Except for a few stray reporters and their crews still wrapping things up and some deputies, things were beginning to settle down into a dull hum. The curious onlookers had finally gone to bed, probably exhausted by what they'd seen.

About twenty feet from the house, Cameron stopped and turned around to take in the scene. A gloomy cloud of uncertainty had wandered not only over the Foley house but also over the entire town of Faith, casting its shadow, leaving everything unsettled, uneasy, and—worst of all—unsaid.

Five murders and one suicide in just a few days—all in a town that, before this, had never seen even one suspicious death. A deputy lay dead, the victim of a sadistic murder. Next, a teacher slaughtered like a piece of meat while she was still alive. Now, Ben Foley, a boy who had appeared as normal as could be, had waged bloody war on his entire family before ending his own life.

What the hell is happening to this town?

Cameron turned away from the house, trying to do the same with his mind, then felt his past catching up with him again, paying yet another unwelcome visit. He'd moved back to Faith so he could come home, start anew and forget the pain he thought he'd left behind.

But it seemed that the harder he tried to resist or ignore it, the harder it seemed to come right back at him, lingering, much like a bad stain. Every time he saw someone's life come to a tragic end, it was just like going back and reliving that horrible day all over again.

Cameron was learning that the past is a lot like a shadow on the ground behind you. Just because you can't see it doesn't mean it's not still there.

Chapter Fourteen

Abrams Medical Center
Albuquerque, New Mexico

Kyle Bancroft was examining a patient at her Albuquerque office. That was when it started.

A torrent of images blew through her mind at warp speed, each one leaping over the next, like bending back the pages in a book, releasing them, then watching them flutter down. Some passed as nothing more than a blur, while others looked like amateur video—a grainy quality—random, dark, unstable. The lens would zoom in on something, then abruptly jerk elsewhere. She could barely keep up with it all.

But they weren't all that way. In fact, some were just the opposite, so vivid, so real, that Kyle could almost reach out and grab them. Unfortunately, those were the ones she could have done without.

Panic breaking out everywhere. Feet pounding frantically across a convulsing floor. People scattering in all directions. It was unparalleled hysteria, and it was everywhere, like a herd of animals running for their lives. Only these didn't look like animals; these were humans.

From whom or what were they all running?

If the pictures weren't enough to unnerve her, the blaring racket surely would. Just as indiscriminate as the images, it would start loud and clear, then cut out intermittently, like a stereo with a faulty wire.

ON-OFF-ON-OFF.

Kyle thought she'd heard screams but couldn't be sure. The noise kept rising to ear-splitting levels, then falling, making it hard to distinguish. Bits and pieces of sound—they were everywhere—exploding in her ears. Intense and rhythmic, the vibrations resonated throughout her body. She could feel them in her bones, her throat, and inside her head too, like the pounding of a drum, incessant and brutal.

With each passing moment, the experience grew even more intense. Soon the vibrations gave way to a forceful rattle, becoming so powerful it almost knocked Kyle right off her feet.

Then it was all gone. Vanished. Swallowed by silence.

But the unexpected calm offered little comfort for Kyle. After all the noise, the confusion, she felt smothered by the stillness.

"You okay, doc?" It was her patient, twenty-three-year-old Amanda Shively. She'd noticed Kyle's face had turned a ghostly shade of white.

"Yeah, fine. Just dizzy for a moment is all," Kyle replied, blinking hard a few times and forcing a less-than-convincing smile.

Then it started again.

Thundering, quaking sensations charged through her body with the speed and intensity of a fast-moving locomotive. The images returned as well, now flickering at an even more hurried rate than before and brighter too—it reminded Kyle of a film projector spinning out of control.

Flip, flip, flip—they just kept coming.

Kyle flinched. The visuals were more violent now.

A woman lay on the ground, curled into a ball, a halo of blood surrounding her head. Even more blood trailed past her, smeared across the floor—a child's finger-painting—in shades of crimson.

And silence again.

"Doc?"

Kyle looked at her patient, puzzled, as if seeing her for the very first time. To Amanda, the doctor appeared disoriented. Kyle's voice was soft and breathy. "Can you excuse me for just a moment, Amanda?"

"Sure thing. You gonna be okay?"

Kyle ignored the question, stumbling toward the door then out into the hallway and toward her office.

Once inside, she dropped into a chair, letting her face fall into her hands. A few stray images still flickered in her head, but much slower now, almost as if nearing the end of the film reel. She sat completely still for a moment, face still buried in hands, trembling, allowing whatever was in control of her mind to run its course.

A few seconds later, it was all gone.

Cautiously, she looked up to make sure everything had really stopped this time. All she could hear was a distant and faint ringing. Kyle scanned the top of her desk, spotted a half-filled water bottle, grabbed at it. She began pouring it greedily down her throat as if she hadn't had any in days, squeezing the sides so hard that it began to collapse inward. After finishing, she placed it down, spread her fingers apart, and stared at them; she could *see* her pulse pounding through the tips.

Her mind had ground to a halt, but her body was still reeling.

Kyle knew what was happening. She'd experienced this before, but nothing quite so powerful. Intense, yes, but overwhelming and incapacitating? Never.

For as long as she could remember, images had often dropped into her head as if from nowhere. Like scattering raindrops—some she caught, others fell past. Usually, however, it would be one or two, not hundreds, not like this. Often, the visions revealed things about to occur or ones that already had, but again, never in such a disruptive or unsettling manner.

This time she couldn't ignore it.

This time it meant business.

Kyle hurried from her office and across the hall, sneaking into the bathroom. Once there, she grabbed on to the sink as if it were the only thing keeping her upright.

"Jeez, Kyle, you look like hell," she said, barely recognizing the reflection staring back in the mirror.

She ripped a handful of paper towels from the dispenser, ran them under the faucet, then pressed them against her face. The coolness felt wonderful on her skin. Kyle sighed as relief passed through her. She felt close to normal again.

Almost.

The only question now: How would she explain her strange behavior to her patient?

Chapter Fifteen

Office of the Medical Investigator
Albuquerque, New Mexico

Ben Foley's remains lay on a stainless steel autopsy table. The child-size body bag surrounded him like a cocoon, zipped tight and topped off with a tamper-proof tie seal. He was nothing more than a number now, one scribbled across the white plastic with a dark marker.

Cameron just stared at it.

It was hard to believe someone so small could inflict harm on such a large scale. *So tiny, so fragile,* he thought, *so broken.* Had he not known better, he could just as easily have mistaken Ben for the victim.

All autopsies in the state of New Mexico came to the Office of the Medical Investigator, located at the University of New Mexico School of Medicine in Albuquerque. For Cameron, that meant a three-hour-plus trip. Although he didn't normally attend autopsies, he knew he couldn't afford to miss this one. Too much was riding on it.

Now he stood at the head of the table observing, along with Assistant Chief Medical Investigator Russell Gavin standing at the broadside, and his assistant, Shelia Murphy, to his left. A microphone dangled loosely overhead to record the doctor's comments while he performed the autopsy.

Cameron shifted his attention away from Ben's body and around the room, but the picture there wasn't much better; in fact, in some ways, it seemed worse—three other bodies lay off to his right, two more on the left, each in various stages of examination…and decomposition.

Without thinking, Cameron breathed in deeply, then realized it was not the best idea, as a strong odor of ammonia, blood, and decaying flesh filled his lungs. He forced the air out quickly, turning his attention back to Ben, back to the body of an eleven-year-old killer.

Investigators had removed his clothing at the scene, bagged and tagged as evidence. All lint, fibers, or other substances that had managed to cling to it would be collected and catalogued for the investigation.

Cameron was intent on staying professional, on not letting memories and feelings from his past cloud his thinking about this case. It wasn't that he didn't think about what had happened to his son—that was with him all the time. It was that he couldn't allow it to intrude.

"Ready, doctor?" Sheila asked.

Gavin nodded. He cut the seal on the bag, drew the zipper down toward the bottom, and reached into the opening with both hands. Working from top to bottom, he pulled the two sides apart.

If Cameron thought seeing Ben's body in the closet had been the worst of it, he was in for a rude surprise; this topped it. Before, in the dimly lit closet, the boy had been crouched down, his body oddly twisted, and a good part of it barely visible. Now, laid out flat under the bright fluorescent light, there was nothing left for the imagination—it was all right there in front of him. Ben's body was coated in a layer of dried blood, everywhere, and in some spots, caked thickly.

Standing only inches away, Cameron could see with alarming clarity the kind of damage a .30/30 round can do when it intersects with flesh and bone. The gun blast had blown the back of Ben's head apart, shattering the skull like an eggshell. This caused the facial features to collapse, leaving them spongy and unrecognizable. Scattered across his face were cuts and bruises, the heaviest of which were on the right forehead, nose, and left cheek. Cameron studied the cracked stretch marks on the boy's lips. He knew expanding gases from the gun barrel had caused them when it went off inside his mouth.

The odor took things a step further—it reminded Cameron of rotting meat. Not only could he smell it in the air, he could taste it on his tongue. Cameron swallowed hard, trying to fight back his nausea, felt a tingling sensation in the pit of stomach as it began to churn.

Gavin spoke suddenly, his voice much louder than seemed necessary considering the intimate surroundings. "The body is that of a white male, appearing consistent with the stated age of eleven years. Four foot one, eighty-five pounds, with a birthmark observed in the small of the back, approximately a half inch in diameter. No other identifying marks or features."

Using his fingers, the doctor reached into Ben's mouth and pulled it open easily, helped by the gun's powerful discharge—it had broken the lower jaw, leaving it hanging loose. Then he lowered his head and looked inside. "There's extensive destruction to the oral cavity, with the hard palate nearly gone. Several attached molars show a grayish-black soot deposition, and the tongue is covered with multiple purple contusions ranging from one-eighth to one-half an inch at its lateral aspects."

The doctor pulled his hand away, and the mouth remained open. He closed it and examined the rest of Ben's body, lifting the arms and checking a few other less exposed areas. "There do not appear to be any other signs of injury or damage to the body's exterior."

He stepped back an inch or two and frowned, staring at Ben's body for a moment. Then Sheila moved in and placed a body block under Ben's spine, causing the arms, head, and neck to fall back and the chest to protrude forward, making it easier for the doctor to cut his incisions.

Using a scalpel, Gavin made a deep, V-shaped cut going from shoulder to shoulder, then another that cut vertically, looping around the navel and continuing on toward the pubic bone. He pulled the two chest flaps open, immediately launching an even more potent odor into the air, a combination of human feces, trapped gas…and more blood.

Oblivious to Cameron's discomfort, the doctor went to work immediately and began by inserting a syringe into the ascending aorta to extract blood samples. He would do the same with the bladder, in much the same manner, only this time removing urine samples. Both would be sent off to the lab for analysis to see if Ben had any drugs in his system or an illness relevant to the case.

After that, one by one, he began removing and inspecting organs. Later, in the interest of saving time, he would weigh them all at once.

"The heart appears to be free of abnormalities," Gavin said, "as do the lungs, intestines, liver, and spleen."

He removed the stomach, which he placed on an adjacent table. After dumping its gray, soupy contents into a plastic measuring cup, the doctor began the dissection process. Suddenly, he stopped.

"See that?" he said to his assistant, still looking down, pointing.

Sheila leaned over with interest. "Yep…sure do."

Gavin directed his voice toward the microphone. "The gastric mucosa reveals extensive ulcerations along the greater curvature of the stomach."

Cameron leaned in, trying to figure out what was happening.

Gavin, catching this, looked over at him to explain. "Although possible, the condition isn't common in a child his age. We're going to have to do some further microscopic evaluation here."

Cameron responded with a nod.

The doctor turned back toward the body and began taking small tissue samples from the stomach, placing them into small, plastic containers.

After examining the remaining trunk organs, Gavin nodded to Sheila, who moved the body block up a few inches toward the back of the neck.

There was no need to cut the skull open—the rifle round had done that work for him, shattering the back of Ben's head, leaving the insides in plain view. After making a few small incisions, the doctor grabbed on to the scalp, then peeled the face flap down and away from the skull, much like a latex mask. He examined the underlying bony surface, then moved toward the back of the head.

The force from the gun blast had obliterated most of the brain, transforming it instantly into pulp and bone fragments. Using a gloved hand, the doctor reached in and scraped out the soggy, mashed contents. After that, he scooped them into a weighing pan, where he examined them.

Gavin continued calmly. "The cerebellum and brain stem are largely intact, as are portions of the posterior occipital lobes. The calvarium is extensively fractured. The remaining brain fragments are a pulverized, gelatinous, and partly clotted subdural mass—about ten milliliters' worth."

He stepped back. "Cause of death: intraoral gunshot wound to the head. Manner of death: suicide."

He walked to the head of the table where Cameron stood, removing the latex gloves from his fingers as he spoke. "The toxicology tests normally take several weeks."

Cameron nodded, still staring at the body. "Those stomach ulcers you mentioned...you said they're not normal."

"Ulcers in children, while not entirely common, do occur, but the vast majority of patients are adults."

"Meaning?"

"Meaning, the most common cause of ulcers in adults is *H. pylori*, or *Helicobacter pylori*, a bacterium often associated with peptic ulcers. Of course, we also see them in people who abuse alcohol or crystal meth."

"But in kids?"

"In kids it's different. Theirs tend to be more of a gastric nature, often brought on by certain medications. Do you know if the boy had been taking any, or if he'd been previously diagnosed as having stomach ulcers?"

Cameron shook his head.

The doctor shrugged. "No worries. The tox screen will tell us if he'd been taking anything, and I'll have a look at his medical records to see if he had a history of stomach ulcers as well. Easy enough to find out."

"What kinds of medications would cause them?"

"Most common are the anti-inflammatory drugs—over-the-counter meds—things like ibuprofen or aspirin and a few others."

"So if Ben was taking aspirin or some other pain reliever, they could have given him the ulcers?"

"Not necessarily," the doctor said, shaking his head. "Not if he was just taking them on isolated occasions. Now, if he'd been popping them like Tic Tacs—well, *then* we'd have cause to be suspicious, but ulcers as widespread as what he had? A few days' worth of use isn't going to do it. Those look pretty severe. It takes *a lot* of something over a *long* time to cause that."

"But what that something is we don't know yet, right?" Cameron asked.

"Not until we get the toxicology results," Gavin repeated patiently.

"Anything else that could've caused them?"

"Hypothermia can produce a condition that resembles ulcers," Gavin said, rubbing his chin while thinking aloud, "but not much chance of that happening this time of year, and certainly not in *this* situation. Besides, those kinds of hemorrhages look smaller, and Ben's are much larger."

Cameron looked up toward the ceiling, thinking. "You know, come to think of it, I don't remember Ben having any sort of medical condition. I was his Little League coach—all team members had to get physicals in order to play. I would have been told if he did."

"I'll double-check his medical records, just on the slight chance it got past you, and the lab will take a closer look at those ulcers under a microscope, as well. We should be able to come up with some answers."

Answers, Cameron thought as he left the building and headed toward his car—the autopsy hadn't provided any. It had only raised more questions.

He was getting used to that.

Dead men tell no tales. Cameron shook his head. *But what about boys? Tell me, Ben—tell me what really happened that night...*

And while you're at it, tell me...what's happening to this town?

Chapter Sixteen

Sheriff's Station
Faith, New Mexico

When it came right down to it, Faith's top cop, Frank Donato, was a no-nonsense, no-frills sort of guy. That notion seemed obvious, judging by his office decor—or lack thereof. Defying any sense of comfort or style, it lent itself to the bare-bones school of design. No feng shui here.

Back in the day, the walls were probably a cheery mustard color. Not anymore. Years of soot and grime had left their mark, leaving them a shade or two past the tune of dried egg yolk. Adding to the overall mood were tattered metal blinds hanging slightly lopsided in a solitary window, slats bent and buckled, along with a thick coating of dust. On a bright day, the sun poked through them, striping the dusty air with intense light and giving the word *filthy* completely new meaning.

Frank reached into his drawer and grabbed a roll of antacids. Using his teeth, he pried one loose, then began gnashing on it.

He looked up at Cameron. He wasn't pleased.

"So tell me," he said, still chewing as he spoke. "With human carnage becoming a normal part of the landscape around here,

I'm feeling a bit confused—exactly how does Ben Foley fit into all this?"

"He doesn't," Cameron said, lowering himself into a chair across from his boss with an accompanying sigh. "That's the problem. Nothing does."

"I thought we were getting closer to having things figured out."

"Not since the Foley murders. They changed everything."

Frank leaned back, and his chair complained with a loud squeak. He crossed his arms and looked at Cameron. "Okay, amigo, now's the time for some good old-fashioned detective work. Thoughts?"

"On the slight chance these could be nothing more than isolated coincidences—"

"Hold on," Frank said, with an expression that mixed frustration and sarcasm. "Isolated is one thing. But coincidence? Doubt it. This *is* Faith we're talking about, right? Five murders here would be about as coincidental as a turd in a shithouse."

Cameron cringed at the parallel but allowed the theory. "Okay, going with the idea they're isolated, then, we already have two killers, right? How 'bout a third?"

"Ryan kills Alma. Ben kills his family…so who killed Witherspoon?"

"*That's* the question."

"And the answer?"

"Your turn. You tell me."

"Okay," Frank said, "try this one on for size: What if they *are* all related? What if Ben and Ryan were working together? You hear stories about it…kids going on murder sprees."

"Sounds like a bad episode of prime-time TV," Cameron said. "Oh, and while we're there, the news media's back in town. In full force."

"We can thank Ben Foley for that one. It's a surefire way to get the talking heads down here flapping their yaks."

"The yaks were flapping all right. You'd've thought their jaws were on fire."

Frank shifted in his chair, shifting his thoughts. "How 'bout Foley's autopsy? Anything new there?"

"Preliminary toxicology report came back this morning. Negative for controlled substances."

"Interesting…"

"Yep. The boy was clean."

"So we know he wasn't high, just garden-variety crazy."

Cameron wasn't sure if Frank meant it as a joke or an observation. "There *was* one thing unusual. Ben's stomach—it was covered with ulcers."

He caught on right away. "That's kinda strange. Kids ever get those?"

"Medical investigator says they can, but not the same way adults do. Usually it's from a reaction to medications."

"Medications? What kind?"

"Taking a lot of the over-the-counter anti-inflammatory drugs'll do it."

"So the kid maybe had, like, an Excedrin headache?"

"No, not exactly. He needed to be swallowing a helluva lot of 'em over a long period of time to cause the kind of damage he had."

"But we know that wasn't the case, since the tox screen came up negative. Right?"

"Yes and no. The test is preliminary," Cameron cautioned. "It only screens for the presence of alcohol or drugs, and only in a general sense. Takes longer for the specifics. But even so, if he took 'em a long time ago, chances are they wouldn't show up now, anyway."

Frank grunted his displeasure, thought for a few seconds. "ME got any theories about what else might've caused 'em?"

"Threw out a few other scenarios. Seemed unlikely."

"So, in a word, nothing."

"No. Not right now, at least. He *is* checking on Ben's medical history to see if he had some sort of preexisting condition. That might explain it."

"Okay," Frank said. "So we have a kid who wasn't high, had no detectable illness other than stomach ulcers—which, by the way, we have no idea where they came from—who suddenly wakes up one night and decides to off his entire family, *then* himself? I'm not buying it." He shook his head, put on his glasses, scanned a few pages of the report. Then he looked back at Cameron over the tops of his lenses. "You knew this kid?"

"Thought I did..."

"How well?"

"Enough to know he wasn't a killer."

Frank removed the glasses, gazed out his window. The bright sunlight made him squint. "Well, no disrespect to your judgment, but we've got three bodies lying across town in a morgue who'd like to tell you otherwise."

Frank was right. There was no denying that.

"What about at the house?" he asked. "Anything *at all* there to indicate why he might've done it?"

Cameron threw up his hands. "If the kid was hiding a secret, he was doing a damn good job of it."

"Okay, so tell me this: How do we get from point A to point C? Something's missing here, and I don't like it."

"Not exactly thrilled about it myself, Frank. From all accounts, the kid was well mannered and well behaved. Never got into a lick of trouble in school *or* back at home, just like Churchill."

"Just like Churchill..." Frank said, contemplating the similarities. "Same shit, different shovel, except that's really the only connection we have between the two, and it isn't much of one. How about the family?"

Cameron shrugged. "That's where the similarities end. Ryan came from a broken home. His grandmother raised him."

"Oh yeah? How'd that go?"

"Not very well. Had a chat with her, a real piece of work Bobbi Kimmons is. Did her best, but kinda get the feeling she starved the kid where genuine affection was concerned."

"And Ben's family?"

"Complete opposite. About as normal and nice as they come. Spoke to them several times last summer during Little League." He let out a humorless laugh. "Get this—they were actually concerned he wasn't aggressive enough for contact sports, too shy, too reserved."

"He obviously overcame *that* problem," Frank said, "with flying colors."

Cameron shook his head. "I know one thing—from where I stand, the kid didn't have it in him."

"So then why'd he do it?"

"The answer's out there somewhere," Cameron said, standing up. "I'm gonna go have a talk with his teacher."

Frank crooked an eyebrow. "Think she knows something?"

"Not sure. But I do: she was the last person to see him alive—at least the only one who's still here to talk about it—and that's gotta count for something."

Chapter Seventeen

Eisenhower Middle School
Faith, New Mexico

Susan Swift was grading papers at her desk when Cameron walked into the classroom.

"Sheriff Dawson, please come in." She stood up behind her desk and reached across it to shake his hand. Everything about her—although quietly stated—reflected a well-bred quality, something hard to replicate if you weren't born into it. She wore a navy button-down sweater draped loosely over her shoulders.

Cameron scanned the room for an adult-size chair, a rare find in those settings, and spotted one in the corner. "Thanks for meeting with me," he said, grabbing and bringing it to the front of her desk.

"I'm afraid I don't know if I can offer you anything useful," she said, her voice wavering a bit, "but I'm happy to help any way I can."

Cameron nodded, sat down.

After a moment of silent contemplation, she said, "We're having a difficult time coping with what's happened here, teachers, the kids…everyone."

"One student dead, another missing...and a teacher...murdered. It's a lot to take in."

"Alma..." Susan said, shivering, as if a cold draft had just blown into the room. She pulled her sweater closer over her shoulders, shook her head with sadness.

Sensing her discomfort, Cameron cleared his throat and slid the pad from his shirt pocket. "I know all this is difficult, but unfortunately there's no way to avoid it. I hope you can bear with me."

"Of course," Susan said, nodding and staring vacantly at the stack of papers on her desk.

"What I need to know is if you saw any significant changes in Ben's behavior before all this happened. Did he seem bothered by anything? Agitated in any way?"

"No," she said. "Not that I could see."

"How about signs of violence or aggression? Ever see Ben show any?"

"*Goodness*, no." She reached for the top button on her blouse and fumbled with it. "Ben wasn't a confrontational kid at all. I don't think I *ever* saw him angry...about anything."

"What about the day of the murders?" Cameron asked. "Observe anything unusual?"

"No. Same as always. The quiet kid we all knew," Susan said, her voice trailing off. She paused, then added, "Maybe a little more subdued than usual, but that was because of the flu."

"The flu?"

"Yeah. He was coming down with a case."

Cameron crossed his legs and started writing. "Can you tell me more about that?"

She shrugged. "Nothing unusual, really. You know how kids are. They're always catching things."

He flipped a page and continued taking notes. "Symptoms?"

"Said he had a sore throat, that he felt achy." She stopped to think, chin in the palm of her hand, elbow resting on her desk.

"His nose was runny too, and he seemed feverish. You know, typical symptoms."

"Observe anything else?"

"No, just a bit quieter than usual, is all," she said.

"Something bothering him?"

"I'm more inclined to think it was because he didn't feel well. I ended up sending him home."

Cameron stopped writing and looked up at Susan. "What time was that?"

"Oh…" she said, gazing at the clock. "I'd say it was around two-ish."

"Who came and got him?"

"His mom. She usually does every…" Susan stopped herself, shook her head. "Sorry. I meant she *did*…anyway, she picked him up about an hour earlier than usual. It was late when he started feeling ill. I could have just kept him here, but I started getting worried. He was looking pretty awful."

"How so?"

"Pale. And I could tell he was feverish just by looking at him. Perspiring, too, with the chills. Flu symptoms are like that, you know—they tend to come on pretty fast."

Cameron looked up at her from his notes and nodded. "Any other kids come down with similar symptoms, before or after Ben?"

"No. I was worried about that. Usually one of them brings a bug into the classroom, and before you know it, everyone has it. I was hoping to dodge that one by sending him home right away."

"How 'bout his home life? He say anything to you during the day, or even previously? Any problems going on there?"

"I don't think so. Ben just wasn't that kind of kid. In fact, I doubt I ever saw him upset about anything. Shy, yes, but he always seemed happy, content. You know?"

Cameron nodded. He did know, firsthand. "What about classmates—problems with any of them at all?"

"None that I'm aware of," Susan said. "Ben was pretty quiet most of the time, kept to himself, almost like he tried to make himself invisible."

"Invisible?"

"Perhaps that's the wrong word. Let me rephrase: he did his best to stay out of everyone's way, didn't *want* to be noticed..." She stopped, thoughtful. "Like he was always lingering somewhere off in the background? But no, never any problems with other students, not as far as I could tell, anyway. Seemed most of the time they hardly even noticed he was there."

"A loner," Cameron suggested.

"Well, yes. Except I hate to use that terminology. Has such negative connotations."

"What about friends? Who'd he hang out with? Meet anyone new recently?"

"No. Like I said, he kept to himself—didn't seem to have many friends."

"Many—or *any*?"

She reconsidered, then shrugged. "I guess *any*, from what I observed. Now, outside of here—that may have been another story. Really, I don't know what his social life was like once school let out."

"What about his parents? Had you met them?"

"Oh, yes. Several times. Open house, PTA. You know. Things like that."

"Impressions?"

She shrugged. "Very, *very* nice people. I spoke with them once or twice about Ben's shyness, how I was trying to help him overcome that. They seemed appreciative...grateful that I wanted to help him."

"Concerned," Cameron confirmed.

"Very much so."

He paused, nodding, thinking. "I know Ben was a quiet kid, but had he shown any sort of fascination with violence lately?"

"No. Not anything I could see."

"Not even with things on TV…movies…music, even?" Cameron asked. "Kids are exposed to a lot these days."

"Yeah, I know what you're saying…" She bit her lower lip. "But see, I'm trying to think of how to best explain this. You have to understand something: I've been dealing with kids almost every day for the past six years. You start to recognize the troubled ones. It becomes second nature for teachers. If Ben had any problems, I think I would have noticed. He just didn't. He was a very considerate, sweet child."

A considerate, sweet child who gunned down his entire family and then himself, Cameron thought and then realized he'd had similar notions about Ryan Churchill.

Susan was still talking. "I know that sounds crazy in light of what he did, but that's how he always seemed around here."

"Okay," Cameron said, moving on. "What about schoolwork? Any problems there?"

"Ben had a little trouble grasping things at times. I attribute that…or I *attributed* it, rather…to his shyness. I got the impression he was afraid to speak up, ask questions and get involved in class discussions. As I said, I was trying to help him with that. His grades weren't exemplary, but they were acceptable. I always felt he had the ability to do better, though. He just needed to step a bit farther out of his shell."

He'd done that, Cameron thought, only had gone *much* too far. It wasn't adding up; there had to be more. He flipped his notebook cover, then stood up. "You've been a lot of help, Miss Swift. Thank you taking the time. I know it isn't easy."

"I'm happy to help," she said.

"If anything else comes to mind—"

"I'll be sure and come by or call."

"I'd sure appreciate it."

As they walked together toward the door, Susan appeared to be struggling with something, then stopped. "Look, it's probably not my place to say this."

"Go right ahead," he urged.

She paused, sighed. "I don't know what came over Ben that day to make him do what he did—I honestly don't—but I can't help but feel someone or *something* must have influenced him. Quiet, well-mannered children don't just wake up one day, murder their families, then kill themselves. Look…you and I both know Ben was *not* a violent kid, and I think we're both qualified to say that. There just *has* to be more to this."

More to this…Susan Swift's words were still echoing inside Cameron's head as he turned the key to his ignition. Then he thought about what she'd said before that: *someone or something must have influenced him*.

Someone else? He'd thought about Ryan but had never considered it further. And other than Ben and his family, there was no evidence of anyone else in the house. Still, he wondered about outside influences—could someone *somehow* have manipulated him into murdering his family? Did he go into that closet to kill himself because of the guilt he'd suffered afterward? Possible, but again, not a shred of evidence to prove it.

All he knew was that up until the murders, Ben showed no signs of anger or hostility and had no inclination whatsoever toward violence.

Good kid on the outside, but inside—*that* seemed to be a completely different story.

Just like Ryan.

Chapter Eighteen

45687 Monument Path Way
Albuquerque, New Mexico

A thick stench charged the air, a vile combination of urine and perspiration that lingered, growing stronger with each passing minute.

Kyle stood before an elongated hallway; it went on for what seemed like forever. At certain moments, the walls looked so white they were nearly blinding.

Stainless steel gurneys sat parked along the narrow corridors, one for every door, each containing a wafer-thin mattress. She gazed down the hall at all of them lined up so neatly in a row, like a traffic jam made up of shining mirrors, each one reflecting onto the next.

The whole place had a hollow, abandoned quality, one she could feel lurking behind every corner—an anxiety-producing aura thick as gutter mud and just as dirty.

Then there were the sounds, an endless array of throaty, guttural moans that seemed to come from nowhere and echoed down the cavernous corridors, almost as if bleeding through the walls; they filled the air, playing out like some eerie, torturous symphony.

Even the lighting flooded the air oddly, covering everything like a thick, soupy vapor—a yellowy haze, drifting apart, then multiplying like resinous smoke.

Kyle was lost in some sort of otherworld.

Just then, she felt a presence over her shoulder, as if someone had walked past her. A rush of cold air danced down the back of her neck, making the tiny hairs along it quiver. A voice, high-pitched and raspy, spoke softly into her ear. It was thin, barely above a whisper. A child's voice: "Empty hearts, empty souls."

Startled, Kyle spun around, but nobody was there.

A chill shot up her spine. She turned back again, only to find a pair of sallow, green eyes bathed in a milky film, staring directly into hers.

The dream was so disturbing, so vivid, it shook Kyle right out of her sleep. Lines of sweat raced down her cheeks, and her nightshirt was soaked. Her body was raging like a furnace, even though her skin felt ice cold to the touch.

It was happening again.

Just as she reached to turn on the lamp, the bulb popped, exploding into a big bright flash of light, then went dark. She fumbled her way to the wall switch, turned on the lights and peered at the alarm clock: three a.m.

Kyle was accustomed to the dreams. She'd been having them since she was a little girl, but these seemed different, more powerful.

"It's a gift," her mother told her when she was young. "A gift from God." She, too, had the gift.

"Like a present, Mommy? A birthday present?" Little Kyle's brown eyes widened.

"Something like that, except it doesn't come with pretty wrapping and a bow. Presents from God don't come that way."

Kyle glanced down at her tiny folded hands, then up to her mother, shrugging the way little girls sometimes do. "A present without wrapping paper?"

She pushed Kyle's little nose and smiled. "You'll understand it better as you become older, but for now, just know it's nothing to be afraid of. It's a good thing."

"Why did God give it to me?" she persisted.

Her mother placed a gentle hand on Kyle's shoulder. Her voice sounded confident, reassuring. "So you can help people."

"Help them how?"

She paused for a moment, trying to figure out how to explain such a complex idea to such a young girl. "Let me see." She gazed up toward the sky. "Let's say a good friend of yours from school..."

"Like William?" Kyle asked eagerly.

Her mother raised her eyebrows and nodded. "Yeah, okay, like William. Say he was going to make a bad decision."

"What kind of decision?" Kyle challenged, tilting her small head sideways. Silky braids bounced onto narrow shoulders.

"Well...let's say he decided not to wear a jacket to school because it was sunny that morning. But you had a dream the night before about a big storm that was coming." Her mother stretched her hands wide apart in an effort to illustrate enormity. "A storm that nobody'd predicted. You might call William that morning to warn him."

"So he wouldn't get all wet?" She covered her mouth with her hands and giggled.

"Exactly," her mother said, laughing along, grabbing Kyle and wrapping her arms around her, kissing the top of her head.

But her mother had never warned her about anything like this.

Kyle pulled open her nightstand drawer, grabbed her journal, and began writing down every detail she could remember, something she'd learned to do when the more confusing dreams came.

This one certainly qualified. *That creepy hospital*, she thought, as the hairs on her arm began to tingle, *both empty and noisy at the same time.* She could still hear those raw, tormented moans echoing down the hollow halls—so much pain and agony.

"Empty hearts, empty souls." She said the words aloud, looked up from her journal to think for a moment and then committed them to paper, still wondering what they meant.

Just then, an image jumped into her head: those haunting eyes, staring directly into hers. She trembled.

So dull and lifeless, a sickly color. And murky, like a cloud of mud stirring restlessly in a lake. She knew those eyes. She'd seen eyes like that many, many times before, both in dreams and in the walking world.

Those eyes belonged to the dead.

On her back and in the dark, she stared up at the ceiling, wide awake. This dream was a message. From whom, she had no idea, but she did know one thing: it was important. These kinds usually were, the ones that pulled at her consciousness, stretching it far beyond limits she never knew existed.

Even more important about the dream, she knew *someone* had lived it. Was it the little girl? Was she recounting some horrible, traumatic experience, one that ultimately led to her death?

And was she reaching out to Kyle for help?

Chapter Nineteen

Felice's Diner
Faith, New Mexico

Felice's was a cornerstone in Faith.

Clattering, bustling, and unpretentious, the affable little diner was a part of the town's history. For many, this was more than just a place to eat; this was place to gather, to catch up on the latest gossip and on each other.

The restaurant's specialty was enchiladas, a crowd-pleasing favorite among the locals and a must-have for first-time visitors. The menu also accommodated those preferring the more conventional, stick-to-your-stomach comfort foods, like meatloaf, chicken-fried steak, and mashed potatoes smothered in gravy.

When time permitted, Cameron and Frank started their mornings there, discussing the day's affairs while filling their stomachs.

Now they sat in their usual corner booth, each with hot coffee and white frosted cinnamon rolls laid out before them, warm, sticky, with the steam still rising.

Cameron had been picking at his roll for the past ten minutes without taking a single bite or saying a single word. Absently holding a fork in one hand, he stared out the diner's window with vacant eyes, seeing nothing.

Frank glanced at him briefly, shrugged, then tore into his roll, chewing around his food as he spoke. "Eat your breakfast, son. You'll grow up to be a big strong boy."

Startled, Cameron glanced down at his plate, suddenly realizing where he was and what he was doing. He poked at the food a few more times, a conciliatory gesture, but made no attempt to actually eat it. Finally, he spoke. "I don't need food. I need sleep."

"You and everyone else." Frank took another bite, chewed without tasting, then tossed the rest of the roll back onto his plate.

"The Churchill kid," Cameron said, gazing out the window again.

"What about him?"

"How's a thirteen-year-old boy manage to slip out of town without being noticed?"

Frank nodded silently.

"And he doesn't have any resources," Cameron continued. "No means of transportation, no money to speak of."

"Unless he stole some," Frank replied. "But with everybody on the lookout for him, I don't see how he could take a piss without *someone* hearing about it."

"So where'd he go?"

"Good question, Detective Friday. Care to wager on some answers?"

Cameron looked at Frank for a few seconds, thinking before he spoke. "Two kids, five murders."

"Huh?"

"Thinking about a connection between the two boys again. They're both juvies."

"Okay. 'Cept they were two years apart, and eleven-year-old boys don't hang out with thirteen-year-olds. Strictly against code," Frank said. "There might as well have been twenty years between them. We're talking about two different worlds."

"True, but still, two kids committing murder in the same town—especially in this town—it's enough to make you think."

"There's that," Frank conceded, ripping the top off a sugar packet and dumping it into his coffee. "How 'bout the teacher? What'd she think?"

"The same thing everybody else has: Ben was a nice kid, not violent, everyone's shocked, it's the same story at every turn." He paused. "There *was* one other thing. She said Ben was sick the day of the murders."

"Sick how?"

"With the flu."

Frank shook his head. "I'm not making the connection."

Cameron shrugged. "It's the middle of May. Flu season ended months ago."

Frank considered it for a moment. "Coulda just been a cold."

"No, she said he had classic flu symptoms. Fever, sore throat, chills."

"The ME report mention anything about it?"

Cameron shook his head. "Not standard procedure."

"Can't they go back and check now?"

"Missed the boat, I'm afraid. Have to do it within twenty-four hours after death. Beyond that, the virus is undetectable."

"So basically, we're screwed," Frank said.

"Could be."

"We know for sure you can't get the flu this time of year?"

"*I've* never heard of it. Gonna see Dr. Grayson over at Faith Community just to be sure, though. And I'll also see if there's been any other reported cases in town."

Frank nodded noncommittally. "So what do you think it means, this flu?"

"Not sure, but Ben's teacher mentioned something before I left the school, something that made me think. She said he wasn't capable of pulling off something like this, acted like there was some other outside factor."

"Outside factor? Like what?"

Cameron shrugged. "Don't think *she* even knew, other than he didn't have it in him, and that he lacked the motivation or know-how to pull off something this extreme...except maybe with the help of another person."

"Back to the idea of Ben and Ryan working together?"

"Not completely. Not yet, anyway. We need something more definitive to connect them, something more concrete."

Frank sighed. "Okay, so suppose Ben *was* working with someone—and not necessarily Ryan—how do you pursue it?"

Cameron leaned back in his chair and stared at his boss for a few seconds, his confidence on the rise. "Ever study geometry, Frank?"

"Sure, a long time ago." He waved a hand. "Longer than I care to think about."

"Getting back to your original question, the one about how to get from point A to point C—the most essential rule in geometry is also the most basic: the shortest distance between two points is a straight line."

"So where's our straight line leading us?"

"To the most obvious." He stared at Frank for a few seconds before speaking again. "To the Foley house."

Chapter Twenty

45687 Monument Path Way
Albuquerque, New Mexico

"Quite a dream," Joshua said, looking down at the steaming cup of coffee in his hand. "Heavy on the weird, though. What do you think it means?"

"Not really sure," replied Kyle. She was gazing through her kitchen window. The heat outside was unbearable, especially for May, but from inside her comfortable, climate-controlled house, one would hardly know it. "Somewhere, there's a message. I just have to figure out what it is."

"A message," he replied, thinking about it before raising the cup to his lips. He tried to take a sip, winced and decided against it. "How about this for a message: stay away from creepy hospitals with empty gurneys?"

Kyle tried to laugh, but all she could manage was a weak groan. This was no laughing matter. Not now. That voice and those eyes—they still haunted her. Her mind trailed off for a few seconds, then came back. "Empty hearts, empty souls… What do you suppose that means?"

"Got me there, Sis." The best he could offer was a shrug and his patented smile, the lopsided one that, through the years, had been his get-out-of-jail-free card for parents, girlfriends, and just about everyone else in between.

It hardly mattered the two were only half-brother and sister. They were just as close as any full-blooded siblings could be. Joshua had been only three when his father married her mother, and Kyle was born two years later.

Like her mother's, Kyle's gift was common knowledge among family members. It revealed itself at a young age, and for Joshua it wasn't anything unusual.

Kyle always used it to help others, even him.

When he was sixteen, Josh had planned a much anticipated deep-sea fishing trip in California. He'd been looking forward to the weeklong excursion for months, but just a day before he was supposed to leave, Kyle started to get a bad feeling about it that she couldn't explain.

Hesitant to cancel a trip he'd been long looking forward to, Joshua didn't take her warning seriously; but Kyle begged him not to go, telling him flat out that if he didn't, he would die. He cancelled the trip.

The following week when he turned on the television, Josh learned of a collision between two fishing boats off the coast of La Jolla, killing seven people. Josh was supposed to have been on one of them.

It was the last time he ever doubted one of Kyle's warnings.

That trust grew, and eventually, he was able to use it to his professional advantage. Once he became a police detective, Josh began enlisting her help in solving some of his most difficult cases, making her his unofficial consultant, a secret weapon of sorts. And it started paying off. His track record solving cases began to improve.

But using a psychic to solve cases wasn't just taboo in the department; for most, it was pure nonsense, pure and simple.

Joshua decided early on that nobody could know Kyle was helping him solve cases; her work had to remain a secret, just between the two of them. Often, when people asked how he caught a break, he'd tell them either an anonymous source had come through or that he'd just followed a hunch. That seemed to take care of it.

Kyle turned her head away from the window and looked at her brother. "What happened at my office was awful. Something, or *someone*, took control of my mind, like they were trying to show me things, leading me somewhere. Josh, I lost complete control. That's never happened before."

"What do you think's going on?" he asked.

"Not really sure." She paused for a moment, thinking. "This girl—at least I think it's a girl—she's trying to reach me, to tell me something."

"Are we talking about something that's already happened, or about to?"

"A combination of both, I think. Nothing concrete, just a feeling."

Joshua grinned. "Well, we know about your feelings. They've been right a time or two."

"But the girl…such a mystery to me. She's dead—I know that much. What I can't figure out is why. I'm thinking maybe all this has to do with her death. After all, one of the places she took me to looked like a hospital."

"She could have died there, right? Or even been killed?"

"Could be, yeah." She shrugged. "I don't know for sure, and I won't—not until she tells me more."

"And when do you suppose that'll be?"

Kyle laughed humorlessly. "It's anyone's guess. I'll tell you one thing though—her timing really sucks. She comes at the worst times."

"She's in a different time zone. Cut her some slack."

"Well, she's in Albuquerque now. She needs to adjust her watch accordingly."

He chuckled. "Make sure you tell her that next time."

"I would, except she never gives me the chance. Doesn't like to stick around for long enough."

"What's her hurry?"

Kyle shook her head. "Don't know yet. I get the feeling she's scared."

"Scared of you?"

"Scared of something. Just don't know what. Not yet, anyway. I think that's why she only shows herself in brief spurts. It's like she's on the run."

Joshua was tracing the pattern on the tablecloth with his finger. "Look, I know I don't have to tell you this…"

"But you will anyway." She reached across the table and placed her hand on top of his. "It's okay. You don't have to worry."

"You'll forgive me if I do."

"Of course. You wouldn't be Josh if you didn't."

"Just tell me you'll be careful. This stuff…sometimes I think you take it too far."

"You know I will."

"Promise?"

Kyle nodded once and smiled. "Promise."

CHAPTER TWENTY-ONE

Old Route 15
Faith, New Mexico

There were several things Cameron knew.

One, Ben's behavior had appeared unchanged right up until the murders—or at least until he left school that day.

Two, he had not been under the influence of any kind of mind-altering substances when he murdered his family.

Three, he appeared to display symptoms associated with the influenza virus, even though flu season had already come and gone. He also had stomach ulcers.

Then there were the other two murders to consider. Alma was dead, and the only plausible suspect, Ryan Churchill, had vanished. But most troubling to Cameron, and weighing heavily on his mind, was Bradley Witherspoon. Still no viable suspect in that case, other than Ryan, Ben, or possibly both working together. Certainly, they'd each proven themselves capable of committing gruesome killings, but hard as Cameron tried, he couldn't find a common link among the three.

He had no evidence. All he had was a tremendous headache.

And a lot of anxiety. Cameron may have been back in Small-Town USA, but he was no longer the person he'd been when he left. A lot had happened since then, and now he had years of solid police work under his belt. Whatever was going on in Faith, Cameron knew he had the skill and know-how to get to the bottom of it. It was time to kick this thing into high gear.

He just needed more time and a few more leads.

And while he couldn't talk to Ben, he could try the next best thing: go back to where the boy had lived and see if he could dig up something, *anything*, that might provide an answer. Just as he'd told Frank, the shortest distance between two points is a straight line. He knew that line moved through the Foley house. What he didn't know yet was where it started, or ultimately, where it ended.

It was time to find out.

The place sat just off the Old Route 15—which in Faith was a flat, narrow blacktop flanked by farmland on either side. Modest but adequate, the Foley house was an old two-story farmhouse with wood siding, a shake roof, and a sufficient amount of land surrounding it.

Everything seemed different to Cameron now as he parked in front of the house. It was daytime and minus all the people who had earlier converged on the scene. Peace seemed to be settling in. It almost felt as if nothing had ever happened.

Except, that is, for the few telltale signs still standing as a reminder. The yellow tape had been torn down, but not all of it: a few loose strips hung from shrubs and fences, flapping in the wind like tiny birds' wings. In addition to that, the place had begun taking on a vacant, abandoned quality. Every window was shut tightly, every shade pulled down. Envelopes spilled out the front of the mailbox, stuffed to its limit with unclaimed mail, and in the yard, weeds were starting to sprout.

As he stepped out of his car, Cameron spotted the next-door neighbor near her driveway raking weeds. She gazed over at him with narrowed eyes, then quickly dropped her head and continued working.

For someone in law enforcement, that kind of obvious avoidance is a clear invitation.

With each step Cameron took toward her, the faster and more furiously she seemed to rake, almost as if doing so would keep him away.

"Morning," said Cameron. "Need to ask you a few questions about the Foleys."

The woman spared him a glance and went back to her raking, poking violently at the ground as if it had done her wrong. Then, in a singsong voice, she said, "Already talked to a deputy the night of the murders. Got nothing else to add."

"I need to talk to you again," he insisted.

Silence.

Cameron sized her up: mid-to-late fifties, bright red hair—a shade you find in the discount aisles, not growing naturally on heads—and skin seared by the sun, the color of a raw steak; it stretched across her face, a texture not unlike Saran Wrap.

"Ma'am?" Cameron persisted, pulling out his badge.

She stopped raking, let out a dramatic, bothered sigh and inspected the badge as if questioning its authenticity. Unimpressed, she grunted, then turned back to her work.

He cleared his throat, loudly.

"I keep myself to myself," she said with a hiss, as if scolding him, still raking, still avoiding. "Said I don't know anything."

"Did you know the Foleys, ma'am?"

"'Course I knew 'em. They were my neighbors," she said, stabbing at the ground, not looking up.

"How well did you know them?" he asked.

"Not very well."

"But you knew them, maybe had some conversations with Mrs. Foley?"

She stopped raking, rested the palm of her hand on the top of the handle and gave him the benefit of a full stare. Over-enunciating each word to show her displeasure, she replied, "Like…I…said…I…keep…myself…to…myself."

Short of firing a shot his way, the woman was about as uncooperative as anyone could get. Cameron knew the only game she'd understand was hardball.

Batter up.

"Ma'am, the last thing I want to do is *bother* you, but I'm not here trying to sell broom handles. Three people have been murdered right next door to this house—*your* house. That makes you a material witness."

He paused. "Now, we can do this the easy way, and you can take a few minutes to talk to me, or I can bring you down to the station and maybe get a warrant to search your home as well. It's up to you. Which sounds better?"

The woman looked up into Cameron's eyes. Her face was hard and stiff—except for lips that quivered almost undetectably. She jabbed her rake into the ground and sighed, then removed her gloves, picking them off one finger at a time, as if they were the cause of her annoyance.

Cameron clicked his pen and held it to his pad. "Your name?"

"Della. Della Schumacher," she replied grudgingly.

"Last name is spelled?" He didn't look up.

She spelled her last name.

"You said you knew the family. How well?"

"Not very. We were *just* neighbors." Apparently that didn't make for intimate relationships.

"What about Ben?"

"We talked occasionally," she said, dismissing the notion as if irrelevant.

He looked up and met her eyes. "Define occasionally."

Della spoke and sighed at the same time. "Ben took care of Snowball once or twice while I was away visiting my sister in Phoenix. It was no big deal."

"Snowball?"

"Yeah, my cat. I paid him a few bucks to do it."

Cameron looked around the property.

She followed his gaze. "She's not here. Haven't seen her since the murders. All that commotion—the bright lights, the reporters everywhere, they scared her away."

Cameron shifted to another subject. "What kind of a kid was he?"

"Ben?"

No, the cat, he thought. "Yes, Ben."

"Normal." She stopped and snorted. "Or at least I *thought* so."

"Thought?"

"Well, it's obvious he *wasn't*. He just *seemed* that way. It was all an act. The kid was a murderer. Probably killed all those others, too."

"In what way did he seem normal?"

"Good lord!" she said. "I don't know!"

"You just made the statement. You *must* know."

She rolled her eyes, then thought about it, as if the act itself took great effort. "He was respectful of his elders—that's rare these days. Kids don't have manners no more." Her face turned sour. "Of course, shooting his family kinda blows *that* theory all to hell, now, don't it?"

Yeah, thought Cameron, *it sure does*. "Observe anything about Ben's relationship with his family?"

"No. I don't think so."

"You don't sound very sure," he prodded.

"Look. Like I said, I keep myself to—"

"Yeah, you keep yourself to yourself. I get that."

Della narrowed her eyes and jutted out her lower jaw. "Is there anything else? I have work to do."

So do I, thought Cameron. "What about on the day of the murders?"

"What about it?"

"See or hear anything unusual?"

"*Like I said*, I barely knew the kid. I only seen him coming and going to school…things like that. They seemed like okay kids—both of them." Then she mumbled under her breath, "Never figured the boy for a cold-blooded killer."

"So you only saw Ben coming and going to and from school? That was it?"

"Yeah. That and sometimes when he was doing his chores around the house."

"What kind of chores did he do?"

She clamped her hands firmly to her hips and tilted her head almost completely sideways. "Now how in the world would I know that? It's not like I stand there all day watching him. I only saw him 'cause I was making my tea. I'm *not* a nosy neighbor."

"Right. You keep yourself to yourself," Cameron mumbled, still writing on his pad.

"Exactly." She angled her head, chin up, to see what he was writing.

"Did you see him at all on the day of the murders?"

She moved her gaze to the ground, scratched her head, mulling over the question. A spasm of cooperation flourished and then faded. "As a matter of fact, I did."

Cameron stopped writing and looked up at her. "Where did you see him?"

"He was fumbling around. Over in that shed there." She pointed past his shoulder to a rundown outbuilding.

Cameron glanced in the direction she'd pointed. "That your shed?"

"Yeah. It's mine. I don't have enough to fill it up. I let them use it…" She stopped herself. "Or I *did*."

Cameron flipped to a fresh page. "What did they use it for?"

"Tools, lawn equipment, things like that."

"How often did you see him go in there?"

"Every now and then, I suppose."

"How about you, Ms. Schumacher? You go in there?"

"Yeah," she said, nodding. "Occasionally. I've got some canning supplies stored away."

"When's the last time you were there?"

Della shrugged. "Don't know. A few days before the murders, maybe. Why?"

"You see what he was doing in the shed around the time of the murders?"

"I was making my *tea*," she reminded him. "It's not like I stand at the window watching everyone. I have better things to do."

"So you just saw him going inside? While you were *making your tea*?"

She caught his sarcasm, narrowed her eyes and glared at him. "Yes."

"And never saw him leave?"

"Correct."

"What time of day was it?"

"Dunno. Towards the evening, I guess."

"Anything else after that?"

She eyed her rake. "Uh-uh."

Cameron closed his notepad. He wasn't going to get much more out of her, not now. Della Schumacher knew a lot more about her neighbors than she cared to let on, regardless of how many times she repeated her worn-out mantra. Cameron also suspected something else: she was a lot closer to the Foleys than she let people think.

"Thanks for your time, Ms. Schumacher," he said, staring at the shed, eager to be there, eager to be finally sifting through clues. "Mind if I just go take a look in there?"

She shrugged. "Whatever."

"Thank you. I'll be in touch if I need anything else."

"Mmmm. Looking forward to that."

Cameron headed toward the shed, wondering just how much Della Schumacher had really seen the night Ben Foley killed his family.

Chapter Twenty-Two

Old Route 15
Faith, New Mexico

Cameron turned his attention to the storage shed. Someone should have checked it. He contained his frustration: it wasn't on the Foley property, and nobody knew Ben had been using it.

Now it had new significance: a place where Ben could have stored his belongings, maybe even hidden them.

The shack was rundown, with wood the color of cigarette ash, and the slats appeared buckled in spots where one could peer inside.

Cameron tried but saw nothing in the dark, formless shadows. He reached for the handle and pulled the door toward him. As he did, a thick ray of sunlight shot through the opening, filling the room with a glow and igniting airborne dust particles, which glistened and flickered.

Then, something else: a rancid stench, so strong that it made him dizzy. Cameron stepped back a pace and pulled a handkerchief from his pocket, covering his nose and mouth. He moved into the shed, looking around as he did.

It took a moment for his eyes to adjust, but once they did, a white, shapeless object caught his attention near the back wall. Cameron shifted his gaze toward it, squinting, allowing his focus to sharpen.

Then his mind made the connection.

It was Della Schumacher's missing cat, Snowball.

Dangling in midair. From the ceiling.

Dead.

Cameron moved cautiously into the room, careful not to touch anything. A rusty chain snaked its way around the animal's neck, tied off with a hasty, rudimentary knot. In its mouth, a pair of pliers protruded, rammed down its throat and pulled apart as wide as they could go. Cameron grabbed the flashlight from his gun belt, aiming it at the hanging animal carcass. He examined its coat. Once pristine and white—as her name had suggested—it was now anything but, covered in a thick layer of dried, caked blood.

Hung up, he thought, *and dead.*

Again.

Just like Witherspoon. Just like Alma.

Trailing his flashlight down along the abdomen, Cameron looked closer. What had appeared to be gashes on the cat's stomach were in fact words, carved directly into the skin.

DIEFUCKING CUMSLUT

A malicious, calculated act, and a message, no doubt meant for Della Schumacher. *Christ, it had to be.* She and Ben were the only ones who ever went in there. Cameron wondered if he'd planned to kill her, too.

There was another side to Ben Foley—that much now seemed obvious—one of which nobody had been aware.

Except for his family—they'd found out in the worst possible way.

As had Della's cat.

How could I have not seen it? he wondered. *How, with all my years of training, my exposure to Ben during the summer, could I have missed it?*

Another thing now seemed very clear. Ben had passed over to the dark side at least several hours before killing his family. But how *much* longer? Hours? Days? Weeks, even? Most important, did that now make him a more viable suspect in the Witherspoon murder?

Then there was still the matter of Ryan Churchill. Were the two boys working in tandem?

One of them was dead, the other still out there. Somewhere.

Something was starting to stink, Cameron thought, really stink.

And it wasn't just the cat.

Chapter Twenty-Three

49 Old Route 15
Faith, New Mexico

Della Schumacher was inconsolable.

Her only companion had been mutilated and butchered, and if that wasn't enough, the sheriff's department was holding its body as evidence in a murder case. That didn't sit well with Della. She stood behind the yellow crime tape wringing a tattered tissue, one that had long outlived its usefulness. With eyes rimmed in red and bottom lip quivering, she listened as Cameron tried to explain why she could not have Snowball back—at least not yet.

"Who does this? Who kills a helpless animal?" She stopped for a moment, glared at him, her eyes squinting, her voice biting and accusatory. "And why won't *you* let me see her?"

Cameron hadn't told Della the exact manner in which Ben had killed Snowball. He also didn't tell her that she herself might have been Ben's next intended target. He didn't see any point in getting her any more upset. Ben was dead, and the threat no longer existed.

She continued her tirade, lapsing into sobs and speaking through tears. "I want my Snowball! I need to bury her!"

"Ms. Schumacher—listen to me—I'm sorry. She's part of the investigation. We'll try and get her to you as soon as we can."

Cameron placed his hand on the woman's shoulder, but she rejected the gesture, flicking at it, as if shooing away a bug.

Back in the shed, Snowball's mutilated corpse lay splayed out on a sheet of white paper, with Jim Avello processing it.

"Do me a favor," Cameron said, glancing back at Della. "Get the cat wrapped and out of here."

Avello looked over at the sobbing Della Schumacher, shrugged, then covered the carcass with the paper.

Outside, a car door slammed.

"Great," muttered Cameron, looking out from the shed.

"What?" Avello asked.

"Frank."

The sheriff wasted no time as he approached, walking directly up to Cameron. "What *now*?"

"We've got a mutilated cat and an obscene message written across its chest—*carved* across it." Cameron nodded to Avello, who opened the paper, exposing the body.

Frank looked at it, then shook his head with disgust. "Left by our current young citizen of the week."

"Looks that way," Cameron replied.

Frank put a palm on the back of his neck, rubbing it as he looked around. "This kid have any other relatives?"

"Nobody in town."

"We need to find them."

"Why? Think they were hiding a secret?" asked Cameron.

"I think they were hiding a monster."

Cameron put his hands on his hips, slowly shaking his head. "Something's not adding up."

"Huh?"

"It doesn't make sense. There's no way he could have hidden this from everyone. If it'd been anyone else I might believe it, but this kid, I knew him, and it just doesn't fit."

"Well, we need to *make* it fit then," Frank shot back, "and fast. People are dying, and the ones who aren't dying are scared half *to* death."

Chapter Twenty-Four

Abrams Medical Center
Albuquerque, New Mexico

A surge of air washed across her skin, like someone passing by.

Kyle felt the tiny hairs on the back of her neck dance, then woke up, startled. She looked at the clock. It was late.

Exhaustion had finally caught up with her. She'd been sitting at her desk in her office, pushing paperwork, pushing her limit, when her eyelids started feeling heavy. She'd laid her head down just for a minute or two—or so she'd thought.

Before she could get her bearings, someone, or *something*, whispered into her ear, startling her, causing her body to pitch. Stunned, she looked around the room but saw no one.

She'd felt it, though: an ice-cold breath of air spilling across her cheek.

"*Kyle*!"

It knew her name.

Before she could respond, another sound came, then another, and another, each one overlapping the last, picking up speed and darting around the room.

Suddenly the place was abuzz with furious and audible activity, random noise that bounced off walls, swooped in rapidly and skirted past her head at a dizzying, frenetic pace. As the presence grew louder, Kyle grew more dizzy, more disoriented. She didn't know where to look, what to do.

Static. Then the whooshing sound of air rushing in, zooming out, followed once again by the whisper.

"*Kyle,*" it said again, snapping at the air like a whip. It was that child's voice, the same one that had been haunting her for days.

She turned around, tried to find the source, but as she did, it swooped in from the other direction, catching her off guard, the cold air grazing the back of her neck as it streaked by.

"*Kyle! Help me!*" it said, still in a whisper but with more urgency now, a whistling, whirling noise trailing it.

"Tell me how!" she shouted, looking around helplessly. "I'm trying, but you won't tell me!"

"*Please! Hurry!*" it pleaded.

Then, silence, but only for a moment. The whooshing started once again, and again, the voice spoke to her.

"*Anyyyyyyy,*" it said, sounding more like noise than words.

"Any?" Kyle shouted out to the invisible, blaring presence. "Any what?"

Another brief pause, then, "*I'm…*" more static, more wind, and crackling. "*Anyyyyyyy…*"

What did it mean? So much movement, so much interference; she couldn't make any sense of it. Kyle closed her eyes and placed her fingertips against her temples, concentrating.

A loud gust of wind began to circle around her, creating an even louder whistling noise. Then it seemed to move away, like a jet lifting off through the sky, swallowed by clouds.

And then—nothing. The girl was gone.

Kyle dropped her head into the palms of her hands.

As usual, the child came and went too quickly, almost as if someone were chasing her. *But who? And why?* If only she could make one lasting connection with the girl, something to give her a starting point, a foundation.

Frustrated, Kyle picked up her pencil, threw it onto her desk.

Then she looked down, and up, then quickly back down again. Something caught her attention, something on her desk. She zeroed in, halfway not believing what she saw but halfway knowing that there was no mistaking it.

Scribbled across the prescription pad, in the rudimentary handwriting of a child, was one word:

Bethany

Kyle didn't know whether to laugh or cry.

I'm Beth-any! That was what she was trying to say!

The girl had a name, and Kyle had her connection; she was on to something.

Now, if she could only figure out what that was.

Chapter Twenty-Five

Community Hospital
Faith, New Mexico

In any larger city, Faith Community Hospital would be barely adequate. To the people who lived there, however, it was just fine.

Much like the rest of Faith, the hospital hadn't changed much through the years. Located just off the main highway leading into town, it had once been a private home, converted later to a medical facility. One of the community's wealthy elders had donated it after he passed away. Although the building was large for a home, it was tiny for a health care facility. That didn't seem to matter much: having a hospital in town made all the difference. Before that, folks had to travel to the neighboring town of Truth for medical care, a good forty-five minutes away.

As luck would have it, a year after it opened, a large, anonymous donation rolled in. Shortly after that, authorities had shut down a private medical clinic in the neighboring city of Parker after an investigation revealed inadequate care bordering on abuse. Their loss ended up being Faith's gain. Officials gave the former clinic's equipment to the burgeoning young medical facility. In addition, the donated money went toward adding on a new wing. Before they knew it, Faith Community was alive and thriving, although it never managed to look like anything more than a cozy rest home. But that wasn't a concern—it could have looked like a McDonald's for all they cared. What mattered was that Faith finally had a hospital all its own.

Cameron pulled into the tiny lot, parked his car and headed inside.

A petite girl in her late teens sat at the front reception desk. Her posture was flawless, her smile leaning toward this side of overkill; it seemed put on, the size and shape of a lemon wedge. A perky greeting followed.

"Good afternoon, Sheriff! How may I direct you today?" she asked, each syllable dramatically overenunciated, her enthusiasm sticky and sweet.

Cameron glanced at the nametag, which said she was Becky. "I'm looking for Dr. Grayson."

"Very well, Sheriff," she replied, flashing a big, toothy grin. "I'll let him know you're here."

Cameron smiled politely and nodded.

"A Sheriff Dawson here to see Dr. Grayson? Yes, of course," she spoke into the phone, then hung it up and turned back to Cameron. In one breathless sentence, she said, "If you'll just walk straight forward and follow the red line all the way down past the patient lounge and turn right at the swinging doors his office is the second door on the left he's waiting for you have a *wonderful* day!"

Cameron nodded with some amusement.

Robert Grayson was a portly man in his mid-to-late fifties, with plenty of hair on each side of his head but none in between. He wore blue-and-white running shoes that looked as if they'd plodded their share of miles on the hard hospital floors.

"Sheriff Dawson," the doctor said, offering his hand and a smile.

Cameron shook the hand. "Appreciate you meeting with me, Doctor."

"Not at all. My pleasure…really."

His office was a cramped space, no larger than a generously sized broom closet, the walls covered in books. Grayson motioned for Cameron to sit in a chair, then settled into his own, a faux-vinyl, high-backed reclining type. He leaned forward, removed his glasses, and gave Cameron his full attention.

"I need to ask you about the flu virus," Cameron said, clicking his pen and scribbling on his pad to make sure it was working. "Did some research online but still need to fill in some of the gaps, if you can help."

"Certainly," the doctor said, a little curious. "What would you like to know about it?"

"It's in reference to the Foley murders."

"I know plenty about the influenza virus," the doctor said, scratching his head, "but how that could be connected to a murder… Afraid you've lost me there."

"It may not be connected at all, but some things aren't adding up. Ben appeared to be coming down with the flu on the day of the murders."

"Okay," Grayson said, waiting.

"Wanted to know how common is it to get it in the summer—the flu—if it's even possible."

"It can be," the doctor said, then hesitated, "but not entirely common. Typically, the so-called flu season occurs in the late-winter, early-spring months. In colder climates, it can lapse a bit further. But here in the desert…not very likely."

"But it *can* occur?"

"It can. But it's rare. If it does, it's usually because someone brings it back from overseas, someplace else where they're in the midst of their own flu season."

"Not many folks in Faith are world travelers," said Cameron.

"No, I suppose not," the doctor said, reflecting. "And they would need to have come back at least ten days prior to Ben's first onset of symptoms. That would be the incubation period."

Cameron made a note to check the local travel agency and see if anyone had, in fact, booked a trip overseas recently. With online ticket sales, it was a long shot, but still worth checking.

"So the likelihood that Ben caught the flu here, it's not very good."

"Well, not very likely, but not entirely impossible, either. There is one other feasible scenario to consider—an outsider passing through town could have had it."

"Not many world travelers passing through Faith, though."

Dr. Grayson smiled. "Or travelers of any kind, for that matter."

"And Ben needed to have at least some kind of close contact with them, anyway—wouldn't he?"

"Yes, that's how the virus is most commonly spread, through direct contact, whether it be with the infected person himself or something he touched previously. But again, the window of opportunity has to be factored in as well."

"Is it possible he had something else?"

"Well, anything's possible, I suppose, but if he had symptoms indicative of influenza, and I'm assuming he did…"

"Sore throat, fever, chills?"

"Textbook indications of the flu. If that's what was going on, then I'd imagine that's what he had," the doctor said. "When people come down with the influenza virus, especially children, it's pretty obvious. Not many other ailments appear the same, other than a cold, which, of course, is much less severe. Do we know for sure if he was running a fever?"

Cameron looked down at his notes. "Teacher said by the looks of him, he was. But he never saw the nurse. Went home early. After that, well…we don't know *what* happened."

"Assuming he ran a fever, I'd say it was a case of the flu. Which brings us, I suppose, back to how he contracted it."

"Just wondering here..." Cameron said, scratching the back of his head and looking down at his notepad, "any other reported cases in town recently?"

The doctor shook his head. "No, can't say I've heard of anything like that."

Cameron made a quick note, then looked up. "One more question," he said. "Can the flu affect brain functioning?"

The doctor tilted his head slightly. "As in, causing someone to commit murder?"

"Something like that."

Grayson smiled grimly. "Highly unlikely. Influenza is a disease of the upper respiratory tract. It doesn't really go anywhere else, unless it develops into meningitis. That's when the virus spreads into the spinal cord or lining of the brain. Even so, I've never heard of it driving someone to murder. That would be so far out in left field...I just don't see it. Besides, the symptoms of meningitis are frequent vomiting and severe neck pain. If anything, the victim becomes weaker, more incapacitated—not stronger and more violent. Besides, it sounds like Ben was in the very beginning stages of contracting the flu. Not much chance he already had meningitis at that point."

"Yeah," Cameron replied, "the teacher said it seemed to come on pretty fast."

"Had they tested for flu or a meningitis infection during the autopsy?"

Cameron shook his head. "Not a standard procedure, and I'm afraid by the time we found out about it, our window of opportunity had already closed."

"I see...then I'm afraid I don't know if I can offer anything else. For what it's worth, the symptoms you describe *are* indicative of a standard case of influenza virus." He thought for a moment. "I can check the medical journals on the slight chance there's something about other conditions that might mimic influenza symptoms..."

Cameron shrugged as he stood up. "Anything would help."

The receptionist seemed delighted to see him again, waving as though they were old friends. Cameron waved back with a thin smile. If there were a law against perky, he thought, Becky would be a first-class felon.

Chapter Twenty-Six

45687 Monument Path Way
Albuquerque, New Mexico

Kyle opened her eyes to a veil of darkness. It surrounded her, smothered her.

Her muscles pulled tightly against the back of her neck, and she could feel her pulse throbbing in her wrists. A short, vivid image had flashed through her mind, coming and going as quickly as the jump of a flame.

A voice, a name, and now a face. Kyle recognized her immediately.

It was the eyes. Green, but not the kind one might expect; the kind that you see when food spoils, a grimy, putrid shade, one that looks like it would stink. Behind them, an amber glow raged like two flaming jewels scorching through a quarry of darkness. Although the image hadn't lasted long, barely a few seconds, there was enough for Kyle to absorb and commit to memory.

Bethany was a tiny waif of a child, with soiled, unkempt hair and a face not much cleaner. In fact, a layer of viscous, wet filth seemed to cover her entire body.

And there was something else—it was her expression: calm, except for a lingering impression of fear running just beneath the surface, barely detectable. Kyle knew the look, had seen it on many other occasions before on the faces of different children, ones who had not only died but who also had done so under cruel and tragic circumstances.

Something horrible had happened to Bethany.

"Follow me," she'd said, gesturing for Kyle to come toward her.

Follow her where?

Kyle wondered; but just like all the other times, Bethany disappeared before revealing the answer.

Why does the child vanish so quickly, if she wants me to follow?

The whole event happened just as Kyle had wandered into that intermediate stage, the one where the line between waking and dreaming often blurs—the one when *they* often liked to pay their visits.

Still, all she had was a jumble of disturbing, bloody images, along with a dirty little girl who appeared very timid, very scared, and very much *not* of this world.

It was a start, but hardly enough to go on.

Frustrated, Kyle rolled onto her side, her desire for answers wrestling against her need for a good night's sleep. As it turned out, she would get neither.

Just outside her bedroom door, she heard a creaking noise, like footsteps. Kyle knew every sound in that house, every clank, thud, and squeak, and she could tell the exact spot from which that one had come.

Somebody was inside her house.

Chapter Twenty-Seven

45687 Monument Path Way
Albuquerque, New Mexico

Kyle pulled the nightstand drawer open, reached in and wrapped her hand around the rubbery grip of her revolver. She'd bought the weapon years ago to protect herself against a patient-turned-stalker. Now she was thankful to have left it there.

She heard a sharp thud outside her door and froze, afraid to move an inch, fearing even the squeak of a mattress might draw attention. Tightening her grip around the trigger, she held steady, waiting and watching.

But after several minutes of silence, Kyle saw and heard nothing.

Slowly, she eased her way out of bed, gun at her side, padding softly toward the door. Using her other hand, she turned the knob just enough to disengage it from the jamb, then pulled it open a crack so she could peer through.

The hallway was empty.

She moved on to the foyer, treading lightly, concentrating on every step, her senses heightened, her mind on high alert.

Suddenly, Kyle heard commotion coming from the living room downstairs and froze. She walked to the edge of the staircase, looked down and drew a steadying breath.

When she reached the bottom of the steps, she immediately felt the air turn frigid. She'd wandered into a patch of ice-cold air so chilly that it turned her breath to steam as it left her mouth. A wave of goose bumps wriggled up her arms; still, she moved on.

But not quickly or easily. Along with the chill, a commanding resistance penetrated the air—something thick, soupy—and the harder she pushed against it, the stronger it seemed to become, like trying to defy a powerful water current. Laboring with each step, she struggled her way through it.

Kyle had experienced this phenomenon before but never to such an extreme. *Cold spots*, she remembered, *an indication of energy from a lingering paranormal presence.*

Slowly, she lowered the gun down by her side, knowing it would do her no good; you can't shoot the dead.

She put the weapon away in a drawer and headed toward the living room.

Turning the corner, Kyle had the uneasy feeling that someone was standing directly behind her. She spun around but saw nothing. Still, she couldn't shake the intense impression of another's presence.

A loud crash interrupted the thought, but it wasn't coming from anywhere near her; it was coming from up near her bedroom.

Kyle looked toward the top of the staircase, then back down and across the living room. Noises were coming from all over the house. First upstairs, then downstairs, now upstairs again. She was chasing ghosts, chasing her fears, and getting nowhere.

Anger replaced fear as Kyle turned to climb the steps again, but upon reaching the top, her emotions quickly changed. She stared with disbelief at her bedroom door.

Closed. She knew she'd left it open.

But that wasn't all—the doorknob was cold to the touch, icier than a tombstone in the dead of winter. Even worse, when she tried to pull her hand away, she found she couldn't—her fingers stuck to it, fused like glue.

They were also quickly turning numb, which set off a wave of panic. Then her skin started to burn. Closing her eyes, Kyle leaned in slowly, and with force, pulled back quickly, breaking free and landing on her backside.

Kyle sat motionless on the floor for a few seconds, catching her breath, while at the same time trying to figure out what to do next.

Slowly, she got back to her feet, eyes trained on the door. Putting her hand inside her sleeve this time, she wrapped it around the knob, turned it, then pushed the door open. To her surprise, when she let go, it swung out violently, slamming against the wall. Startled but determined, she stepped forward, peered into her bedroom.

And saw nothing.

But she felt something: a hard slap across her face. She screamed, then heard more noise off in the distance, the sound of bells, hundreds of them. The sounds quickly graduated until finally reaching ear-shattering intensity.

Kyle finally gave in to her panic. Things were moving too fast. She didn't know where to look or what to do next.

All of a sudden, the bells cut out at the same time, and there was complete silence.

Before she could gather her thoughts, she heard a child screaming, followed by a cold, tingling sensation that felt like icy water on her spine. Something, or *someone*, had just passed through her body. She had an idea who it was.

Kyle swung her head toward the window; it was wide open, although she knew she'd closed it earlier, and even though the wind was blowing in, the curtains were blowing *out*.

Just then, a powerful gale picked up speed and barreled toward her, lifting furniture inches from the floor, then slamming it down forcefully and violently. Things were falling off shelves; others did worse, flying across the room, one book missing her by inches as she dropped to the floor.

A brutal storm was raging inside her bedroom, inside her house. Determined to get to the window, Kyle picked herself up and pushed forward, struggling against the wind, the noise. When she finally got there, she caught the curtains with her hands and pulled them inside; as soon as she did, all the commotion instantly came to an abrupt halt.

The air was as calm as could be.

Kyle stood silent, gazing out at the bottomless night, wondering what she'd just experienced, and why. She closed the window and the drapes.

Then she crawled back into bed, burrowing beneath the covers and closing her eyes. But only for a few seconds. She jumped when she felt her toe pressing against slimy, cold flesh.

Someone was in her bed with her.

She screamed, swung her head to the right, and found a pair of flat, listless eyes staring back, only inches from hers.

Bethany lay right beside her, on her back, head turned toward Kyle, stringy, filthy hair clinging to her skin like wet, muddy grass. Kyle was peering into the eyes of a corpse.

She jumped from the bed and screamed, "What do you want?"

Bethany gave her the answer, coldly, impassively, and with only two words: "Help me."

"Help you what?" Kyle pleaded.

The child lay silent for a moment, a death rattle coming from her throat, dull, expressionless eyes still fixed intently on Kyle's. "Five days," she said, then paused. "You only have five days."

And then the little girl was gone.

Chapter Twenty-Eight

Highway 10
Faith, New Mexico

It didn't take long for the other shoe to drop, and when it did, there was a loud, resounding thud, one that could be heard for miles.

Another victim.

This one turned up along the highway, about ten miles past the Fill 'n Grill Service Station and Diner. With the next sign of civilization more than twenty-five miles away, it was the perfect place to dump a body. The victim, a young female, lay inside a drainage ditch, barely visible from the road. A broken-down motorist had the misfortune of finding her first.

Deputies had already taken photos, bagged the hands for evidence, and cordoned off the scene by the time Cameron arrived to investigate. He slid down the steep embankment to take a better look, making sure only to step where there were no existing footprints or tracks.

She was lying stomach-down, with her head twisted awkwardly off to one side. Animals appeared to have gone on a feeding frenzy, chewing off part of her nose and an ear. In addition to that, the skin on her cheek had been gnawed all the way down to the bone. There were flies too, lots of them, crawling over her face, across her lips, and in and out of the open, rotting wounds.

Slowly, Cameron moved his gaze along the rest of the body. Brand names from head to toe: Tommy Hilfiger blouse, Lucky Brand jeans, and shoes courtesy of Kate Spade; she was no vagrant.

Nor was she a local. Although occasionally seen, designer brands were as uncommon as they were impractical in an agricultural community like Faith.

Cameron pulled a pair of latex gloves from his pocket and snapped them onto his wrists, then reached down and gently pulled back her hair. As the silky strands parted, he saw a dark bruise on the throat, then lighter ones moving upward toward the back of the neck. Strangled, in all probability, although not necessarily; choking someone to death is harder than it looks on TV, and many attackers often move to a quicker, easier method. It would be the medical investigator's job to determine the exact cause of death.

When Cameron rolled the body over, a foul odor hit him, so strong he had to turn away just to catch his breath. The stench of death; he'd smelled it when he first arrived. Turning the body faceup seemed to unearth its full potency, a volatile combination of urine, feces, and decaying flesh. The pounding heat hadn't helped matters much, either.

He knelt over the body, covering his mouth and nose with his hand, and took a closer look. Just below the rib cage was a gaping hole. He pressed his fingers against it and could see into the body cavity. The intestines were chewed through, and beyond that, so were several other internal organs. Animals hadn't wasted any time working on her insides.

Cameron shook his head. He'd left Amarillo to get away from violent crime.

He looked back down at the girl. Deputies hadn't found any personal effects—no purse, wallet, or ID of any kind, and with the face in this condition, making positive identification would be a chore. He hoped at least the hands were still intact and the fingerprints readable.

Before leaving the immediate scene, Cameron stepped back a few feet, taking one last look at the victim. *Who is she?* he wondered. *How did she end up here?*

Then he remembered what he'd learned while working homicide back in Texas: *Never put yourself in the victim's shoes; put yourself in the suspect's.*

He stood up and scanned the ground—no signs of a struggle there. It seemed unlikely she'd been murdered at the bottom of the ditch. Somebody had probably killed her elsewhere and dumped her here. Somewhere out there, maybe just a few feet away or perhaps even farther, was the primary crime scene where it all went down, where the victim came face-to-face with both her killer and her own mortality.

Cameron felt sadness tugging at his gut as the image of his son floated before his eyes. He pushed it away. Still, it was a reminder: he'd just been looking at somebody's daughter. Painful, the thought, but also it kept him grounded, allowing him to view victims as actual people, not just cold, nameless corpses. Whether or not their hearts still pounded or lungs drew air was irrelevant; they were all still human beings. All had a history—every one of them did—and most had loved ones who cared about them. Their lives mattered.

Cameron moved up the incline, careful to travel the same path he'd used coming down.

When he reached the top, something caught his attention: drag marks in the dirt. Perhaps even more telling, upon closer inspection, he discovered what appeared to be tiny drops of blood mixed in with them. The trail went from the side of the road to the edge of the trench. Cameron remembered a few cuts on the victim's arms. Most likely, the source. Just as he'd suspected, she was probably killed elsewhere, then dragged from a vehicle and dumped there.

Then it hit him.

Ben was already dead by the time this girl was murdered. As for Ryan Churchill, he was too young to have a driver's license; besides, the victim's condition here was tame compared to that of the others, and the method of killing couldn't have been more different.

Cameron knelt down and picked up a fistful of sand. Opening his fingers, he watched as the tiny granules slipped through them, falling quickly to the ground. He looked up for a moment, squinting in the bright sunlight.

Ben Foley was dead. Ryan Churchill was still missing. And in their wake, a shocking revelation: someone else was out there.

Another monster.

Like the grains of sand slipping through his hand, so too was the sense of comfort, of security everyone in Faith had always known, even taken for granted. Nobody was safe anymore.

The sound of screeching tires jolted Cameron from his thoughts. He looked up to see a news van slamming on its brakes, skidding forward several feet and almost plowing right into his car. He shook his head with disgust as he watched the crew pour out from the van.

Once again, the vultures had landed.

Chapter Twenty-Nine

Highway 10
Faith, New Mexico

Cameron watched as the side door of the news van burst open. A petite, blonde woman appeared, wearing a suit the color of a traffic cone. Pinned to her lapel, a gold number *9* shimmered in the afternoon sunlight, the same one splashed across the side of the news van.

As if executing a parachute drop, the tiny woman leaped from the vehicle with excitement, literally hitting the ground running. She immediately headed toward the crime scene with the determination and vigor of an Olympic sprinter, arms pumping, and clutching the microphone as if it were her torch. A chubby cameraman waddled behind her, barely successful in his attempt at keeping up.

The reporter stopped abruptly at the edge of the embankment, staring down at the corpse, her expression more one of exhilaration than concern.

"Psssst! Quickly!" she whispered loudly to the cameraman, poking her finger in the direction of the body, and oblivious of the crime scene investigation happening all around her.

Deputy Avello moved in. Placing a firm hand on her shoulder, he pointed her to the area behind the yellow tape.

Head tilted, mouth agape, and ego visibly bruised, she reached for her cell phone and called the station. Her cameraman stood faithfully behind her like a trained dog, waiting for his next command. Avello remained in front of her, arms crossed, determined, and immovable.

Just then, another news van came sliding into place right behind the other. More people filed out and ran toward the scene. Confusion quickly turned to chaos, and Cameron decided enough was enough. He stepped directly into the TV reporter's personal space, but with little effect; she continued her phone conversation as if he weren't even there.

He stepped even closer.

Unable to ignore him now, she raised her index finger into the air in a *just a minute* sort of way.

Cameron responded by shaking his head in an *I don't think so* sort of way.

She placed her hand over the mouthpiece and shot him a terse look. "Do you *mind*?" she demanded.

"Actually, I do," Cameron said firmly. "Please move back *behind* the yellow tape—that is, unless you'd prefer I arrest you for disturbing a crime scene."

She jumped back to her phone call. "I gotta go, Chris… Call you back in a few, hon…uh-huh… Yeah. Sure will. Okay."

Cameron cleared his throat loudly, then pointed toward the yellow tape. "We're conducting a murder investigation, and *you* need to step back."

"And you would be…?" she asked in a tone that managed to be both dismissive and condescending.

"I would be Cameron Dawson, assistant sheriff, and I'm asking you to step back—now."

The reporter's face suddenly changed, blossoming into a pleasant shade of *kiss-up*. Seizing the moment, she thrust her microphone into Cameron's face. "Sheriff Dawson! Great to meet you! Can we get an on-camera with you right quick?"

"Actually, Miss…" He paused and waited for her to say her name.

"Casey Gold, Channel Nine News," she said quickly and eagerly, then pushed the microphone closer.

Cameron was about to speak but stopped and pushed the microphone away. "To be quite honest, Ms. Gold, I have nothing for you. We arrived here shortly before you did, so we're hardly prepared to give any interviews. Please move aside *now.* We have a job to do."

Disarmed, but only for few seconds, Ms. Gold's indignation rose. So did her tone of voice. "We have rights too, you know!"

Cameron had more important things to do than deal with an overzealous reporter. He'd already wasted too much time here. "Miss Gold, listen to me very closely. Your rights end where that yellow tape begins. If you continue to be a nuisance here, I'll arrest you on a variety of charges ranging from disturbing evidence to disturbing the peace. It'll make great headlines, good video too… and just in time for the five o'clock newscast. Now get behind the tape before I put handcuffs on you."

Casey shot Cameron a dirty look, then, pivoting around on one heel, marched toward the crowd, shaking her head in disbelief. Other news people who had slowly crept around her followed closely behind.

Cameron stood, arms crossed, eyes following them as they walked to the outer perimeter. He kept them trained on the group as he spoke.

"Avello," he shouted.

The deputy looked up, giving Cameron his full attention.

"Stay on top of these people, will you? Arrest anyone who gets in your way. This is a murder scene, not a damned circus."

Chapter Thirty

Sheriff's Station
Faith, New Mexico

"She was nineteen years old. From Ruidoso. On her way through," Cameron told Frank.

Frank looked up from the mound of paperwork on his desk with interest. "Coming *from* Ruidoso, or going *to*?"

"On her way to Albuquerque," Cameron said, "and headed for the University of New Mexico."

"A college kid," Frank said with a nod. "Makes sense. But if she was driving, where's the car?"

"Found it shortly after we found *her*, just a few miles up the road from where she got dumped. Parked along Old Highway 80. Suspect probably ditched it there after getting rid of her, then headed out on foot. Nice car, too, a BMW. Purse and ID were inside."

"Find anything else in there? Blood? Hair?" Frank asked.

Cameron shrugged. "Deputies are processing it."

"How 'bout signs of a struggle?"

"Some blood on the ground nearby."

"Could be our primary murder scene, then," Frank agreed. He paused, rested his chin between his thumb and index finger, thinking for a second or two. "Who was she?"

Cameron slid a manila folder across the desk. "She wasn't just any college student. She was a college student whose mother just happens to be state sena—"

"Senator Connie Champion," Frank interrupted, reading from the report, then letting the folder drop onto the desk, "*Christ*...it can't be."

"It is," Cameron affirmed. "Felicity Champion was murdered within our city limits, or at the least, dumped here. Now she's *our* headache."

"That's one huge fucking headache," said Frank. He removed his glasses, then rubbed his temples. "*Jeez-us.* This means the feds. Guaranteed they'll be here, if they aren't already."

"If they're not, the media will sure as hell sound the alarm," Cameron said.

"And if we've got a serial-kill going on here," Frank added, "they'll *have* to step in."

Cameron shook his head. "Not so sure we do."

"Then what *do* we have?"

"I was at all four crime scenes, Frank. While there's similarities with a few, each one's different in its own way. Alma's killer was methodical, organized down to the last detail. Even the manner she was killed...it was very clinical...and he brought his own weapon."

"And with Witherspoon," Frank added, "while he was also left hanging, the weapon and methodology are still very different."

"Exactly. The rage, the anger, and he improvised."

"And this one?" Frank asked.

"This one's at the other end of the spectrum. Utter chaos. A complete mess," Cameron said. "Everything scattered, every which way. Looks like she was strangled and that was it. No toying with the victim like we saw with Bradley and Alma. It was quick."

"Mercifully quick," Frank observed, "compared to the others."

"Yep. Killed her then dumped her. Strangulation's not a speedy process, but she died a hell of a lot faster than the others did, no question about that. The whole thing was about as disorganized as they get."

"Then we have the Foleys," Frank said. "We knew *that* never fit in with any of this."

"A textbook case of mass murder."

Frank leaned back, scratched the side of his head. "The idea of a serial killer was never really a sure thing anyway—just one of the possibilities."

"And now we have more crimes to compare it to. I think we can safely rule it out."

"Okay, but what about Ryan doing Alma and the last one? Methods were different, but there's still a common connection, both female."

Cameron gazed across the desk at Frank, thinking a few seconds before speaking. "It might have worked, 'cept for one thing. The Champion girl was killed, then taken to another spot and dumped, right?"

"Okay, I know Ryan wasn't old enough to drive yet, but not having a license—that never stopped anyone here before," Frank pointed out. "This is the sticks. Kids get behind the wheel long before they ever reach sixteen."

"But not Ryan. I checked with his grandmother, and she confirmed it. Remember, Frank, he has dyslexia. Don't know if it affects driving, but Granny tended to be a little on the overprotective side. He never set foot or ass behind the wheel of a car. She made sure of it."

Frank shook his head, apprehension spreading across his face like a slow-moving shadow. "*Four* separate murderers."

"Dollars to doughnuts—I'd be willing to bet on it."

Frank stared at Cameron, dumbfounded. "Holy… Fucking… Shit."

"So the next question—"

"Is who did this one?" Frank said. "And don't forget Witherspoon."

"Witherspoon's still the wildcard. But this…this one may give us our break."

"A break how?"

"Well, for one thing, the killer was all *kinds* of sloppy—didn't bother to cover his tracks. We've got a lot to go on here, lots of physical evidence."

Frank gazed out his window, rubbed his forehead, then frowned as if seeing something he didn't like.

Cameron noticed. "What?"

"Dead bodies popping up like damned daisies around here," he said, shaking his head, "and now a senator's daughter…"

"We gotta think fast on our feet here, Frank, gotta find a way to keep the media from crawling up our asses."

Frank put his glasses on, peered over the tops at him. "In case you hadn't noticed, they're *already* climbing up our asses. Motherfuckers get any farther, they'll be poking at my rib cage."

"Okay. What, then?"

Frank paused for a moment, deliberating, tapping his pencil on his desktop. "I think it's time for a news conference, let everyone know *we're* running this show. Not the citizens, not the media, not the feds."

Cameron breathed deep, then let the air out while nodding. "Fair enough."

"But we need to figure out how much we want to release to the media. That's always a slippery slope. We want to keep the bastards informed, but we don't want to let them ruin the investigation. And they'll not only ruin it—they'll try to run *away* with it, if we let them." He lifted his hand, looked down at his calendar.

"Let's say tomorrow...tomorrow night. That'll give you time to prepare."

"Prepare," Cameron repeated, suddenly realizing Frank had just slapped a bull's-eye on his back.

"Relax," Frank reassured, waving a hand, "it'll be a piece of cake."

"Easy for you to say."

"Better get busy, Cam. We're changing gears here, shifting into damage control."

Chapter Thirty-One

Office of the Medical Investigator
Albuquerque, New Mexico

Felicity Champion's murder gained instant and national media attention. In the process, it had the same effect on Faith, something nobody there wanted.

More and more, members of the press—both television and print—were spilling into town. They were everywhere: in the grocery store, on the streets, and—much to Cameron's dismay—parked outside the sheriff's station, their newly designated command post.

The problem wasn't just that the press was there, more that they didn't seem to understand boundaries. Nothing was sacred, not even places of worship. Church members were horrified Sunday morning when they filed out of services only to find a firing squad of television cameras aimed directly at them and recording their every move. Five murders in about a week—along with the constant fear that any one of them could be next—was bad enough. Living under this high-powered microscope only exacerbated the effect.

With the press conference that evening, time was becoming Cameron's worst enemy. He felt like he was racing against it and losing. In addition, he was tired. Unfortunately, there was no time for that, either.

The latest victim being a senator's daughter complicated matters further, adding more stress to the mix. All eyes were on him. As a result, he felt he had no choice but to attend Felicity Champion's autopsy. That meant yet another trip back to Albuquerque. He wasn't looking forward to that. He'd already seen her animal-ravaged, decomposed corpse once; he didn't need to see it again.

As it turned out, an overturned semi on the highway forced a sudden change in plans. With the road jammed for several miles, by the time he finally arrived at the medical investigator's office, Russell Gavin was already wrapping things up.

Cameron entered the autopsy room. Once again, the increasingly familiar smell of decomposing flesh, blood, and nonspecific cleaning agents flooded his senses.

"We really have to stop meeting this way," Gavin remarked with a hint of humor.

Cameron returned a thin smile. His exhaustion prevented him from doing better. It had been a long trip. This was no picnic, either.

The doctor got down to business. "We have a few interesting things going on here. You're going to want to know about them."

Cameron nodded and crossed his arms, stealing a quick glance at Gavin as they moved toward the autopsy table.

When they got there, Cameron stood and stared—wordlessly—at Felicity Champion's lifeless, naked corpse. Long incisions, deep and bloody, crisscrossed her torso. One ran across her neck and chest, and another started between her breasts, then moved down, ending at her pubic bone—all stitched back together now, crudely, with what looked to be nothing more than common household string.

Cameron moved his gaze up toward her face and stopped there. With her mouth slightly ajar, eyes closed and relaxed, she looked so peaceful; all this in spite of being sliced by the medical examiner's knife, ravaged by animals and by time, and worst of all, put here at the hands of a murderer.

She shouldn't have to leave the world this way; nobody should.

Gavin was still talking. Cameron struggled for a moment, trying to find his way back to the present.

"You were right," the doctor said, nodding toward the body. "Your girl was strangled. That'll be the cause of death. The broken hyoid bone was enough to confirm it…some pretty severe hemorrhaging of the neck muscles too. But it wasn't done with a rope or any other device, for that matter. The weapon here was somebody's bare hands."

"The marks on the neck?"

"Yes," Gavin replied, "and judging by their severity, death came slowly."

"Dead bodies don't bruise," Cameron said, his eyes pensively drawn to the corpse.

Gavin glanced up at him. "Exactly. So we know those bruises were inflicted quite some time before she expired."

"What about thumb prints on the neck?" Cameron asked. "Able to pull any?"

"No luck there, I'm afraid. It would have been nice—"

"But a long shot, I know. Anything else?"

"Now here's where it gets interesting," Gavin said. "We did manage to find some other physical evidence."

"You did?" Cameron asked, brightening a bit. "What kind? Where?"

"A very short fiber, actually two of them—nearly identical. One embedded under a fingernail, the other on the victim's blouse, sticking through a buttonhole."

"Know anything about them yet?"

"Not really. I'm afraid a fiber is just a fiber until it's examined and analyzed under a microscope. We're sending them off to the lab. But the color *does* appear quite unusual, which could turn out to be a decent break for you.

"The *color*?"

"Lime green. Real bright. Almost fluorescent."

"Not very common."

Gavin laughed. "I'm no fashion expert. I haven't a clue what's in style these days. But even I'd have to agree with you there."

"How long before we know something?"

"Not sure. All depends on their caseload—you know how that goes—but since we're dealing with such a high-profile case, I'm hoping we can streamline things a bit, maybe get an answer for you sooner rather than later."

"Perfect," Cameron said. "Anything else?"

"Actually, there is." Gavin said, an inkling of apprehension creeping into his voice.

Cameron sensed the tension, then waited for what had caused it.

Gavin paused for a moment, cleared his throat. "What's interesting is that she wasn't *just* strangled."

Cameron's confusion caused him to flinch. "Didn't see any other signs of trauma—I mean, besides a few cuts on the arm and what the animals did to her. Did I miss something?"

"Yeah, about that…those weren't animal bites."

"Not animal bites?" Cameron said, confused. "What then?"

"Not what…*who*."

Cameron shook his head.

Gavin studied Cameron's face for a moment, thinking before speaking. "Those were caused by another human."

Chapter Thirty-Two

University of New Mexico Hospital
Albuquerque, New Mexico

Morning.

It had been a long night. It was going to be an even longer day. A tonsillectomy scheduled for ten, gallbladder removal at one—all in a day's work for Kyle, but this day wasn't feeling like one of her best.

Playing hide-and-seek with Bethany into the wee hours of the morning had left her feeling worn down, empty-handed, and most of all, deeply troubled.

You only have five days.

Until what? Kyle wondered.

The date didn't seem to hold any meaning, but she had a feeling she'd soon find out.

She pulled into the hospital parking lot and managed to land a preferred space right up near the front, marked "Doctors Only." One fringe benefit, at least, she thought, for suffering through all those years of medical school.

~

Sierra Conley lay in bed with Kyle at her bedside, her mother seated in a chair right behind them. The elfin six-year-old might have been diminutive in stature, but not in attitude. Her precocious manner was larger than life, as was her loud, penetrating voice. A fringe of slick, black hair cut straight across her forehead, the rest forming a frame around a set of full, round cheeks, which seemed too large for her smallish face. She reminded Kyle of a dwarf-size clown.

"When do I get to eat the eyth cream?" the pint-size youngster queried.

"Sierra!" her mother scolded sharply.

"It's okay," Kyle said with a patient, polite smile. "Kids always ask me that when I take out their tonsils. Can't say I blame them—it's the only thing they have to look forward to. Can you open up *real* wide for me, Sierra, honey?"

The child instantly dropped her jaw and shot her tongue out in a manner that appeared automatic and involuntary. She'd already become familiar with the routine.

"How long will the surgery take?" her mother asked idly, legs neatly crossed, a flawlessly manicured fingernail tapping against the arm of her chair.

"Breathe deep, Sierra." Kyle placed a stethoscope against the child's chest, listened, moved it again, then pulled the instrument from her ears. "No more than a few hours, probably less, if everything goes well."

"And how long to recover?" asked Mrs. Conley, wrapping her hand around her Starbucks cup. She raised it to her mouth, took a sip.

"I have thoccer in three weekth!" the child reminded her mother.

"Sierra, please!" she said with a snip. "Let Mommy talk to the doctor!"

Kyle winked at Sierra, smiled, and then addressed the mother. "She should be good to go by then. Takes about ten days on average, maybe two weeks, worst-case scenario. It just depends how quickly she heals. Every child is different."

Sierra's mom nodded, then gave a lukewarm smile.

Had Kyle not been looking at Mrs. Conley, she probably would have missed it; however, because the woman's chair was right beside the door, Kyle had a clear shot over her shoulder and directly into the reception area.

There were people, lots of them, mostly nurses, some pushing patients in wheelchairs, others working behind the counter and processing paperwork. Amid all the confusion, all the people, was a little girl, one who appeared strangely out of place: filthy nightgown, dirty, tangled hair, gaze fixed straight ahead. But the face was hard to miss—as was her expression, as blank as a china doll's.

And those eyes.

The dull, vacant stare was enough to put anyone on edge, but the child's movements were downright unnerving. Slow, choppy, robotic...

And backward.

Bethany's legs moved as if walking forward, yet she was traveling in reverse. Besides that, her body jerked with a series of spastic, repetitive actions, like a broken mechanical toy.

People seemed to be walking directly through her, or perhaps she was walking through *them*. Kyle couldn't really tell. It almost seemed as if the girl were wandering within some other dimension superimposed onto the present.

Suddenly, everyone around her began moving in slow motion. Then they all shifted into reverse. Bethany stood in the middle of the action appearing unaffected, maybe even unaware of what was happening around her. The child pulled to an abrupt stop and in one long, drawn-out movement, turned her head directly toward Kyle, looking into her eyes as she spoke: "We died in there." The words flowed from the small girl's mouth, but the voice was not Bethany's.

It was someone else's. Deep, growling, labored…and clearly male.

Kyle shot back on her feet, eyes wide. She ran to the doorway and shouted out to the child, or the man, or whoever was talking to her. "Who did? Who died? *Please*, tell me who died!"

Bethany began to disappear, her image dissipating into the air.

Just then, an orderly pushing a gurney moved past Kyle, but the person lying on it was no ordinary patient. Bethany looked up at her, face stoic. "Four days" was all the girl said as she disappeared down the hall, the only sound, a squeaky, repetitive noise coming from the wheels moving beneath her.

Kyle looked up to find everyone staring at her, confused.

They weren't the only ones.

CHAPTER THIRTY-THREE

Roosevelt High School
Faith, New Mexico

Just back from the autopsy, Cameron stood in the middle of the empty high school gymnasium.

Neat little rows of folding chairs—scores of them—lay out before him, covering the slick, wood floors like an unwavering army of steel. Up front, an old walnut podium stood as the focal point. Soon, the press would arrive, as would the citizens of Faith.

Game on. All bets off.

He placed his pad on top of the podium and studied his surroundings. It had been years since he'd been here. Back in high school, the gymnasium seemed like a second home to him.

And he'd had Sarah.

The memories came rushing back at him. They'd met toward the end of their junior year. Sarah was, without a doubt, the most beautiful girl in school. In fact, she was the most beautiful girl Cameron had ever laid eyes on: long, wavy blonde hair kissed by the sun; eyes the color of tanzanite; with her soft, delicate skin blending it all together like a brushstroke to canvas. She looked as though she'd be more comfortable walking along the golden, surf-kissed beaches of California than the hot and dry deserts of New Mexico.

Cameron finally got up the courage to ask her out, and she politely turned him down.

Sarah's maturity far exceeded her years, and things that mattered to most kids that age meant little to her. She had no interest in dating the school's basketball star, especially one who ran with a crowd most considered wild, immature, and heavily driven by ego.

Hardly accustomed to girls turning him down, Cameron also knew that Sarah was in a class by herself. Smart, pretty, sweet—she was all of those things and more. But there was something else about her, something he couldn't explain. Maybe it was the way she carried herself, her confidence, her sense of purpose. Whatever it was, he found it irresistible and knew he had to do whatever it took to win her heart. Cameron Dawson never gave up, and the word *no* only made him more determined.

With each subsequent rejection—there were five—his resolve only seemed to grow stronger. Finally, on his sixth try, Cameron hit pay dirt. Much later, Sarah would claim she only acquiesced so he'd stop bugging her.

But Sarah quickly discovered that Cameron Dawson was nothing like the image he'd worked so tirelessly to protect. There was more to him than that, much more, and before she knew it, Sarah found herself falling in love.

They married right out of high school, despite admonishments from both sets of parents. The couple did manage to keep one promise they'd made to them though, that they wouldn't have a child until they were sure they could provide for one. About a year later, Cameron landed a job as a deputy with the Faith Sheriff's Department. Soon after that, the two decided it was time to start a family.

Dylan Wade Dawson came into the world on a cold December night—at least by New Mexico standards—just days before Christmas. For Cameron and Sarah, he was the only gift they needed.

The boy became the center of Cameron's world; in fact, Dylan *was* his world.

The two were inseparable, and Cameron spent every free minute he had with his son. Together, they attended ball games, went fishing on the lake, took bicycle rides in the park. Cameron wanted Dylan to experience all there was to see in the world and did his best to make it happen. Things Cameron had done hundreds of times before now suddenly seemed different. Seeing them through his son's young eyes somehow changed the context, transforming them into fresh, new adventures.

That was before everything changed, before that day, one that wasn't just a turning point; it turned his whole world upside down.

"Ready to go?" Frank asked, startling Cameron, driving him back to the present.

"Ready as I'm gonna be," he replied, trying to appear casual and unaffected.

Frank walked toward him, feet hitting the hardwood floor and sending an echo throughout the gymnasium. He placed a hand on Cameron's shoulder. "You look like you just saw a ghost, son."

Haunted by one is more like it, Cameron thought.

Chapter Thirty-Four

45687 Monument Path Way
Albuquerque, New Mexico

She was back in that hospital again, wandering through its long, unsettling hallways, feeling lost and alone. Everything looked out of focus, almost warped, as if shrouded in a smoky, yellow haze. Kyle worked her way through a seemingly endless maze. The slick, frosty floors felt like ice beneath her bare feet.

Although the place looked and felt empty, Kyle knew she wasn't alone. She may not have been able to see them, but she could hear them. Once again—those agonizing moans, slicing at the air and coming at her from every direction.

She tried pulling on the doorknobs, but there was no use; somebody had locked them. She even tried knocking—pounding—but to no avail. The rooms were inaccessible.

The voices began to grow louder, whirling through the air, their volume swelling like an orchestral crescendo. Kyle couldn't tell if they were protesting her attempts to open the doors or crying out for help. Either way, the noise was unbearable. She stopped, knelt in the middle of the hallway and pressed her hands over her ears.

Then they were gone.

As Kyle pulled her hands away from her head, she could still hear lingering fragments of noise, distant echoes drifting down the halls, like air swallowing up smoke.

She stood, walked forward a few steps, and as she did, heard something else: shallow, gurgling gasps, barely audible, weak, and anemic. She wandered farther down the hall, trying to follow the sound, to find its whereabouts, but its source seemed too elusive, too vague.

Kyle turned another corner and there, suddenly, was Bethany. The child's eyes locked onto hers as if pulled in by some strange, commanding, and magnetic force. Bethany said nothing, her only sound a sick, burbling noise, as if struggling to breathe. The death rattle.

There was something else terribly disturbing about the girl: the odor she gave out was foul. Kyle's sinuses started burning at once, her eyes watering.

She knew that smell. It was the stink of death.

Kyle advanced a few steps forward, but as she did, the little girl responded by stepping back the same number, all the while keeping her eyes trained on Kyle's. She stopped. So did Bethany. She moved forward one more step. The girl moved back one as well.

In utter frustration, Kyle screamed out, suddenly, "Tell me what you need! I can't help you unless you let me!"

As if on cue, the chorus of moans started up again in the background, like waves of misery and pain, one rolling on top of the other. For the first time Kyle realized they were actually saying something, but she couldn't make out the words: there was too much noise, too much confusion. She strained to listen, but the harder she tried, the more confused she became.

The sounds grew even louder, and while she wanted to block her ears again, this time Kyle fought off the urge, forcing herself to listen. At just that moment, one voice seemed to break apart from the others, escaping the confusing cacophony of ear-splitting clamor and falling away from all the commotion. It was a man's voice, the same one Kyle had heard coming from Bethany's mouth the other day at the hospital.

"Make it stop!" it shouted, agonizing, begging.

"Make what stop?" Kyle cried out, looking around.

The girl's explanation came not in words but in actions. She nodded, and Kyle's body instantly jerked violently, as if something had pummeled her, knocking her off her feet and slamming her hard onto the floor. A few seconds later, lying on her back, she felt a cold, prickly sensation against her skin. Something was tightening around her chest, causing it to constrict, making it difficult for her to breathe. The pain intensified, and she tried to scream but couldn't gather enough air to produce even a whisper.

She was suffocating.

Kyle began to panic. Then suddenly her arms slammed down at her sides, as if forced by some invisible entity. Once again, a tight, ratcheting sensation began, squeezing them tight against her body.

"Why are you doing this?" she screamed out to Bethany.

The little girl's face remained fixed, expressionless, and as stiff as an effigy. Then her eyes rolled up into her head. Kyle's own eyes widened too, like those of a terrified child forced into the front seat of a rollercoaster.

A blinding, silvery light ignited behind Bethany's eyes; they looked like diamonds aimed into the sun, causing Kyle to squint. The light was powerful, the energy electric. Gradually, the glow began to fade. Bethany's eyes were like mirrors, replicating everything they saw.

Then the eyes came to a standstill, and Kyle could see something forming inside them. The effect was similar to looking through binoculars—two openings, one image. Splinters of light moved together, flickering and turning until they formed the picture.

Kyle knew exactly what it was.

Chapter Thirty-Five

Roosevelt High School
Faith, New Mexico

The high school's parking lot was an overflowing sea filled with news vans, satellite dishes, and people—hordes of them—all scurrying in all directions. A broad sense of uneasiness seemed to swirl through the air like waves of nervous emotion, causing tempers to burn, impatience to flourish.

Closer to the school, things seemed even worse.

Cameron elbowed his way through the massive gaggle of press congregating outside the gymnasium. It was chaos in every sense of the word. Black, dusty cables poured out from news vans, snaking their way along the glittery asphalt and into a multitude of propped-open gymnasium doors. Outside the school's main entrance, television reporters basked in the hot glow of spotlights while carrying on conversations with cameras perched atop battered, aluminum tripods.

Inside, it was much the same but magnified even more by the lack of space. Reporters, residents, and just about everyone else squeezed their way inside, filling the gymnasium until there was standing room only.

When Cameron reached the podium, he looked out into the crowd, then down at the thick tangle of microphones and cables shooting from every direction and seemingly from every news media outlet in the state—all pointed in toward him like an octopus with a hundred arms.

Cameron began by reading a prepared statement, including basic facts about the murders of Bradley Witherspoon, Alma Gutierrez, the Foley family, and Felicity Champion, daughter of Senator Connie Champion. He left out the speculative aspects of the case, as they were still unconfirmed.

Not a second after he finished, Casey Gold shot up from her chair like burnt bread from a toaster. She waved her hand back and forth over her head in large sweeping motions and began talking, even though Cameron had not yet called on her.

"Is it true you think that all the homicides are unrelated?" she shouted.

Cameron glanced at Frank, who was standing along the wall watching and shaking his head nearly imperceptibly.

"We can safely assume the Foley and Gutierrez murders were committed by two different people," Cameron responded. "However, we have no viable suspects in the other cases so far." It was the truth.

A wave of collective chatter passed through the crowd.

"We heard you think there may be *four* different killers," insisted Casey.

"I believe I've already addressed that question. Next, please?"

"Assistant Sheriff," said a male reporter from the back, "have you been in touch with Senator Champion, and if so, has she made a statement for the public?"

Cameron cleared his throat. "I've spoken to the senator personally."

The crowd mumbled, appearing pleased.

"I offered her our sincerest condolences and informed her we're actively working this case and are determined to find her daughter's killer. I also told her we will keep her apprised during every phase of the investigation."

"What was her reaction?" This from another reporter on the opposite side of the room.

Cameron paused and looked to Frank for encouragement. This time, the sheriff nodded his head slowly as if to say: *you're doing fine.*

Cameron looked back into the sea of faces, pens, and pads. "The senator was extremely gracious, despite her tragic loss. She seemed pleased that I called and thanked me for doing so. It was not a lengthy conversation. She has a lot on her mind, and I think it's only fair we give her the opportunity to grieve for her daughter. Next question, please."

A female reporter stood up. "Do you believe the murder might in some way be connected to the senator's job? Maybe an angry constituent?"

"We have no evidence to support that—however, we're certainly looking at all possibilities during the course of our investigation."

Cameron continued answering reporters' questions for a while longer, then turned the discussion over to Mayor Robert Redman, who fielded questions from residents. Most wanted to know what was being done to keep them safe. It was a peaceful discussion, and for the most part, everyone seemed as satisfied as they could be, considering the circumstances. When it was over, Cameron thanked everyone for coming, relieved to be finished.

But if he'd thought he could just walk away after that, Cameron was sadly mistaken. Immediately, Casey Gold came scurrying toward him, waving her hand and looking like she was about to miss a train. The same heavyset cameraman was right behind her, waddling along, trying to balance an increasingly cumbersome camera on his shoulder.

"Just a few more questions, if you don't mind, Deputy," said Casey, with a wide grin that revealed a lipstick-smudged tooth.

She swung the microphone into Cameron's face, missing him by just inches.

He hadn't appreciated her behavior before and didn't now, either.

"Actually, I *do* mind." He pushed the microphone away and spoke stiffly. "The press conference is over, and I believe you already got the chance to ask your question. And it's *assistant sheriff*, not deputy. You're a reporter. Get your titles straight."

He continued walking, trying to put as much distance between them as possible, not bothering to turn around to catch her reaction.

Unfazed by the abrupt dismissal, Casey continued following right behind him. "Okay, *Assistant Sheriff*," she said in a deep voice that mocked him.

Cameron stopped, shot her a stony look and then continued walking.

"Just one quick question," she begged, peddling beside him and trying to keep pace.

Finally, he stopped, sighed deeply and gave in. Casey Gold, Cameron had decided, was a lot like a bad cough: she wasn't going to go away quickly or easily. "All right. Let's get it over with, then."

Casey's eyes lit up with delight, and she signaled for her cameraman to come closer. Immediately, the reporter snapped into action. Gone, suddenly, was the catty, high-pitched voice that had grated on Cameron nerves. Instead, her delivery became smooth, authoritative, and deep.

"Assistant Sheriff, why are you hiding specific details about these cases from the public?" she asked, her voice gradually growing louder, more hostile. "Six people have been murdered. Don't you think they have a right to know what's going on?"

For a few seconds Cameron said nothing, realizing she'd just set him up.

Casey leaned over and whispered into Cameron's ear, "Payback's a bitch." Then she stepped back with an eager smile. "Assistant Sheriff? Comment, please?"

Cameron shot her a look that did not hide his annoyance or his anger, but let it fade, reminding himself he was on camera. "Naturally, in any investigation, there's going to be evidence that's sensitive and won't be released if it will jeopardize the case—"

Casey stepped closer, interrupting him with the stomp of her foot, while at the same time moving in for the kill. Her cosmetics polluted the air with their thick, sweet smell, a cross between Aqua Net hairspray and pancake syrup. A crowd began forming around them. "How much longer do you think you can put off the public by throwing out these canned, overprepared statements that, in reality, amount to nothing?"

Cameron bit down hard and felt his jaw tighten. His temper flared. He'd had it. "We are not *putting off the public*—that's absolutely ridiculous—you know it as well as I do, *Ms. Gold*. And we are *not* throwing out any canned phrases. This is a murder investigation—"

"And being a murder investigation," she interrupted, nodding her head to make her own point, with a shadow of a smile, "the people of this town have the right to know what's going on. Are you *even* aware how frightened they've become?"

"What kind of question is *that*?" asked Cameron, outraged. "Of course I'm aware. How could I *not* be aware of—"

"People bolting their doors at night? Parents afraid to send their children off to school? And this is all you can offer them? This worn-out, hollow statement that *this is a murder investigation*?" Her face suddenly softened, her voice taking on a tone that feigned diplomacy. "Come on, Sheriff. Surely, you can do better than this. As one of the chief law enforcement officers in this town, I think you owe them more."

"Like I said before, we're doing everything—"

"What? What *are* you doing? Tell me…what? Better yet, tell the good people of Faith what you're doing. But please…tell them the truth. They deserve *at least* that."

Everyone around them was staring. Cameron felt the sweat trailing down the side of his face. The bright light from the camera wasn't helping matters; it felt hot against his skin, like tiny daggers. But before he could speak, he heard another woman's voice rise from the crowd, slicing cleanly through all the commotion.

"I have a question for you, Ms. Gold," the voice said, calm and confident. "When are *you* going to back off and let him do his job?"

The cameraman swung around, taking the spotlight out of Cameron's face, allowing him to see again. But he could barely believe his own eyes.

The crowd parted as Senator Connie Champion approached, her smile so confident, so icy, it gave even Casey Gold pause. The reporter shifted her head toward her, eyes wide, hands clenched into tight fists, like a child caught in the act.

Champion stepped out in front of Cameron. She might as well have had the words "I mean business" written across her forehead. She did.

In an attempt to save herself, Casey halfheartedly floated the microphone toward the senator, as if presenting her with a rare opportunity to speak.

Champion, not the least bit impressed, pushed it away with one broad stroke of her hand, then leaned forward so only the reporter could hear. Her voice was unmistakably calm yet unmistakably stern. "Ms. Gold, perhaps we should talk about Chicago." She raised an eyebrow, then added, "You remember that, don't you?"

Casey's eyes widened with surprise, her once-loud, booming voice now deflating to nearly a whisper. "I…I don't know what you're talking—"

"Two years ago in Chicago? Champion said, moving in a step closer. "Where you used to work? That ugly incident with—"

Before the senator could finish, Casey turned to her cameraman. Eyes closed, jaw jutting out, she dragged her index finger across her throat, signaling for him to stop rolling.

The spotlight powered off so fast it looked as if the bulb had blown.

The senator placed her hand on the trembling reporter's shoulder, leaned over and whispered into her ear, "Now run along, dear."

Then she stepped back and smiled, as if admiring her own work.

"Now, if you'll excuse me," she continued, "I need to speak with Sheriff Dawson. In case you hadn't heard, my daughter was murdered, and he's trying to find the killer. That is, *if* you'll let him."

Cameron fought hard to keep his mouth from falling wide open.

Connie Champion had arrived in Faith.

Chapter Thirty-Six

Sheriff's Station
Faith, New Mexico

The senator was sitting across from Cameron's desk when he walked in and placed a cup of vending-machine coffee in front of her. She looked up at him and smiled her thank-you. He nodded and settled into his chair.

A few seconds of silence lingered before she cleared her throat and spoke. "I actually hadn't planned on coming here. But then I realized that sitting at home and thinking about my daughter wasn't doing me a bit of good." She stopped, looked down at her hands, and shook her head, her voice decidedly softer now. "My husband…he's devastated. They were very close."

"It's rough," Cameron said, "for both of you."

The senator grasped her cup but did not lift it, staring at it, nodding. "I understand his grief. I really do. I guess what I'm having trouble with are his feelings of utter helplessness."

"It's a normal reaction," Cameron said. He was thinking about his own past, his own helplessness.

"Don't get me wrong," she said, looking up, raising a hand. "It's not that I don't feel the same way at times. I do. It's just that he and I, well…I suppose we just handle our emotions differently."

"The death of a child," Cameron said, "something like that—it can cause stress on even the strongest marriages."

She laughed mirthlessly. "You say that almost as if you've seen it happen. But I suppose in your line of work, you probably have."

Cameron nodded and smiled noncommittally.

"As for me, well, I guess I just prefer to stay active. Seems to help, keeps me from wandering into those dangerous corners of my mind."

"Dangerous?"

"Oh, you know: Should I have done this? What if I'd done that? Second-guessing myself…the way a mother often does." She shrugged and shook her head. "All that self-doubt—it does no good, just leaves you feeling empty inside…and then devastated. It's a vicious game we all play with ourselves at one time or another, I suppose, but rarely does it serve any purpose: In the end, you end up losing. *Stinking thinking*, I call it, you know what I mean?"

Boy, did he.

"Anyway…I knew if I stayed at home, that's just where I was headed. Then I heard about the news conference and I figured: What the hell? Maybe I could help out in some way. I suppose my timing was good."

Cameron didn't say anything, his run-in with Casey Gold still leaving a nasty aftertaste.

"I wouldn't let that incident with Gold get you down, by the way," said the senator, as if reading Cameron's mind, in a soft, reassuring manner, one clearly intended to offer him solace. "She's a shark, and a dirty one at that."

"No argument there," he replied, hand around his cup, staring at it, nodding.

"If it's any consolation, you're not the first to get snagged by her claws," she said, "and I suspect you won't be the last, either.

She pulled the same stunt with me some time ago while I was visiting in Albuquerque…caught me completely off guard. Seems to be her specialty."

"She does it well."

"Hardly to her credit. The only way to battle her, I've found, is to fight back with equal measure. You just have to know how to push the right buttons to shut her down. In this case, knowledge was power."

"More coffee?"

"Oh, heavens, no," she said, raising a hand in protest. "I shouldn't even be having this one. I'll be up all night…although, with everything going on, I doubt I'd be able to sleep, anyway."

Cameron had never met the senator before. He'd only seen her on television every now and then. Meeting her in person now, he could see how she'd become such a powerful politician. She was clearly a woman of substance—extremely bright, exquisitely attractive, and brimming with class.

She tipped the empty cup toward herself, staring into it, then looked up and met his eyes. For the first time, Cameron saw her sorrow, could feel it, and the moment felt awkward.

The senator looked down into her lap, then ran a hand across the fabric of her skirt with a smoothing motion. When she raised her head again, she seemed to emerge a different person, reverting back to the strong, confident woman he'd seen earlier at the press conference. "I'm hoping you'll be as forthright with me as I'm being with you. I need to know you're doing everything you can to find my daughter's killer."

"I told you in our phone conversation that I plan on keeping you informed throughout this investigation, and I want you to know I meant it. You have every right to know what's happening."

"Thank you," she said, nodding. "I appreciate that."

He paused, looking at her appraisingly. "At the same time, I need your reassurance that certain information will remain just between us. It's crucial if we're going to find your daughter's killer."

She nodded once. "Understood."

He looked down at his hands, rubbing them together, biting his lower lip. Connie looked at him curiously.

It took him several seconds to speak. "I know what you're going through right now. With your daughter, I mean…"

"Trust me, nobody knows. Nobody can, until it—"

"I lost my own son." Cameron blurted it out.

Connie's expression instantly turned blank.

"I lost my son," Cameron said again, this time much softer, with regret. "It was several years ago."

"Oh, no…my God…I'm *so* sorry." And she was. Tears began to fill her eyes. Even with the pain of her daughter's murder fresh in her mind, she was able to consider someone else's.

Cameron cleared his throat, made an attempt to appear strong. "But I'm not telling you this because I'm looking for sympathy—it's because I want you to know I understand what you're feeling right now. *Really* understand. Not many people can say that to you and mean it…I can." He looked down into his lap and stopped for a moment. His voice softened. "I just wanted you to know that."

"Thank you," Connie said, her voice barely a whisper. She closed her eyes and nodded, trying to hold her composure. "Thank you for telling me. Thank you for this."

Chapter Thirty-Seven

45687 Monument Path Way
Albuquerque, New Mexico

Kyle continued staring at the image in Bethany's eyes.

The woman was dressed all in white; she was falling, plummeting, and twisting through the air, her body moving into positions one was never meant to go. The farther down she spiraled, the faster and more exaggerated her movements became.

Just for a second, Kyle made eye contact with her—it was a dark, eerie moment. The woman's expression couldn't have been clearer; she was begging Kyle to save her, but she couldn't—she, too, was a prisoner, her body tightly bound by restraints she could feel but not see.

The woman's body slammed into concrete, producing a resounding, hollow thud. Kyle could hear it…and feel it. The vibration curled through her own body.

Kyle woke herself up screaming. It took her a few minutes to realize she wasn't in her dream anymore, that she was safe.

Her arms felt like they were on fire. When she looked down, deep red indentations marred them, the exact spots where they'd been bound to her sides. *Just a dream*, she told herself, knowing it was much more than that. The sense of danger, the helpless feelings of vulnerability; they all seemed so real, and the welts on her arms proved it.

It was time, she'd decided, to begin sorting through all the shattered fragments: the locked doors, the empty hallways, the moans, the human stampede, and the woman in white falling to her death. She needed to start making sense of it.

The setting was clearly some sort of hospital, but what kind of facility was it, and where? She thought about the restraints, the tormented moans. Was she inside a sanitarium? If that were the case, then there was still one element missing: the patients. She'd never seen one.

She only heard them.

Her mind kept coming back to that woman falling through the air, her eyes begging for Kyle to help spare her life. Hard as she tried, she couldn't shake the image. Had she fallen, or had someone pushed her? The sound of her body slamming into the pavement kept playing over and over in Kyle's head.

That hollow thud.

And what about the voice she'd heard *pleading* to make it stop. Make what stop? Bethany hadn't told her—she'd shown her. *Are the patients being restrained in a similar manner? Is that why I can't see them?*

The deceased never crossed the line between life and death unless strongly compelled to do so. In Kyle's experience, it was always about unfinished business.

Unfinished business indeed, she thought. Bethany seemed to have plenty of it.

Now all Kyle needed to do was figure out what that was.

Chapter Thirty-Eight

Sheriff's Station
Faith, New Mexico

Connie Champion sat with her hands neatly folded in her lap, listening intently, while Cameron laid out the facts surrounding her daughter's death.

He took a deep breath. "I have to warn you there are some… aspects…of your daughter's case that will be hard to hear."

She nodded. "I only need to know what's pertinent to catching her killer. I'll let you decide what that is."

"Fair enough," Cameron said, and told her what he knew. Connie seemed to take it calmly. She listened but didn't say much. Halfway through, Cameron paused for a moment, as if considering a thought.

"Something wrong?" she asked.

"I'm going to step out on a limb a bit here," he said. "I didn't want to say this during the press conference, but not because I was being deceitful. It was because I didn't want to speculate about things I can't yet prove."

"What kinds of things?"

"I'm sure you're aware of what Faith's crime rate was like before all this."

She shrugged one shoulder. "There was none."

He nodded. "Six murders in this short a period of time—that's enough to raise worries in any small town, but in a place like this, where there's never been even one—"

"So what are we talking about here?"

"What I'm talking about," he said, "is that Casey Gold may be a nuisance, but she wasn't that far off. I just didn't want *her* to know it."

"You mean about there being different killers?"

Cameron shrugged. "Can't prove it, but there seem to be enough variations in each to make me wonder."

"And you have no idea what's going on? No idea at all?"

"No. At least not yet. I've searched the national databases looking for something similar, something that might've happened elsewhere—patterns…*anything*. No luck. Same thing when I spoke to other agencies." He drew a deep breath, exhaled heavily. "I've got a lot of work ahead of me."

"I can provide you with any assistance you need," the senator said. "All you have to do is ask. I hope you know that."

Cameron nodded. "I do, and I appreciate it. Right now, the media's my biggest headache. Can't seem to get them out of my way."

Connie was still for a moment, thinking. "Maybe I can help you."

He laughed faintly. "No way to control the media."

"True. If I could do that, it would make *both* our jobs *a lot* easier. No, we can't—but I *can* get them to be a little more cooperative."

"I'm all for that. But how?"

"Every major news organization in the state and beyond has been trying to get me to sit down for an interview the past few days. I've turned them all down. Just haven't seen the need for it. Now I do. But they're going to have to help *me* before I help them."

"Help you how?"

"As far as I'm concerned, anyone who gets in the way of *any* of these investigations is interfering with finding my daughter's killer. I can't have that. I'm going to ask for their full cooperation. If they do that—if they stay out of your way—they get full access, a one-on-one interview. If they don't, they get nothing. No second chances."

Cameron grinned.

Connie studied his face with interest. "You know, you should smile more often. You look like a completely different person when you do."

Cameron hadn't even realized he'd been smiling; still, he knew she was right. He also knew that *different person*, the one she was referring to, no longer existed.

He'd been gone for years now.

Chapter Thirty-Nine

Cameron could remember the exact day he lost his mind—it was the same day he lost his son.

Eight years earlier
Amarillo, Texas

The Texas Panhandle was miles away from Faith, and for Cameron, worlds away from the small-town life he'd come to know—a place where the southern plains and desert meet. A place where he and Sarah had decided to start a new life.

Covered in oil and gas fields, meatpacking plants, and flour mills, Amarillo's landscape was a far cry from the aesthetic beauty of Faith; but for Cameron, it offered something else, something he craved and needed.

Like many boys growing up in small towns, he wanted more excitement. Things in Faith moved too slowly, and to him, slow meant dull. There was more waiting for him out there in the rest of the world, and from were Cameron stood, Texas seemed far enough.

Young, ambitious, and a bit naïve, he hungered for a law enforcement career that would provide new excitement, new challenges. Cameron was tired of breaking up bar fights and rounding up teenagers who raised hell to relieve boredom. And while hardly a hotbed of criminal activity compared to larger cities like Houston or Dallas, there was enough in Amarillo to keep him busy.

Professionally, the change proved to be a good one. Cameron found himself moving up quickly through the ranks. Two years in and he was promoted to the burglary unit, a year later, homicide. His career was steadily on the rise, and so was his income. Soon, he and Sarah decided it was the perfect time and place to raise a family.

Autumn had arrived—Texas-style—and suddenly there was a chill in the air. As the mercury slowly inched its way downward, thoughts of the upcoming holidays came more into focus, along with the inclement winter, sure to follow close behind.

The morning was crisp and clear as Cameron drove his son to school. For Dylan, entering the first grade was exciting. Kindergarten just seemed like practice. This was the real deal. Now he would be like the big kids.

As they drew closer to the school, Dylan rifled through his backpack, making sure everything was in place; it was the fourth time he'd done so since leaving home.

"Do you think we'll study astrology?" the child asked, brimming with excitement. He was talking so fast, Cameron could barely understand him.

"I think you mean astronomy, son, the study of the stars," he corrected. "Astrology is where you get your horoscope."

Dylan looked down at his knees, considered what his dad said and then popped his head up. "Yeah! Astronomy! I wanna learn about the planets and stuff. What about painting? Will I get to paint, too?"

"Slow down, buddy, you're moving too fast," he said, reaching over and tousling his son's hair. "You'll find out soon enough."

Dylan reached into his pocket to make sure he still had the lunch money his mother had given him. As he did, his backpack fell between his knees and onto the floorboard, causing a pencil to spill out and roll under the seat.

"Uh-oh," Dylan said, unbuckling his seatbelt and scanning the floor.

"Over by your right foot, son," Cameron said, pointing and splitting his attention between the boy and the road.

Dylan looked down. "I don't see it, Dad."

"You're looking at the left foot, buddy—it's the other one."

"Oh, I see now," Dylan said, looking at the other foot, spotting the pencil, then grabbing it.

"Got it?" asked Cameron.

Then something strange happened. Dylan looked up at his dad in the most peculiar way—a loving, thoughtful smile, one filled with a depth of emotion that seemed uncommon in a child, especially one his age.

But the impression would be quickly erased by what happened next: the sudden and loud screeching of tires, followed by an explosion of glass shooting through the air like confetti.

A truck had slammed into them.

Cameron grabbed the steering wheel and tried to stop the car from spinning, but as he did, it collided head-on with a telephone pole. The impact folded the vehicle down the middle, giant shards of jagged steel wrapping around them like a metal blanket.

The frightening sounds faded into silence, and everything went black.

~

Cameron woke up hours later in a hospital bed, his mouth dry and his vision blurred. "Dylan?" he blurted out.

"Do you know what day it is?" The nurse's voice was soft and calm.

He looked up and saw the young woman leaning over him with a smile. She placed a gentle hand on top of his.

"Tuesday?" he guessed, eyes still adjusting to the light and trying to find their focus. "No, Monday…it's Monday." Dylan's first day of school, he remembered. "Dylan? Where's Dylan?"

"Good," said the nurse, ignoring his question, her accent thick Southern. "How about your name? Can you tell me that?"

He looked over to his side, trying to focus on the hallway outside his room, and then back up at her. "Cameron…Dawson."

"Good. Do you know where you are, Cameron?"

He blinked twice. "I'm in a hospital. Where's my son?"

The nurse reached over and placed her hand on his wrist to take his pulse, then wrote a few notes on the clipboard near his bed. "I need you to hold real still for a few seconds. Can you do that for me, sweetie?"

Cameron started to panic. "My son…where's my wife?"

She pulled back and fixed her gaze on him. "She's fine. Everything's fine. Just relax. I need you to try and stay calm, hon, so I can help you to feel better. Do you think you can do that for me?"

Cameron nodded reluctantly.

She looked up at the machine beside his bed, down at her watch, and then wrote something else on the clipboard.

Cameron tried to move. When he did, he met up with a sharp, stinging pain in his side. He moaned.

"Those are your ribs; several of them were broken in the accident."

The accident. The memories were starting to come back to him now.

The nurse turned and grabbed something from the cart. "We'll see if we can't get you something for the pain. Broken ribs can be hell."

He closed his eyes for a few seconds. It hurt to breathe.

The nurse reached for a small paper cup and held it up. "I'm going to give you a little something so you can sleep."

He took the pill.

And within minutes, everything went dark again.

~

The next morning, bright sunlight bore through the window, hitting Cameron's face and jolting him from his sleep. He squinted to protect his eyes from the harsh glare.

His wife was standing over him.

"Sarah…" he said, his voice rasping. "Dylan. How's Dy—"

"Shhh. It's okay." Sarah reached for his hand, interlacing her fingers with his and squeezing gently. "It's all okay now. I'm right here."

She looked tired, worn down. Her eyes were puffy and red, like she'd been crying. "Are you all right?" he asked.

"I've been worried about you, is all." She nodded as she spoke, forcing a thin smile. "How are you feeling?"

"Okay…I think." But he felt disconnected, confused.

Time passed. A doctor came to see him, followed by a woman wearing a nametag. JOAN SHIPLEY, *it read,* BEREAVEMENT COUNSELOR.

"No," Cameron said, slowly shaking his head while reading it, the panic steadily rising through him. "No!" He looked up at Sarah for reassurance. She was crying. Then he moved his gaze all over the room, as if searching for Dylan.

"It can't be," Cameron said, begging for it not to be true, tears filling his eyes. "It can't…it just can't…he was just…"

"It's true, Cameron." Sarah moved closer, tears rolling down her cheeks. "Our baby boy, he's…" She embraced him and broke down, rocking him gently, pressing her face against his. He could hear her sobs, felt her warm tears turning cold on his skin.

"I'm sorry, Cameron," the doctor said. "We tried to save him. His injuries were just too severe."

"WHEN?"

The doctor took a deep breath, then let the air out slowly. "About an hour after we got him here. We did our best."

Cameron stayed still for a moment, but it didn't last long. He grew agitated and tried to get out of the bed. The doctor rushed toward him. Two passing orderlies ran into the room to assist and to keep Cameron from hurting himself. Even with broken ribs, holding him down proved difficult.

This was a different kind of pain, and it had a strength all its own.

In the end, the doctor had to administer a sedative.

Everything went black again.

~

Cameron slept into the next day. When he came to, it took him a few seconds to realize his nightmare existed not in his sleep but in the waking world.

He soon learned the details of the accident. A truck driver, in a hurry to make a delivery, had run a stop sign and slammed into their car.

The district attorney planned to file reckless driving and manslaughter charges, but that made little difference. Even though the other man was at fault, Cameron still felt tremendous guilt over Dylan's death. If he hadn't taken his eyes off the road, been more attentive, he might have seen the truck coming and avoided the accident.

Sarah didn't blame her husband for their son's death; she knew Cameron's theory was flawed. It was easy to look back and think of what he should have done, she told him, but in reality, you rarely get the luxury of carefully weighing things out before doing them. Life moves too fast. It's only later that you can begin untangling the chain of events and applying any sort of logic to them. She tried to convince Cameron there was nothing he could have done to change the outcome, that nobody blamed him for Dylan's death, but Cameron knew she was wrong: one person did blame him; that person was himself. In his eyes, he was just as responsible for his son's death as the other driver was.

Eight months after the accident, Cameron still hadn't been back to work. He just didn't have any energy left. He could barely function at home; how could he possibly perform at his job?

Sarah did her best to help him, but with little success.

The threads continued to unravel. He stopped responding to Sarah, acting as if she weren't even there. She tried her best to salvage the marriage, but she was living with someone she no longer knew.

A year later, she reached her breaking point.

"I can't live like this anymore, Cam," Sarah said as they sat on the front steps of their house, both of them staring ahead into the distance. Silky strands of sun-streaked hair danced around her face as the wind blew against them. She pushed them away with her fingers. "I've tried. You know I have." She paused, tears glinting in her eyes, then her voice dropped to a whisper. "I miss him too, Cam."

Cameron sat, looking straight ahead, saying nothing, face stoic, except for his eyes, which blinked rapidly, as if deflecting the impact of her statement.

"You can't bring him back, Cameron. Nobody can. You've got to face that. And you've got to stop blaming yourself." She placed her hand under his chin and gently turned his face toward hers. "You gave that boy life. You didn't take it away. Can't you see that?"

Tears welled in his eyes, the first sign of emotion she'd seen in him in a long time. He squeezed them shut, forcing the drops to roll down his cheeks. Still, he was silent.

Sarah wiped the tears from his cheek with her thumb, then she turned forward again, locking her hands around her knees. "I have to go, Cam. I need to grieve the loss of my son too. I've been so busy taking care of you and your needs, I've almost forgotten I even have any."

"I'm sorry." He blurted the words out, almost as if the act were involuntary.

She turned to face him. "Stop being sorry! You did nothing but love that child from the day he came into this world, and you gave him love until the second he left it. Dylan would never have blamed you for this, so stop blaming yourself."

Hearing his son's name felt like a knife going into his chest. "I can't." He brought his face down into his hands and sobbed.

She took a deep breath, didn't say anything for a long time. "I love you, Cam. I always will. If you know anything, please, know that. But if I don't do this, I'll die too, and I refuse to let that happen." She looked down at the ground, shaking her head. "I...I have to go now."

He knew she was right. He couldn't blame her; in fact, he was surprised she'd stuck it out as long as she had. Love had kept her there, but even love has its limits.

Sarah stood up and turned to walk away. She stopped and spoke without looking back at him. "Do yourself a favor, Cam. Free yourself. Free yourself from the guilt, the shame. It's time."

The woman he'd fought tirelessly to win over so many years ago, the one he'd sworn he could never live without, not even for a moment, was now walking right out of his life.

He never saw her again.

~

Cameron had given up on life, and life, he figured, had given up on him.

Sarah had been gone for several months. Now, the larger city he'd once yearned for seemed even bigger. Emptier, too.

On yet another seemingly endless night, Cameron opened his nightstand drawer and pulled out his service weapon. He hadn't turned it in yet. He was, technically, still on disability leave. He stared at the weapon for a long time.

"I have to go now," he finally said, repeating Sarah's words. "Yeah, me too, Sarah. Me, too."

Cameron tightened his grip and raised the weapon toward his head. The weight of the gun seemed heavier than he remembered, perhaps because now he had it pointed the wrong way—toward himself.

He brought the gun closer, finger curled snugly around the trigger. His hands were trembling and his palms wet with sweat as he closed his eyes.

"I have to go now," he said again, breath labored and a tear rolling down his cheek.

He shook his head, offered a final apology to his son, and began to squeeze the trigger.

That was when it happened.

A feeling of warmth quickly wrapped around his upper body, applying pressure to his chest, his shoulders, his neck. It was consuming and yet, at the same time, felt remarkably comforting. It was electric. He'd never experienced anything like it before, as if the chemistry in his body were changing all at once.

A feeling of peace moved through him like a gentle wave. He watched with astonishment as his hand lowered the gun, completely independent of his will. As it touched the nightstand, his fingers began to loosen, uncurling from around the trigger. He let go of it, and when he did, it was as if he were letting go of all the demons keeping him captive for so long.

Their reign had ended.

Cameron had no idea what had caused it, or why it occurred, but he knew it was powerful, knew that something within him had changed. Something remarkable.

He placed his gun back in the drawer and slammed it shut.

All the color in the world slowly began to bleed back in, the gray areas dissolving, leaving behind something of great beauty.

That thing was life.

Chapter Forty

45687 Monument Path Way
Albuquerque, New Mexico

Midnight had come and gone.

Dark clouds lifted apart, then separated as the earth spun its way toward dawn. Sunlight emerged between them, its sharp rays igniting the skies, igniting the world.

Such a beautiful morning. Such a sharp contrast to the way Kyle felt. During the past several days, she'd been sleep deprived, had the daylights scared out of her, and still had no idea why Bethany had invaded her life. All she knew was the little girl needed her help and needed it badly.

It was just before five o'clock, and Kyle had a full day ahead of her, with patients scheduled all the way through; yet, there she sat in bed, wide awake, still trying to figure out this complex mystery involving the little girl who seemed just as mysterious.

Bethany, she thought. *Pretty name*. Kyle wondered where the girl had been living when she died. Albuquerque? Perhaps somewhere even farther away, maybe even another country? Not only did she not know where Bethany had lived, she also had no idea *when* she lived—or died. Without a time of death, checking state records by first name seemed futile. Things would have been so much easier if she could just find two pieces of information that connected in some way.

Kyle sat up in bed and yawned. Then she heard something.

You're exhausted, Kyle. Your mind's shot... Now it's getting the best of you.

But the sounds were just loud enough to convince her otherwise.

Barely audible, yet enough to get her attention, the volume began to climb; once it did, Kyle knew the sounds were real.

She could hear people talking, several of them, the low, rumbling hum of voices whirling through the air. Kyle tried to focus so she could hear the conversations. Within a few seconds, the sound increased even more, and the words became clear.

A man's voice: "Let's get moving, everyone. We only have a few minutes left before it wears off. Let's get this right."

Then a female voice: "Too late, Doctor, he's beginning to come to."

"Already? Shit. Sedate him. Do we have another?"

"I think we have Lewison, just up the hall. He's been parked for a week now. Not sure how responsive he'll be."

"Lewison? I thought he died already."

"Nope. Almost, last week, but he recovered. Don't ask me how. Looks like *that* cat's got *ten* lives."

Laughter all around.

"The timing'll be right if we grab him fast. But he'll only be good for one more round," the female voice said, then added, "It won't be long before he expires."

"Okay. Sedate this one, and park him up the hall. Bring Lewison back in. And let's be quick about it. This is a time-specific procedure. We don't have all day."

"Yes, Doctor."

The sound of people stirring about, metal clanging against glass, and the low rumbling of more voices.

Then, another voice, one Kyle had grown accustomed to hearing: Bethany's.

"Time is running out," she whispered. "You only have three more days."

CHAPTER FORTY-ONE

Sheriff's Station
Faith, New Mexico

"Some kid's in your office," Cameron said to Frank while they stood in the hallway.

"Look again," Frank replied, nodding toward the door. "It's no kid."

Cameron did and realized Frank was right. The person sitting behind the desk, acting as if she owned it, was a woman barely four foot ten, wearing jeans and sneakers, with mousy brown, pageboy-styled hair.

When the two walked in, she glanced up from the folder, almost as if they'd interrupted her, then quickly went back to her reading.

"Meet Special Agent Margaret Kazlowsky," Frank said. Then he leaned in closer toward Cameron and mumbled, "*Fed*."

"FBI," she corrected, raising her hand while turning a page. "Here for the party."

"Party?" Cameron asked. "Didn't know we were having one."

"Judging by what's been going on around here, I'd have to agree with you." She dropped the folder onto the desk, stood up, then walked toward them. "What you *have*—excuse my Polish—is a bona fide cluster-fuck."

"That one of those fancy technical terms they teach you back at Quantico?" Frank asked.

"Nope," she replied. "That's an opinion. Take it for what it's worth."

"Well, you know what they say about opinions," Frank replied. "They're kinda like assholes. Everyone's got one—everyone thinks everyone else's stinks."

Margaret swallowed her words, then flashed a smile, the kind people give when they think they know something that someone else doesn't. "Look, fellas, just between you and me, as far as the bureau's concerned, I'm only here to investigate the Champion murder. That's it. You know how that goes. The folks up in DC, Quantico—all of them—well, let's just say they've got their panties pulled into a tight little wad over this. They want answers, and they want 'em quick. Of course," she added, "there's no rule saying we couldn't help each other out."

"And how would that work?" Frank asked.

"It's easy," she said with a shrug. "A little bit of give and take. You know…two agencies lending a hand, like neighbors helping neighbors. Know what I mean?"

They knew exactly what she meant.

Frank walked back around to his desk, sat down. "Look, I appreciate your offer, Ms. Kazlowsky, but I think we've got things under control on our end."

"Beg your pardon?" she said, stifling a laugh. "From where I stand, things are far from under control. No offense meant, of course."

"None taken, of course," Frank said. "Think you can do better?"

"Not saying that," she cautioned.

"Then what exactly *are* you saying?"

"Like I mentioned earlier, I'm here strictly to look at the Champion girl. But at the same time, if I just *happened* to stumble across information, information you could somehow use…"

"And vice versa," Cameron said.

"Vice versa. *Absolutely,*" she replied with a solemn nod.

"All right," Cameron said after giving it a moment's thought. "I'll bite. You've looked over the cases. Give us your take."

Recognizing the challenge, Margaret said, "Here's how I see it. You got different murders, and when I say different, I mean *different.* Not a snowball's chance in hell any of them were committed by the same person. I'm just not feeling it."

"You're not telling us anything we didn't already know," Frank said. "We came to the same conclusion—"

"Not so fast there, cowboy," she said, hand raised, looking down toward the floor. "Wasn't done yet. What I was about say, is, I think they still *could* be related."

"Related how?" Frank asked. "Like they were all working together? Because we've already floated that theory as well—it sank."

"Didn't say that," she warned. "Didn't say that at all."

"Then what *are* you saying?" Frank asked.

"What I'm saying—what I *think*—is there's a connection. Now, what that connection is, well, it's hard to say…right now, anyway. But I do feel like there *is* one—though a conspiracy theory might be pushing things a bit further than I want to go. However, I *can* say this: you got a peaceful town—or, at least, had one—suddenly going all ape-shit in a hurry… Well, it just doesn't happen. Not like this. Not this fast."

"So what do you think's going on?" Cameron asked.

Margaret walked back to Frank's desk, flipped the folder open, twisting her head sideways to read it. "This first murder, the one with your deputy. Anything new there?"

Cameron shook his head.

Margaret looked at the wall, thought for a moment, then alternated her gaze between the two men. "Something sorta odd about it."

"What is?" Frank asked.

"You've got a seasoned deputy, been on your force a decent amount of time, right?" She didn't wait for an answer. "In good physical shape too, tall, athletic. To get at him, it had to come as a complete surprise—either that or he knew the suspect…or maybe both."

"And knowing the suspect could create a possible motive," Cameron said.

"Yeah. There's that," she said, nodding. "And then there's something else, too. My guess is it's a male, a pretty strong one too—had to be in order to overcome your deputy, even if he *did* take him by surprise, even if he knew him. Once that first hook landed on his neck, the adrenaline would be pumping. He'd put up a hell of a fight, and it would have taken a lot of strength to control him."

"Okay," Cameron said. "What else?"

She flipped through a few more pages. "Profile-wise, I'd say he's probably in his mid-to-late twenties, probably unmarried, and probably local."

Cameron looked at Frank, slowly nodding. Both knew what the other was thinking.

"Okay," Cameron said, "so you've made your point—rather well, in fact. What would you need from us?"

The smile grew more confident. "Exactly what I just gave you: your insight, information—anything—pertaining to the Champion murder."

"I can do that," Cameron said. "The senator and I have been in close contact."

"Yeah. I know that…" She stopped herself. "I mean, I've *heard* something to the effect."

"Bet you have," Cameron said.

She shrugged. "It's my job to know these sorts of things."

"So where do we go from here?" Frank asked.

"Let me get busy on this," she said. "Let me poke around town a little, start putting some things together, speak to my people up in Quantico, too. I may be able to work up a better profile on your cop killer."

"Okay," Cameron said, "but do me one favor."

"What's that?"

"Keep things on the down-low if you can. This town's up to its ass in alligators. An FBI agent snooping around and asking questions—that'll just give 'em more to be nervous about. And we can't afford that right now."

"No worries there. I'm real good at flying under the radar—*way* under. It's one of the benefits of being vertically challenged. People hardly ever notice me—that is, unless I open my mouth." Then she giggled.

Cameron and Frank laughed too.

"If you need me, I'm staying over at the Graybill Motel on Third Street." She reached into her back pocket, pulled out a card, passed it to Cameron. "Cell number's on there. Meantime—completely unrelated here—can you tell me where a gal can go to get some good Mexican food 'round here? I'm starving, been craving it ever since I got here. Must be a southwest sorta thing. Hit me as soon as I rolled into town."

"Felice's," Cameron said, "over on Main. Doesn't get any better than that."

"All righty then. Once I get some fuel, I'll be ready to roll." She gathered her things, looked at Frank, looked at Cameron, gave a single nod.

Then she was out the door.

Chapter Forty-Two

Roses Are Red florist shop
Faith, New Mexico

Judith Hedrick always opened her store at precisely nine o'clock each morning and had been doing so for more than fifteen years. In a world filled with inconsistencies, it was one thing that always remained the same. You could set your watch to it.

Until today.

By ten o' clock, the doors were still locked tight, lights still off, and Judith was nowhere to be found. Concern quickly turned to worry for employees and friends; it just wasn't like her.

Judith was a perfectionist. Along with her impeccable punctuality, she was also meticulous about her shop, paying close attention to the smallest details. All one had to do was set a foot inside to see firsthand why her talent and creativity translated into great business success. Her name had appeared in two national magazines, both of which highlighted her stunning arrangements.

In addition to her extraordinary talent, however, Judith was also extraordinarily generous. She made a comfortable living from her business and was a firm believer in sharing her good fortune. Through the years, she had given a lot to back the community.

When Faith held its Distinguished-Ten Dinner, an award ceremony honoring citizens who contributed most to their town, not only was she honored, she designed and donated all the floral displays and table centerpieces for the event.

Her contributions didn't end there. When Faith's library burned down a week before the first day of school, Judith stepped in. She committed thousands of dollars of her own money and donated a percentage of her proceeds for one week toward the creation of a new library and learning center.

All this made Judith's disappearance even more disturbing.

~

7586 Chrysanthemum Way
Faith, New Mexico

Jim Avello decided to run by Judith's house to check on her. When he did, he noticed all the outside lights were still on, and her car, usually parked in front of her garage, was nowhere in sight.

He approached the front door, hand resting over his holstered gun, and knocked twice. No answer. He rang the doorbell. Still no answer. Finally, he cupped his hands against the stained glass and peered inside. Almost instantly, he saw a rocking chair lying on its side.

Avello reached for the handle. The door was unlocked. He stepped inside. Furniture lay overturned, and there were broken bits and pieces of cherished objects everywhere.

The living room was the crime scene.

It looked like a madman had gone through it. Worst of all, there was no sign of Judith anywhere. Avello radioed for help, and soon, Judith Hedrick's house was buzzing with activity as deputies searched for a body that wasn't there.

~

Avello met Cameron on the front steps outside the house. At almost the same time, an Albuquerque news van pulled up across the street. A lone cameraman fumbled with his gear for a few minutes, then moved toward the house, camera propped on his shoulder. No sign of Casey Gold anywhere.

Cameron knew Judith well. He and her son, Jason, were the same age and had been good friends growing up. Jason's father had passed away when the boy was only ten, and Judith did everything possible to make her son's life a good one despite the loss.

Peanut-butter-and-jelly-and-potato-chip sandwiches on Saturday afternoons—that was what came to Cameron's mind when he remembered Judith. He and Jason used to attend a basketball clinic together, and Judith always had lunch waiting for them afterward. The potato chips were the boys' own addition—they liked the way they made the sandwiches crunch when they bit into them.

Cameron shook the memory off and entered the house. The disarray struck him first: much like her floral shop, Judith had always kept her home immaculate, everything in its place. Despite the chaos everywhere, he didn't see any physical signs Judith had been injured—no blood, no clumps of hair on the floor, nothing. It looked like someone had just thrown things around. Books lay scattered about, far from their shelves, and it appeared as if someone had hurled dishes against the living room wall, pieces scattered everywhere.

Cameron scratched his head. Perhaps it was a good sign that Judith wasn't there. Maybe this was nothing more than vandalism. Maybe she hadn't even been home when all this happened. But if that were the case, where was Judith?

"Sheriff," yelled Avello from the doorway, radio pressed against his ear. "We got something."

"What?"

"Hedrick's car. Blue Toyota Camry. Plates match and everything."

Cameron felt something heavy turn in the pit of his stomach. "What about Judith? Was she—"

"Negative, boss," he said, shaking his head. "Still missing."

Cameron sighed with relief. "Location on the car?" he asked.

"You won't believe it."

"Nothing surprises me anymore. Try me."

"Not far from where the Champion girl's car turned up. Looks like it was driven into a creek."

Cameron was already halfway out the door and on his way to his car.

Chapter Forty-Three

45687 Monument Path Way
Albuquerque, New Mexico

The voices were gone, and so was Bethany.

But it was hardly over.

Images started to come, at first unclear—shape shifting, silvery forms twisting through the air. Then the scene came into focus. Kyle looked closer and recognized a group of medical personnel, dressed in white and gathered around some kind of operating table. A man reached above his head and pulled down a large, domed fixture. He flipped the switch, and the whole room exploded with light, making the white lab coats appear electric.

Pictures that matched the sounds Kyle had just heard.

Over to the right, she saw the doctor and nurse talking. Although she couldn't see anyone on the table itself—too many people blocked her view—she had a feeling she knew who was lying on it. Beyond that group of medical staff lay the patient they would later replace with someone named Lewison.

The images disappeared into a bright flash of light.

Kyle's whole body stiffened. *What were they going to do with him?*

But something about the equipment didn't seem right; it seemed old. She'd been in many operating rooms, and none of them looked anything like this. Besides that, the walls, the floor, even the people looked peculiar.

Worst of all, the nurse standing next to the doctor looked hauntingly familiar.

She was the same one Kyle had watched fall to her death.

The visions were coming together, forming a coherent story. One nurse plunged to her death, another died while being trampled upon during some sort of riot—all at some odd medical facility, a place where patients were heard but not seen, a place where patients were "parked," then left to "expire."

Kyle kept ending up there too.

But where was Bethany, and how did she fit into all this?

Kyle looked up toward the ceiling as if speaking to the girl, her voice barely a whisper. "Tell me, Bethany—in God's name, *please*—tell me what they did to you."

CHAPTER FORTY-FOUR

Old Highway 80
Faith, New Mexico

"I'm a little confused here," said Frank.

He and Cameron were gazing down into the steep canyon where Judith Hedrick's car lay upside down. "Help me understand how we managed to miss an entire car just a few miles from an established crime scene."

The deputies were now at the bottom, processing the vehicle and combing it for evidence.

"I asked the same question," Cameron replied with an exasperated sigh and shake of his head. "They should have caught it."

"Damn straight, they should have," Frank said. "So does anybody know for sure if the car was here while the Keystone Kops were busy stumbling over one another?"

"Time sequence seems to fit. The girl left home around two on Saturday, which puts her here around five-ish, and as we know, she never made it any farther. Meanwhile, Judith closes her store at four the same day to go out of town. She was supposed to be back this morning to open the shop. She didn't."

"So both of them ended up here around the same time," replied Frank, shaking his head, "and our deputies are idiots."

"I'll take part of the blame for that, Frank. Should have kept a closer watch on what they were doing. Besides the timeline to prove it, we also have logic—a crime scene's the last place anyone would want to leave Judith's car."

Frank turned around to observe the string of news vans lining the road. "Hard to get past all *that.*"

"Plus, the tire tracks leading to the creek don't look fresh. They've been here a while, at least a few days. Which leads to my next concern—"

"Felicity Champion's killed in one location," Frank said, "and her car's left in another. Then Hedrick's car is found not far from that. Shit. Two women, one killer. You said you didn't think so."

"That was before Judith's car turned up here. Kinda hard to ignore it."

Frank put his hands on his hips and gazed out at the road, shaking his head. "Be a hell of a coincidence."

"And pretty unlikely."

"But why would the killer dump Hedrick's car, then leave Champion's out in plain view? Doesn't make sense."

"Don't have an answer for that right now, Frank."

"And something else…if Hedrick *is* dead, where the hell's her body? Anybody go back and check where we found Champion?"

Cameron nodded. "Searched the area for several miles—twice now—plus this one, too. Didn't find anything."

"Without a body, we don't even know if she's dead…and your two-women, one-killer theory goes right out the door."

"True, but still, we can't rule out the connection. Seems like a strong possibility."

"But it doesn't hold water, not unless we find something linking one killer to both crimes."

Cameron moved forward a few steps toward the edge of the canyon, crossed his arms and looked down. “I know one thing. If we’re tracking patterns here, the odds don’t look good for Judith.”

Frank put his hand on Cameron’s shoulder and gazed down with him. “So what’s your next move?”

“The obvious one.” Cameron paused, then sighed. “Dead or alive, we’ve got to find Judith. And we’ve got to find her quick.”

CHAPTER FORTY-FIVE

The Landing Doc Café
Albuquerque, New Mexico

It caught the light from all the way across the room and Kyle's attention at the same time.

She and Josh had just sat down to have lunch at The Landing Doc. The restaurant was next door to the medical building where Kyle's practice was located. It was a favorite spot, and doctors and nurses filled the place daily, starting around noon.

Josh watched as his sister's face went blank, her mouth slightly open. "Hey…hello? Still with me here?"

Kyle said nothing. She was staring across the room.

"Um, Sis?" he said, his voice a little louder this time.

Kyle snapped out of her daze as if someone had just yanked her arm. "That's it!"

"What is?" asked Josh.

"The caduceus."

"Ca-what?"

"Caduceus," she repeated while nodding toward a nurse who was sitting across from them and eating her lunch. "See on her lapel, the pin with the winged staff and two snakes wrapped around it?"

"The medical symbol?" He shrugged. "You see it everywhere. What's so special?"

"It was in my dreams. I didn't remember until now. That's because I'm bombarded with the thing all day long, and I've conditioned myself to ignore it, which is what I did when I saw it... blocked it out."

Josh raised an eyebrow. "And it's important because...?"

"Because everything looked so weird in the dream, you know? The equipment, the medical personnel, even the operating room—it seemed outdated, and not by just a few years, either. It was like I was viewing something from a long time ago."

"How long ago?"

"Hard to say. I wasn't paying much attention to the surroundings...too focused on the people...trying to figure out what they were doing, but that symbol—*it* might tell me."

"Tell you? How?" He stabbed a french fry with his fork, doused it in ketchup, took a bite.

"It looked different from any other I've seen before. I may be able to research it, figure out the time period." She thought for a moment, then added, "It had a big letter *N* across it."

"Letter *N*." He rubbed his chin while stealing another glance at the woman's Caduceus pin. She noticed him staring. Josh quickly looked back at Kyle. "Then you can work your way forward, maybe pick up a few more clues along the way."

"Exactly." She stared down at her half-eaten sandwich, thought for a moment, then looked back at Josh. "And to think it was right there all the time."

Chapter Forty-Six

Felice's Diner
Faith, New Mexico

Cameron walked into Felice's and found Margaret tucked away in a booth, sipping coffee and poring over paperwork.

"Guess the Mexican food hit the spot," he said. "You're still alive…and you came back. Mind if I join you?"

"Please," she said, gesturing toward the empty seat. "Not a bad little place you got here. Not bad at all."

"We like it. Food's great and it's cozy," Cameron said while sitting down.

"Wasn't talking about the restaurant—although their enchiladas are the bomb. Was talking about the town. Has a lot of appeal. Reminds me of where I grew up."

"Yeah? Where's that?"

"Place called Fountain Lake, Wisconsin. It's near the Minnesota border."

Cameron shook his head. "Never heard of it."

"My point, exactly," she said with a smile, then shifting toward more practical matters, "Heard about your missing woman. What a drag."

"Yeah…complicates things, to say the least—speaking of which, got some information you may find useful."

"Oh?" Margaret said, tilting her head slightly.

"Found her car. Hedrick's, that is."

"You did? Where?"

Cameron cleared his throat. "Not far from where Champion's was."

Margaret looked off at the table next to them for a split second, then back at Cameron. "I don't get it. How did they—"

"Don't ask. Long story," Cameron said. "Anyway, it obviously changes the scope of things, creates a possible link between the two women."

"Damn straight, it does. The question now, what's the connection?"

"Hard to say. Too soon to know, really. We searched Hedrick's vehicle."

"Find anything?"

"Some blood," Cameron said. "Lab's got it."

"I'll wanna see whatever they find," she said.

"Naturally."

"Any immediate thoughts?"

Cameron gazed out through the diner's front window, sighed. "Well, of course, judging by the close proximity of the two vehicles, seems possible we've got one perp going after both of them. That would be one. But with Hedrick still missing…hard to say."

She nodded, appearing thoughtful. "Need a body."

"Well, the *last* thing I need here is another murder, but yeah, I know what you mean."

"Strange, though," she said.

"What's that?"

"With all the other crimes having different killers, seems odd a double murder suddenly coming from out of nowhere…"

"True, but odd *does* seem to be the flavor of the day around here."

"Damn Skippy on that." She looked down at the table, thought for a moment, then glanced back up at Cameron. "Well, at least there's one thing may come out of it."

"What?"

"Like I said earlier, I thought they were all related—I just didn't know how." Then she raised her eyebrows. "Maybe this'll tell us."

Chapter Forty-Seven

Sheriff's Station
Faith, New Mexico

The roast beef sandwich tasted like a dry sponge pressed between two sheets of cardboard. After several attempts at eating it, Frank wrapped the whole mess back up and tossed it into the trash.

Cameron walked in, and Frank glanced up with a sneer. "You look happier than you've got a right to be. Don't you know people are getting killed around here?"

"Good afternoon to you, too," said Cameron. "Bad day?"

"I'm a tad under the weather," Frank said, creasing a thick brow. "Six murders and another on the way'll do that to ya. What's up?"

"Got the lab report we've been waiting for."

"You don't say." Frank's expression lightened slightly, but not enough to denote any measure of satisfaction.

"You said you needed more evidence." Cameron held the folder up. "I have more evidence. Remember our green fiber?"

"The one on the Champion girl?"

"That's the one. Turns out it's pretty unusual. Not something you see every day."

"Lime green," Frank said with a grunt. "Hideous color. We knew that."

Cameron pointed to the report. "Not just the color. The material. It's angora."

"Okay. I can't even match my shoes with my belt. Tell me what it means."

"Comes from an English angora rabbit, the softest of all, used to make sweaters—*women's* sweaters."

Frank's expression shifted in an instant, going from annoyance to shock. "You've *got* to be kidding me… Killer's a female?"

"And if that's true, it for sure rules out Ryan Churchill as a suspect."

"Shit." Frank stopped to think for a minute, then suddenly looked up at Cameron. "Margaret know about any of this?"

"She knows we found Hedrick's car. Saw her at Felice's and mentioned it to her. But not this, not yet."

"Better give her an update."

"Will do, boss."

Frank began moving his lips as if counting. "So if all this is true, it brings our total up to four suspects: Foley, Churchill, whoever killed Witherspoon, and now Champion's killer…a woman?"

"Then there's Judith," Cameron said. "Don't forget about her."

"Like I could."

"If *she's* dead, also at the hands of the same killer…"

Frank sighed, heaved himself out of his chair, then went over to gaze out the window. "You check the calendar lately?"

"No. Why?"

"Oh, nuthin'. Just wondering if there's a scheduled apocalypse. I never got the memo."

Cameron cleared his throat. "Something else, Frank."

"What?"

"Daytime temperatures have been close to ninety. Now that we know the killer was wearing a sweater…"

Frank turned back from the window to look at Cameron, shook his head. "Doesn't make any sense."

"Ben had flu symptoms, remember?"

"Yeah?"

"Teacher said he had the chills, one of the symptoms of the flu. When you have the chills, you can't get warm, even when you're wrapped in blankets."

Frank nodded slowly. "Or while wearing an angora sweater."

"You got it."

Frank went back to his desk, then sat down. He ran the back of his hand under his chin several times, as if it might help him think better. "More similarities—they keep popping up."

"Something else here," Cameron said. "Remember the blood in Hedrick's car?"

"Yeah."

"Wasn't hers."

"What the… Who'd it belong to, then?"

"Report just came over the fax." He paused for a long moment. "Felicity Champion's."

"*The hell*? What's Champion's blood doing in Hedrick's car?"

"Got a theory on that." Cameron walked toward him. "Let's say the suspect lures Champion to the side of the road, maybe acts in distress or something. Remember, if the killer's another female, she'll appear less threatening to her."

"And Champion stops to assist."

"Yep. Suspect grabs her, attacks her. Then Judith comes driving by and notices the two struggling, stops to help. I know her—she'd do it in a minute," Cameron said. "She gets out, gets killed in the process as well. Now the suspect has two bodies, two cars, and very little time to get the hell out of Dodge."

"Makes sense," Frank acknowledged. "It'd explain why the scene was so sloppy."

"She puts Champion in Hedrick's car, dumps the body a few miles out, then takes the vehicle back to the scene—maybe to go finish the job, get rid of Judith. Chucks the car into the canyon."

"But what about Champion's car? She just leaves it sitting there? In plain view?"

Cameron shrugged. "Fits the pattern. Suspect was in over her head by then. Didn't know what the hell to do. Probably knew the longer she stuck around, the better her chances were of getting caught. She panicked, realized there was no time to dispose of the other car, took off."

"Okay. I can see her leaving the car behind," Frank said, "but if she took off on foot, what'd she do with Hedrick?"

"That whole area's surrounded by woods. We searched through some of it, but I have a feeling not well enough—that was before we knew Judith went missing. Her body could still be out there, maybe well hidden, not too far away. We need to get back out there, Frank, need to keep looking…*really* looking. If we missed the car, we damn well could've missed Judith as well. Gotta go deeper, find her."

"Indigestion," Frank said. "I'm getting indigestion."

"Time to get busy, boss—sort through all this—make sense of it."

Frank was rooting around in a drawer for calcium tablets as he spoke. "Get some deputies out there, good ones—ones who know what the hell they're doing. I don't want another train wreck."

Cameron nodded.

"Meanwhile, the angora fiber. Let's get that nailed down. It could be the key to finding our killer. I want to know everything about it."

"Already on it," Cameron assured him. "Lab's still trying to narrow down its origins, working on determining what type of dye was used and which manufacturers might have put it in their products. If we can figure out where it was sold, it might lead us right to our killer."

"Good. It's the most solid piece of evidence we have so far. Now let's see where it takes us. Tell me everything you can about it, short of which rabbit it came from and who plucked it."

"Why stop there?"

"All right," Frank muttered back. "Get me that, too."

Chapter Forty-Eight

7586 Chrysanthemum Way
Faith, New Mexico

Deputies launched a full-scale search in the wooded area along Highway 10, the same one where Felicity Champion's body had turned up several days before. Now they were looking for Judith Hedrick, also presumed dead. Then it was on to where both women's cars were dumped. They were leaving nothing to chance this time. If she was there, they were going to find her.

Judith was probably another victim in a bizarre string of sadistic murders in their town. Feeling as though he needed more in the way of evidence—especially since Judith's body still hadn't turned up—Cameron decided her house might be the place to find it.

Unfortunately, time was becoming less of a luxury, more of a challenge. He needed to delegate responsibility if he was going to win this war. With his top man, Jim Avello, leading the search along the highway, he knew things were in good hands, enough to where he could break away and start working some other angles.

~

From outside, Judith's place looked like a dollhouse: small, quaint, and neat. The outer walls were pale olive with crisp, eggshell-white trim. Flowers—lots of them—sprang up everywhere, a riot of color filling her front yard.

On the front door, a cheerful hand-painted sign hung with the words "Everyone's Welcome!" But beneath that, yellow tape stretched across, adding, CRIME SCENE—KEEP OUT.

Cameron nodded to the deputy standing guard outside, pushed the door open, then ducked beneath the tape to enter the house.

Calling the place a mess would have been kind; it was in shambles, worlds away from the orderly manner Cameron knew Judith always liked to keep it in.

He frowned.

Who did this to her?

He moved toward the living room, bending over and picking up books off the floor, reading the titles as he went along, mostly cookbooks. That didn't surprise him. Cameron remembered the wonderful meals she'd prepared for him in the past, back when he and her son, Jason, were friends. He put the books back on their shelves.

Cameron moved into the kitchen and checked the cabinets: empty—every single one of them; every dish thrown across the room, smashed. He moved back to the living room, where most of the broken pieces had landed, picking them up as he went along. Detectives had already dusted as many of the fragments as they could for prints; however, the only ones they'd found had been Judith's. No surprise to Cameron. Most organized criminals these days had the foresight to wear gloves.

He went back to the living room and shone a flashlight under the sofa and loveseat. Nothing there, not even so much as a dust ball: Judith always kept her house immaculate.

Cameron moved into the office and looked over her desktop and through each drawer. Everything there appeared neatly in order.

"Hey, Cam." The familiar voice seemed to come from nowhere.

He turned around quickly, loosening some after seeing who it was. "Hi, Jason. You startled me. Didn't hear you coming."

"Sorry 'bout that," Jason said with a nervous laugh.

"Nonsense. Great to see you." Cameron moved forward to shake his hand. He'd heard Jason was in town. Deputies had called him as soon as his mother went missing, but Cameron had been so busy working the Champion case that he hadn't had the chance to catch up with him yet. "I barely recognized you."

"Been a long time, huh?" Jason said. His grip felt loose and tentative.

"Seems like ages," Cameron replied, suddenly noticing how awkward the moment had become, while at the same time trying to hide his discomfort. "Sorry we have to meet again under these circumstances."

Jason didn't react to the comment. Instead, he broke eye contact with Cameron by switching his attention toward the front entryway. "Hope you don't mind I came inside. Didn't want to disturb any evidence. The deputy let me in."

"'Course not. This *is* your house, after all," Cameron replied. He looked down at the floor, unsure what to say next, then decided to take a stab at the obvious. "I started cleaning up the place. You know how your mom's always been… Just thought about how much it would bother her, seeing things like this."

For the first time, Jason looked around the room. He appeared just as disturbed by the mess as Cameron had been. "She always liked you a lot."

"The feeling's mutual, Jason. She's a special lady," Cameron said, careful not to speak of her in the past tense. "Actually, the cleaning was just an afterthought. I wanted to go over things again, make sure I didn't miss anything."

"Any luck?"

"Not so far." An awkward pause, then a shift in subject. "So where ya living these days?"

"Out in California," Jason said, his voice slightly more animated now. "San Diego. Working for a biotech firm. Not too exciting, but it pays the bills."

"You look *great*," Cameron continued. It was true. He'd shed a lot of the baby fat he carried around as a kid and appeared to be in better physical shape. His complexion, once covered with teenage acne, was now suntanned and clear.

"Thanks…you too," Jason replied. "So what do you have so far on my mom?"

"Not a whole lot, I'm afraid. She most likely disappeared around Saturday evening. Last time anyone saw her was when she closed shop for the day, around four."

Jason nodded, processing the information.

Cameron thought for a moment. "Mind if I ask you a few questions…about your mom?"

Jason nodded and shrugged.

"Wanted to know if you can think of anyone who'd want to hurt her."

Jason laughed a little. "My mom? Naw. I don't think so. Everyone loves her."

"No disagreements? With anyone? Ever?"

"If she did, I never heard about it."

"Not even at her shop?"

Jason shook his head. "It's just not the way she does business. If a customer was ever unhappy, she'd always bend over backward to make it right. That's just the kind of person she is."

"Yeah," Cameron said, nodding, rubbing his chin, thinking. "Had to ask, though. You gonna be in town a while? Can I call you if anything new comes up?"

"Sure. I took a leave of absence from my job. At least until we know if my mom's…" He stopped. "Until something *definite* comes up. My wife's here too. I'm married now."

"That's great, Jason."

"She's back at a friend's house. I had to get out. You know, driving around town, trying to clear my head a bit."

"Understandable."

"I'm staying with the Reddings, over on Helix Street. You can call me over there, if you want."

"Oh, yeah. Of course. I figured that's where you'd be—Chip being your best friend and all." *It should have been me.*

"Yeah. Chip's always been there for me," said Jason. The deadpan expression on his face was difficult to read but seemed to imply blame. Cameron couldn't be sure whether he'd meant the comment as a jab. He decided to change the subject once again. "I'm gonna head upstairs to the bedroom. I need to look over a few things. You're welcome to come along if you want."

Jason mulled it over for a moment, then shrugged. "Okay. I think I will. Maybe I can help you out."

When they reached Judith's bedroom, Cameron suddenly turned around toward Jason, started to say something, stopped, then began again. "You know, I feel real bad about how I treated you in high school, Jason. You were never anything less than a good friend to me, and I screwed it up real bad because of dumb peer pressure. I wish I'd done you better. We do stupid things when we're young. I've regretted it for a long time. I'm sorry. I realize it's little consolation now, but I just wanted you to know."

Jason offered a softened smile and blinked a few times. It was as if he'd been waiting for an apology all these years. He nodded solemnly. "It's okay, Cam. We were just kids. We don't always make the best choices at that age. We grow up, and we learn… that's all. It's history now. Doesn't matter anymore."

But it did. He knew Jason well enough to know he'd been deeply hurt. Now his mother was missing, maybe even dead; still, Cameron felt relieved to have cleared the air, glad Jason had accepted his apology. The moment seemed to offer both men a moment of consolation amid a sea of uncertainly.

Inside Judith's bedroom, Cameron shone a flashlight under the bed as Jason looked on. Once again, not a speck of dust or lint to be found. As he got up off the floor, however, he froze, staring at the wall across from him.

"Cam, you all right?" asked Jason. "You look pale."

Cameron moved around the bed, inching closer toward the wall, blinking hard, wondering if his eyes were seeing things wrong.

Tacked to the bulletin board was a photo of Judith: beautiful smile, arms wrapped around two friends—one on each side—happy as could be.

And wearing a lime-green sweater.

"Cam?" Jason repeated.

"Jason?" Cameron finally said, moving even closer toward the bulletin board, still staring at it. "How long has your mother had the sweater in that photo?"

Jason moved closer too now, squinting, inspecting the picture. "That? Oh, shit, man, for years. It's her favorite. I think she got it in England."

"*I know.*"

"Huh?"

"Never mind. Do you know if the sweater's here now?"

Jason shrugged, hands buried in his pockets, then nodded toward the closet. "It would be in there. Mom always likes to hang her sweaters. Hates bunching them up inside drawers. You know how she is."

Cameron turned his gaze toward the closet, then moved forward, his feet falling heavily, like bags of sand.

"What's going on, Cam? What's this all about?"

Cameron didn't respond. He was sifting through the clothes, searching for the sweater, for an answer he was afraid to find.

It wasn't there.

Cameron took a step back, eyes opened wide, still fixed on the closet's interior. Then he turned to Jason. "I've got to go."

"What is it? What do you have?"

"Jason, I promise I'll get back to you and explain everything, but for now, I have to go."

Cameron ran down the steps and then out the door.

Chapter Forty-Nine

Chrysanthemum Way
Faith, New Mexico

Cameron put the squad car in drive and took off down Judith Hedrick's street at a speed that was neither safe nor legal. Not that he cared. Not right now, at least.

Judith wasn't a victim after all.

She was a suspect.

Judith killed Felicity, used her own car to dump the body elsewhere, then took it back to the vicinity of the murder scene, where she pushed it into the canyon. After that, she took off, heading out on foot.

But even though the logistics seemed to add up, in Cameron's mind the act itself did not. He knew Judith, knew she was a gentle, caring woman, one who would never hurt anyone.

How could this be?

Cameron recalled Felicity Champion's autopsy. Part of her face had been chewed off, not by animals but by another human. *By Judith? The loving mother, upstanding citizen, and proud businessperson?* He shook his head quickly, trying to jar the thought from his mind but with little success—not because he didn't want to—because the sweet woman who once served him peanut butter and jelly sandwiches on Saturday afternoons wouldn't let him.

A murderous cannibal?

He'd had trouble seeing Ben Foley and Ryan Churchill as killers, too.

Still, even if Cameron *could* entertain the possibility that Judith had killed Felicity, what was her motive? There was no connection between them. Felicity wasn't even from around these parts—she was just passing through on her way to Albuquerque. They didn't even know each other.

Or did they?

Cameron's boyhood hero, Sherlock Holmes, said, "Once you eliminate the impossible, whatever remains, no matter how improbable, must be the truth."

While not entirely impossible, it was improbable the two women had ever crossed paths before this—all the more reason, Cameron supposed, to dig deeper, especially after uncovering this most recent bombshell.

He started running different scenarios through his mind: Judith disappeared shortly after closing her shop Saturday. Felicity went missing around the same time. A slight shift in the time frame, and theoretically, the girl could have stopped in town on her way through. It was also possible Felicity had gone by the florist shop. That would have afforded her the opportunity to meet up with Judith.

But even if their paths did intersect there, what would make Judith want to murder Felicity? Had the two women shared some kind of secret connection? One that caused them to come to blows with one another?

He thought about the other cases, trying to come up with a common variable among them. The only logical one was that the three known suspects—Ryan, Ben, and Judith—were also the least likely. None had a criminal history. None had an inclination toward violence.

Thinking back to his Internet research on English angora, Judith's sweater looked a lot like the photos he saw there. That certainly wasn't enough to make her a murderer. But something else was: the fibers—they were on Felicity Champion's body. They were also an unusual color, and worst of all, they matched Judith's sweater. Then there was Felicity Champion's blood in Judith's car. When Cameron added all those up, he had the inescapable truth.

Solid, irrevocable evidence making Judith a viable suspect.

Backed into a corner, Cameron thought. He needed to get himself out of it, had to turn this all around before it was too late. Before another body turned up.

Frank, Cameron thought: he had to let him know what he'd found at Judith's. Grabbing his cell phone, he frantically began punching the number. It rang once, twice, three times, but no answer. *What now?* He dialed Frank's pager.

Just as he finished, his phone rang. Cameron looked down at the number.

"Frank," Cameron said, not even giving him a chance to speak. "You won't believe what I have here."

The sheriff laughed. "I was just going to tell *you* the same thing."

"Unless you have Felicity Champion's killer in custody, I'd better go first."

"Not Felicity's, but Alma Gutierrez's. That count for anything?" He sounded smug.

"*What*?"

"Ryan Churchill," Frank said. "We have him."

Cameron dropped his phone, catching it near his waist. He fumbled, trying to get it back up to his ear. "What? *Where?*"

"Right here. At the station. We've got him in custody."

"I'm on my way." Cameron's tires squealed as he made a 180-degree turn and headed back in the opposite direction.

"Hey! What was your news?" Frank's tinny voice came through the phone, trying to catch Cameron before he disconnected.

"Never mind," Cameron said as he slid up to an intersection, moving his head in both directions to see if it was clear. "I'll tell you when I get there."

"Oh good. More surprises. We don't get enough of those around here."

"You won't be saying that when you hear it."

CHAPTER FIFTY

Abrams Medical Center
Albuquerque, New Mexico

Time to go to the Internet for a refresher course on the caduceus, Kyle decided. It had been years since medical school, where she first learned its extensive history.

It came from Greek god Hermes, who carried a winged staff symbolizing fertility, healing, and wisdom. She read on.

The Caduceus was approved by the US Army in 1902 for its medical corps. It later spread to the civilian population and has been an emblem representing American medicine ever since.

She did another search, this time using *caduceus* and *letter N*. The results were even more telling:

World War II Medical Department, The Medical Corps: For each division, a letter was placed over the caduceus. For example, Veterinary Corps (V), Medical Administrative Corps (A), Sanitary Corps (S), and Army Nurse Corps (N).

Army Nurse Corps: there it was, the context Kyle needed. The scenes she saw in her dreams had taken place during World War II. That's why everything looked so outdated.

On to an image search using *US Army Corps, nurses, uniforms, history.* It gave her more of what she needed. Studying the photos, she could see that in World War I, the uniforms didn't conform to the shape of a woman's body; in fact, they were formless, no curves at all. During World War II, however, styles began to change, and the new look complemented the female body rather than hiding it.

Those uniforms Kyle saw in her visions were definitely from World War II. The skirts still went all the way down to the lower calf, but there was much more shape above them.

Kyle had nailed it.

CHAPTER FIFTY-ONE

Sheriff's Station
Faith, New Mexico

"The kid was wandering around Truth," Frank said to Cameron as they stood outside the canteen, now serving as a makeshift interrogation room. He nodded toward the door. "He's in there."

"*Truth*?" Cameron said. "That's a good seventy miles from here. How'd he get there?"

"Judging by his condition, I'd say he walked," Frank replied. "Kid looks like he's been through a meat grinder. Clothes torn up, blood all over them, cuts and bruises everywhere. Filthy, too, from head to toe."

"Anyone talk to him yet?" Cameron asked.

"Sure. Problem is he won't talk back. Not even so much as a *fuck you*."

"How 'bout the grandmother?"

"Kimmons?" Frank grunted his disapproval. "She split. Left town a few days ago. Apparently couldn't take all the heat she'd been getting over Ryan. Still trying to track her down."

"Okay," Cameron said and took a deep breath. No law prohibited officials from questioning a minor without a parent present. They were okay there. "How 'bout I give him a try?"

"Sure. Take him for a spin." Frank stretched his hand out toward the door. "I've already played the bad cop. Maybe the good cop'll work."

"I do good cop pretty well," Cameron muttered, moving past Frank and heading on toward the door.

"Well, here's your chance to prove it."

~

When Cameron entered the room, Ryan Churchill sat straight up in his seat, flinching, as if moving to avoid a blow. Appearing shell-shocked and tired, the boy wore only a paper nightgown. His clothes had already been removed and were en route to the lab to see if the bloodstains on them matched up with Alma Gutierrez's DNA.

Frank was right. Physically, the kid was a mess—lip busted, face and arms covered with scrapes and dried blood. His wrists were cuffed behind him, hooked on the chair, and his feet shackled as well.

Ryan was trembling, his chair squeaking and the chains around his legs rattling with his movement. Tears rolled down his grimy cheeks, leaving behind murky streaks, almost like running mascara. He looked like wounded prey, counting seconds before being devoured alive.

This wasn't what Cameron had expected. He'd anticipated a coldhearted killer, but what he saw instead was a timid, frightened child. It was hard to believe this was the same kid accused of slicing his teacher from neck to spleen, then robbing her of her life—slowly, one organ at a time—as if it meant nothing.

Basic criminal profiling told Cameron the suspect would be smug and detached, with a self-confidence level bordering on egomaniacal—not the tearful, frightened boy now cowering before him.

"Hello, Ryan," he finally said, his voice calm and quiet.

No response. No eye contact.

Cameron studied him for a moment, then walked over to the refrigerator, opened the door and grabbed a bottle of water. Out of the corner of his eye, he could see the boy watching him. Cameron unscrewed the top, took a long swallow, then turned to face Ryan, who quickly turned his head away.

"Sure is hot outside," Cameron said, staring out the window. He took another swig of water, then looked at Ryan as if it were an afterthought, holding up the bottle. "Want some?"

The boy nodded at the offer but didn't speak, still avoiding eye contact. At least he was responding. It was a good sign.

Cameron reached into the refrigerator, pulled out another bottle, then headed toward the boy, who followed it with his eyes as if it were something rare and exquisite. After twisting off the lid, he held it up to the boy's mouth, allowing him to drink from it.

Ryan greedily clamped his mouth onto the bottle with such force that Cameron lost his grip, dropping it onto the floor. When he brought it back up again, the boy resumed gulping, emptying it within a matter of seconds.

Cameron watched, round-eyed, then said, "Would you like another?"

Ryan nodded.

Cameron took out another bottle and went through the same process all over again. It seemed obvious the boy was dehydrated, hadn't had any water in days. Cameron wondered why nobody'd thought to offer him any.

Four bottles later, Ryan finally seemed satisfied, though he was gasping for air. Drinking had been more important than breathing.

Cameron pulled up a chair and sat across from Ryan. The others had obviously tried the intimidation route and failed, leaving behind a subject who wasn't in the best frame of mind for an interview. Cameron decided to go the opposite route, offering the boy comfort, while at the same time trying to establish a bond.

"I want to help you, Ryan, but in order for me to do that, I need to ask you a few questions. It's important you answer. Do you think you can help me out with that?"

A quick, timid nod, but with eyes still filled with terror.

"Do you know why we're holding you here, Ryan?"

He shook his head. Once again, tears began rolling down his cheeks.

"No idea at all?"

He closed his eyes tight, squeezing out even more tears, which again tumbled rapidly down his cheeks. After that, a sob exploded from his mouth, and Ryan let it all out. He cried, shaking his head.

Cameron waited a few moments, allowing the boy to compose himself. "Ryan, do you know what happened to Alma Gutierrez?"

The boy shot his head up, startled. "Miss Gutierrez?" He scanned the room as if searching for her. "What happened to Miss Gutierrez?"

"Ryan, are you telling me you don't know what happened to her?" Cameron looked directly into the boy's eyes. Fear and confusion stared back at him.

"I *don't* know. Is she okay?"

Cameron paused. "She was killed, Ryan."

Instantly, the boy's expression went from confusion to horror. "She was…? I don't under… Who'd want to…?" He began crying again.

Now Cameron was confused too. "Are you telling me you don't know *anything* about this? At *all*?"

Ryan shook his head emphatically, his bottom lip quivering.

Cameron didn't know what to make of the boy's answer, and he was having a difficult time hiding his surprise. Either the kid was an Oscar-caliber actor, or he knew nothing about Alma's murder, which made no sense. Cameron put his hands together and looked down at them, thinking a few seconds before he spoke. "Ryan, what was the last thing you remember when you saw Miss Gutierrez last Wednesday?"

Ryan sniffled a few times, composing himself, then responded almost matter-of-factly. "I didn't see Miss Gutierrez on Wednesday."

"You didn't? Ryan, are you sure?" Cameron said. "You *never* saw Miss Gutierrez that day?"

The boy said nothing, just sniffled again, nodding his head.

"Ryan. I need you to be truthful with me."

"I *didn't* see her Wednesday," he cried out between gulps of air. "I swear!"

"Where were you, then, Ryan?" Cameron asked, hearing his own voice become more tense. "Where were you when you were supposed to be with her in her office, getting tutored?"

"I..." He stopped, looked around the room, shaking his head and trying to think. "I was...I..." Then he let out a giant frustrated sigh, and said, "I don't remember, but I know I didn't see her. I'd remember it, and I just don't."

Cameron drew a steadying breath and tried to regroup. "Let me make sure I understand you correctly, Ryan. You have no memory of seeing Miss Gutierrez on Wednesday, but you have no idea where you were instead? Can you see how I'd have a hard time believing you?"

Panic had returned to the boy's face, and he labored over each breath he took. "I know...I know it sounds weird. It sounds weird to me too. I...I can't explain it. But it's true—I *swear* it is—and it's not just that. I can't remember a lot of things."

"What do you mean?"

Ryan glanced down at his feet, shaking his head, almost as if they didn't belong to him. "Lots of stuff. It's like there are big spaces in my head. They're missing or something."

"You mean blocks of time you can't remember?" Cameron suggested.

"Yeah." He nodded, relief in his voice.

Cameron studied the boy's face for a few seconds. He didn't know what to think. Ryan *did* look genuinely confused. Could he have killed Alma and had no memory of doing it? Did he even kill her at all? "Ryan, do you remember *anything* that happened that Wednesday?"

"Some," Ryan said. "But I was sick. I wasn't feeling too good."

Cameron was reaching into his shirt pocket for his pen and froze. "Sick, how?"

"I had a stuffy nose. And my throat hurt."

Cameron swallowed hard. "Were you running a fever?"

"My gramma took my temperature. Said it was just a little over ninety-nine. Not bad enough to keep me home, so she made me go to school."

"Okay," Cameron said, feeling his throat becoming tighter. "Do you remember what happened after that?"

Ryan deliberated for a moment, then looked across the table and shook his head. "I don't know. I think maybe when I was on the bus."

"Going to school?"

"No…I mean…yes…I mean…I'm just not sure. Can we stop? I'm really confused right now. I need to think for a minute."

He wasn't the only one.

Cameron paused, then turned his head sideways, looking at a manila folder lying on the table. He reached for it, opened it up, then pulled out a sheet of paper. After glancing at it for a few seconds, he flipped it around and slid it in front of the boy. "Ryan, does this mean anything to you?"

Ryan tilted his head so he could read the paper. When he was done, he looked up at Cameron, confused. "What's *that*?"

"You have no idea?"

The boy shook his head. "Uh-uh."

"It's a poem called 'The Hunted Soul,' by Virgil Morrison. You've never read it before?"

"It's scary. Why would I want to read something like that?"

Cameron scratched his forehead, staring at the paper as he spoke. "Ryan, I have to leave the room for a few minutes."

The boy panicked, his eyes welling with tears. "You're leaving? Why? Did I give the wrong answers? Please, ask me again. I promise I'll try harder. Just don't go."

Cameron sat, speechless. How could this child, this scared little boy, so eager to please, be their suspect? The longer he heard him talk, the more preposterous the notion became. "I promise I'll be right back."

When Cameron came out into the hallway, Frank was still there, waiting to hear what had happened. "So? Did ya get the kid to sing?"

Cameron leaned against the wall, crossing his arms and looking at the ceiling. "Oh…he sang all right. Just the wrong song."

"Did he confess?"

Cameron hesitated, trying to find words. "That kid in there?" he said, nodding toward the door. "If he killed Alma Gutierrez, then he sure as hell doesn't know it." He paused. "And you wanna know something else? To be perfectly honest…neither do I."

Chapter Fifty-Two

Sheriff's Station
Faith, New Mexico

"Would you please tell me what in God's name you're talking about?" Frank asked, practically shouting. "Because I haven't a clue. What the hell did he say in there?"

"He had no idea what I was talking about, Frank—none of it. When I showed him the poem, he looked at me like I had two heads. He was disgusted by the words, said he'd never seen them before."

"And you believe him?"

"I can't explain it. There's this innocence about him, a naïveté," Cameron said. "Trust me—the way he was talking, the fear in his eyes—the kid doesn't have the sophistication to lie like that. There's a disconnect. That kid in there is scared to death."

Frank looked away, throwing his hands up in surrender. "I don't get it."

"Think about it for a minute. Nothing is fitting. I think we're way off track."

"So how do we get back *on* track?" Frank asked. It sounded more like a demand than a question.

"For one, we can't trust the obvious because the obvious doesn't work. Nothing is as it seems...*nothing.* We know that, Frank—we've seen it over and over. And I just saw it in there."

Frank said nothing, leaning against the wall, folding his arms and shaking his head.

"Something strange is going on here, and I have a bad feeling it's gonna get worse...a lot worse."

"What the hell are you talking about? Where are you getting all this?"

"Wanna know where I'm getting it? I'll tell you where: from Ben Foley, from Ryan Churchill, and from Judith Hedrick—that's where; that's what the evidence is telling me. That's what *they're* telling me.

"Wait a minute...*Judith Hedrick*?"

Cameron breathed deep, let it out quickly. "That's what I wanted to tell you before the news about Ryan."

"I don't understand. Judith—she's a victim."

Cameron shook his head. "Judith's not a victim, Frank. She's a suspect."

"A *suspect*? A suspect in *what*?"

"In the murder of Felicity Champion," Cameron said, regret creeping into his voice. "That green fiber—I think it came from a sweater she owned. I think Judith killed the girl, and now she's on the run."

"*What the...*?" Frank said, now sweating visibly.

Cameron pulled the photo from his pocket, the one with Judith wearing the lime-green sweater. He held it out.

Frank snatched it and glared at Cameron before studying it. After he did, he looked back up, wide-eyed. "I don't fucking believe it."

"Believe it, Frank. And as long as we're dealing out the shocking details, I've got another one for you. Try this one: Ryan Churchill may not recall anything about Alma's murder, but there's one thing he *does* remember."

"What's that?"

"Coming down with flu symptoms the same morning she was killed. And that's about *all* he remembers. After that, everything's just a blur."

Just then, Margaret burst through the door and headed down the hallway.

"Christ," Frank said, shaking his head, "there's a shitload of trouble coming down the pike…and it's headed straight toward us."

Chapter Fifty-Three

San Mateo Boulevard
Albuquerque, New Mexico

It was late afternoon, the start of rush hour. Traffic was getting thicker by the minute, patience among drivers growing thinner. As Kyle waited at the light to cross Central Avenue, she began feeling light headed. Almost immediately, the visions started again.

She sat, paralyzed, gripping the steering wheel as if hanging on to it for life. Somewhere in her outer consciousness, she could hear the other drivers sounding their horns, but it didn't matter—they couldn't compete with the noises inside her head.

This must be what it's like to lose your mind, she thought. Was she losing hers?

Red—that was all she could see at first—just red and nothing else. Thick as syrup, deep and velvety, like a rose petal.

The color of pain.

It whirled before her eyes, separating, becoming thinner with each round until disappearing into nothingness. Kyle heard a scream, then an explosion. She felt almost certain it was a gun blast. After that, an image came into focus: a hand pushed against a sheet of glass, moving downward and leaving a long streak of smeared blood behind it.

Then a crackling clap, followed by a blinding light.

Kyle's back felt like it was glued to her seat. She drew her hands up to her face and covered her eyes, trying to clear the images from her mind; her head fell down onto the steering wheel, and her own horn started.

She knew she was blocking the road, knew she was holding up traffic. She also knew there was nothing she could do about it. The raging storm of sounds and images had now taken center stage, taking over her thoughts, taking over her mind.

The images continued to turn at warp speed, materializing as a long, protracted blur. Just as before, every few minutes the thread of pictures would slow to a stop, like video fast-forwarding to a specific point. During one of those breaks, Kyle saw a man's face, eyes closed and head shaking rapidly back and forth. His movements looked bizarre and unnatural, the intense vibrations making his features look distorted and out of shape—less like a human, more like a freak.

Again, the speed picked up, fast-forwarding to the next scene. A smear of colors blazed past her, along with a series of whines and high-pitched squeals. Kyle felt dizzy and disoriented.

Then, almost instantly, she found herself transported somewhere else. It was that hospital again—and again, she was standing in the middle of it.

But this time she was in a different part. Kyle saw blood-splattered walls, tried to get a better look but suddenly heard something behind her. She spun around and found two men attacking one another—no weapons, just bare hands. To her right was a long glass window; it was some kind of observation booth, with a man and two women standing inside. They watched as the conflict escalated—half-interested, half-indifferent—doing nothing to stop the two men as they tried to kill each other.

One of the men reached for the other's throat so his thumbs were just below the Adam's apple. He pushed hard, breaking skin and causing blood to spill down. The other man let out a fierce howl. Kyle screamed too, but nobody seemed to hear her.

With his fingers still lodged in the man's throat, the attacker guided his victim down backward, toward the ground, until he was lying flat. Raising one foot high into the air, and with all the force he could muster, he slammed it hard onto the victim's chest. Kyle could hear cartilage grinding and bones cracking as the wounded man's body skipped a few inches off the ground, then fell back again. A circlet of fresh blood instantly materialized around the victim's head, spreading out onto the floor.

One of the observers glanced down at his watch, as if he had somewhere to go. The other jotted a few notes on a clipboard.

The attacker stood over his prey with an expression of superiority. He was tired, breathing heavily, thrilled by his own accomplishment. His eyes looked unnatural, almost black. Kyle looked away.

Suddenly, a loud horn blasted. Then another sound: a voice. Kyle couldn't make out what it said through the booming echoes, but the attacker did. Obediently, he backed up to the same wall where the observation window was located. Locking his hands behind his back, he eased them into a metal reinforced opening inside the wall. One of the observers leaned forward and reached through, grabbing the man's wrists. When he pulled them back out, they appeared to be locked inside some sort of contraption, a square metal box with openings on the ends, one for each hand. A restraining device, Kyle thought, but she noticed the latch on one side wasn't closed properly. Still, the man stood, compliant.

The loud buzzer sounded off again, followed by a mechanical noise, like heavy pieces of steel disengaging from one another. A giant door slid open, and two males dressed in white emerged. They moved toward the other two men, pushing a gurney, the wheels emitting a loud, squeaking noise—it sounded like a child's hysterical laughter—and maneuvered the assailant onto it.

Kyle looked at the victim, still lying on the floor, surrounded by his own blood. She watched helplessly as he stopped breathing, finally giving in to death.

Nobody seemed to notice the man on the gurney still had one hand free—one deadly hand.

CHAPTER FIFTY-FOUR

Sheriff's Station
Faith, New Mexico

It was time to start facing facts: whatever was taking over the town seemed to be spreading fast, becoming more unpredictable, more deadly, while at the same time, as far as Cameron could tell, going virtually undetected.

What the hell is it? he wondered while driving home from the station that evening.

He needed to find out.

Armed with the news about Judith, Margaret was off running around town, trying to chase down leads. Meanwhile, for him, more time meant the possibility of more lost lives. He couldn't afford another second of it. Nobody could.

Once again, Cameron began thinking about Sherlock Holmes, wondering what he might do in the same situation. And then, as if from the legendary detective himself, he got his answer: *There is nothing as deceptive as an obvious fact.*

The facts need a makeover, Cameron thought, *a new perspective.*

He needed to go back and begin reevaluating every piece of evidence, starting with the most obvious one: although each case appeared isolated, and different suspects kept emerging, there was still a strong chance they were all connected in some manner. Margaret had suspected that, but Ryan's flu symptoms seemed to confirm it.

As it turned out, Judith in the role of suspect rather than victim was not an entirely bad thing. She'd given him one more person to use for comparison—and that could come in handy while searching for similarities among the cases.

Getting back to Holmes, there was one obvious fact in particular that still wasn't adding up, never really had, and that was this flu virus. Ryan and Ben were the only people in town to contract it, and both just happened to be murder suspects.

Quite a coincidence. That alone was enough to cause suspicion, but here was another: the influenza virus is highly contagious. Even if the boys *had* managed to catch a rare case of summer flu, it would have gone around town by now—and it hadn't. All this led Cameron to think that perhaps they weren't really dealing with a virus at all. Maybe, he thought, it was something else, something just mimicking one.

And that wasn't all that was bothering him. If Ryan had in fact murdered Alma Gutierrez, he appeared to have no memory of it. Cameron felt certain that was no act: the boy seemed to be as confused as he was, maybe more so.

Cameron shook his head. Ben was dead, Judith was missing, Ryan was in custody, and the person who killed Witherspoon—whoever that was—seemed as elusive as the facts themselves. That murder seemed to be the missing link, one he had yet to find, one that was still eating away at him.

In the meantime, there were other things to consider. Susan Swift had second-guessed her own theory about what had happened to Ben. Looking back now, her words seemed to resonate almost prophetically. She'd said she thought there must have been some kind of outside element involved, that Ben could never have done such an awful thing on his own. That seemed to be the central theme in each of the suspects' lives: good one minute, evil to the core the next.

But what outside factor? Who—or what—is really in control here?

Now more than ever, it seemed, Cameron was battling against two increasingly fierce enemies, neither of which he could see or hear: one was whatever was turning good citizens into vicious monsters.

And the other was time.

Chapter Fifty-Five

San Mateo Boulevard
Albuquerque, New Mexico

Neither saw it coming: the man they were placing on the gurney pulled out his free hand, grabbed one orderly's neck, and hit him over the head with the metal restraining device. Then he did the same thing to the other one.

It all happened in a matter of seconds.

As the two men lay motionless on the floor, soaked in their own blood, Kyle screamed out, but it did no good; nobody could see or hear her.

The patient disappeared out the door before anyone in the observation booth could stop him. Almost immediately an alarm sounded, followed by an ear-piercing siren.

Kyle heard screaming, turned around and saw chaos everywhere, people running in all directions. Meanwhile, the renegade patient went from room to room releasing occupants, using a key he'd taken from one of the fallen orderlies. Sirens continued to shriek as more patients filed out and even more rushed into the courtyard.

It was a full-blown riot. People scrambled in every direction, not knowing where they were going—either out of the way or just plain out. The ones who didn't move fast enough fell underfoot, their bodies dropping like scattered bowling pins, only to be trampled upon by merciless feet beating a path behind them—crushing flesh, crushing bones, leaving behind a wide trail of blood.

Patients were attacking the staff, attacking one another.

The stampede continued.

White uniforms turned red with blood, as did the floors, the walls, and anything else falling into the path of chaos.

Kyle heard more screaming. She spun around and screamed herself when she saw a man grabbing a woman by the neck and then throwing her into a window. The woman slammed into the glass, plunging through, her cries trailing off as she sailed toward the pavement below.

Kyle recognized her: it was the nurse she'd watched falling in her earlier visions. Now she was seeing that same scene but from a different perspective.

Then she saw another vision from before, the woman lying on the floor, the one with the halo of blood around her head. The picture began to blur and move again, turning into nothing more than a streaking fog of colors.

Then Bethany spoke. "Hurry up," she urged, yet again. "You're running out of time."

"Ma'am? You okay, ma'am?"

Kyle opened her eyes, confused. The entire sequence had lasted only moments, yet it felt like hours. She focused blearily on the person standing on the other side of her car door, tried to say something, but her throat felt dry and gritty. The horns had stopped now, and all she could hear were distant street noises playing in the background.

"You okay, ma'am?" he repeated.

"I—I'm…" She looked up at a plaid shirt and a concerned face.

"It's okay, just hold still. I'm going to call for help." He reached for his cell phone.

"That won't be necessary," she managed to say. "I'm fine."

The man frowned. "Are you sure?"

"I'm a doctor," Kyle said, reaching for her purse, rifling through it. "I have a low blood-sugar problem. That's all. I got weak and passed out because I hadn't eaten all day. I was on my way home to get something, but the traffic slowed me down. I assure you, it's nothing serious." She raised her wallet to show him her hospital ID.

He looked it over and then into her eyes with hesitation. "You sure you don't want me to call an ambulance just to be safe? You look pretty shaken up."

"I'm positive. I assure you." She forced an unconvincing smile, turning the key in the ignition and leaving the Good Samaritan staring, wondering.

After she turned the corner, relief began to settle in, and she smiled. Even though she felt like she'd just been to hell and back, Kyle also knew she'd just figured it out.

She knew what the dreams were about.

CHAPTER FIFTY-SIX

Lane's Barber Shop
Faith, New Mexico

When a stranger passed through Faith, people noticed.

As the morning sun dusted the air with its coppery glow, Lane Smith sat outside his barbershop, drinking coffee and reading the paper. It was his usual routine—that, and keeping tabs on everyone passing in front of him. The old man never missed much.

So when a plain-looking van came slinking down Main Street, it was no surprise that Lane's radar went off. He watched covertly as the vehicle stopped and sat for a few minutes, then slid forward several feet before stopping once more. Finally, a man got out of the passenger's side, looking around to see if anyone was watching him.

Lane narrowed his eyes and widened his interest.

The man reached into his shirt pocket, pulled out a pen and pad, and began writing. Just then, Betty Greenway came walking out of the nail salon and unknowingly headed directly toward the stranger. He looked up, caught her eyes and nodded once, but she seemed to want to get by him as quickly as possible. Once she left his line of vision, the man continued writing for a moment, looked around, then hurried back into the van. After that, once more, it proceeded down the street. Slowly.

All under the watchful eye of Lane Smith.

He lifted his head just high enough to peer over the top of his newspaper, catching the van as it went by, studying it carefully. Lane could barely see inside, but it was clear that neither the men nor the van were from anywhere around Faith.

Lane didn't waste any time in calling Cameron.

"You're overdue for a cut," he complained to the assistant sheriff.

"Too much going on right now," Cameron responded. The last thing on his mind was a haircut. "How 'bout next week?"

"Won't take too much of your time," the old barber said, casually. "Bring that mop of yours in here…say, about fifteen minutes? Be my first cut of the day. Then ya got all day to get back to your work."

Cameron looked at his watch, trying to contain his annoyance. "Like I said, Lane, I've got a few things going on right—"

"All righty, then. So I'll see you in a few," Lane shot back, then quickly hung up.

Cameron stared at the telephone receiver, shook his head. Then he buzzed Betty Sinclair, the department's receptionist and dispatcher.

"Looks like I'll be getting my hair cut in about fifteen minutes," he told her, "whether I like it or not."

Chapter Fifty-Seven

Lane's Barber Shop
Faith, New Mexico

Cameron had practically grown up inside Lane's Barber Shop.

He'd started out sitting on a wooden booster seat and could still remember the day he came in and no longer needed it. For him, it felt like a major milestone.

Now, as an adult, Cameron sat in the same chair, though these days it was a little worse for wear; the leather seat cushion was cracking in spots, the metal tarnished. Not that it mattered. For him, that chair was a part of history—the town's and his own.

The smell of hair tonic and shaving cream swirled through the warm, moist air while Lane cut Cameron's hair. The pleasing aroma always evoked happy memories for the sheriff, times when haircuts meant special occasions: first days of school, birthdays, and Easter.

Cameron found himself enjoying the moment once again, not because of the memories, or even the pleasant smells, but instead because he felt lost in the long-overdue calm surrounding him while Lane cut his hair. The repetitious and rhythmic sound of the snapping of scissors had a soothing effect, and Cameron closed his eyes, allowing himself to relax, if only for a few minutes.

Then Lane broke the mood.

"So how's your parents doing?" he asked, giving the chair a half turn and throwing Cameron from his momentary refuge. "Haven't heard anything from them in a while."

"Doing okay," Cameron said. He looked up into the mirror and made eye contact with Lane. "Still out in Arizona—still enjoying retirement, I guess. Haven't gone out to visit in a while. Get there when I can, but the way things have been going lately... well, you know..."

"Yeah, I hear ya. Well tell 'em I miss seein' their mugs around here," Lane said. He was a large man; the exterior was hard, but the heart beneath was soft.

A long pause followed, filled by the sound of scissors slicing through hair. "You know," Lane finally said, "saw something this morning that didn't look right to me."

"Yeah? What's that?"

"'Bout eight this morning. A van. Coming through town. Looked like it didn't have no business being here."

"What makes you think that?"

"Well, for one, it was drivin' right up against the curb, slower'n a slug in a hurry," Lane said, combing Cameron's bangs forward in broad strokes. "Seemed to me they was lookin' for something."

Cameron squinted as short bristles of cut hair fluttered down past his eyes and nose. "Catch who was inside?"

"One of 'em got out. Looked shifty as *all* hell, if you ask me, like he was fixin' to do something he wadn't supposed to."

"In what way?"

"Dunno...lookin' all over the place...makin' sure nobody was watchin'. Stood there for a spell, writin' something. Then Betty Greenway come walkin' by, and he gets all skittish. Runs back into the van and takes off again. Really strange—know what I mean?"

"Sure," Cameron replied, considering Lane's account. "And the other?"

"A guy. Couldn't see him too good. He was the driver."

"Happen to get a make or model on the van?"

Lane stopped and gazed out the window for a moment, as if watching the whole thing all over again, then went back to cutting. "Older. Not one of them minivans you see all the time. A white-colored Ford…Econoline… Yeah, that's what it was. Plain as could be, almost like it was tryin' too hard to look that way."

Cameron stared out the window. "What about the plates? Get a good look at 'em?"

Lane pulled a thatch of blond hair straight up with his comb, snipped across, then let it fall back into place. "New Mexico. Couldn't see the numbers though. Eyes ain't what they used to be. But they was both wearin' sunglasses—that much I remember. Anyway, whole thing wadn't right."

"Looked out of place," Cameron said.

"Like a nun in a whorehouse."

Cameron let out a half laugh without sound. "I'll check around town to see if anyone else saw them."

"Yeah. Do that. Just a thought…but check with Georgia up the street at the bakery. She keeps a steady eye on things, almost like it's her second job." The barber leaned in toward Cameron, cupping his hand beside his mouth as if telling a secret, spoke softly. "A real busybody."

Cameron resisted the urge to laugh. Lane was every bit as much a busybody as Georgia, just more subtle in his technique.

With one foot, Lane pumped the chair up a level or two, then leaned forward so he and Cameron were almost eye-to-eye. He studied his work, bobbing his head back and forth, making sure the sideburns looked even.

When he was done, the barber removed the barber's cloth, folding it away, careful not to dump hair on Cameron's clothes. Then he handed him the mirror to inspect his haircut.

Cameron held the mirror up, moved his head from side to side. "Nice job as usual, Lane."

"Ahh," the barber shot back, dismissing the comment with the wave of a hand. "You're easy. I could cut your hair blindfolded. Been doing it since you were, what—about three?"

"Something like that," Cameron said.

"Can still remember the first day you came walkin' in here, almost like it was yesterday." Lane laughed. "Actually, running was more like it—all excited to get your first haircut, scurrying across the floor like a mouse on a mission. Was a good two or so minutes before your mother come hurryin' in after you—frantic—thought she lost you. Of course, by then, you'd already climbed up into the chair, hands on both armrests, all ready to go."

Cameron smiled, looked down at the floor, a little embarrassed. "Bet you've got a story for just about everyone in this town."

"Not everyone…but most." He paused, studied Cameron's face. "You doing okay, kid? Don't mind tellin' ya, you're looking a bit on the dog-eared side."

Cameron pulled a bill from his wallet and held it out to the barber. "Yeah, fine. Just real busy, is all."

Lane nodded, looking at Cameron's hand. "You can just put that right back where it came from. Your money's no good here. Haircut's on me."

Cameron put the bill away. He knew the routine. "Thanks, Lane."

"Think nothin' of it, son. Pleasure's mine. Take care of yourself now, ya hear me?"

"I'll try," Cameron said, heading toward the door.

Just before he was out of sight, Lane shouted to him. "Hey. One more thing."

Cameron turned around and glanced back at him.

"Almost forgot. For what it's worth, the guy taking the notes—he was standing in front of Hedrick's shop…and lookin' inside the window."

Chapter Fifty-Eight

Abrams Medical Center
Albuquerque, New Mexico

Kyle sat in her office, trying to regain some of her strength. While excited about the new information, the roadside horror show of the night before had taken more energy than she cared to admit.

Several things seemed almost certain now: Somewhere in this country, around World War II, there was a hospital, one where horrific events had taken place. People were seriously injured, some even killed. In one scenario, a riot broke out after a patient got loose, bringing casualties to the staff as well as to other patients.

In addition, many of her earlier visions had come back for a repeat performance, only now they made sense. That nurse, the one she'd seen lying on the blood-smeared floor, had died during the riot, after the crowd of people trampled her.

As for the falling woman, Kyle now knew that somebody had pushed her through that window. Somebody had killed her.

But she had yet to figure out where this hospital was. From her research, it appeared to have something to do with the US Army, but beyond that, she was unclear.

One thing she definitely *did* know. Seeing that bloody match between the two men—the way the staff just stood there and watched—it wasn't only neglectful, it was downright immoral. They seemed so unaffected by it, bored, even.

What would make a human so indifferent to another's suffering? Kyle had to wonder if it was some form of punishment, or maybe, she thought, something else, some kind of twisted, morbid game they were playing—except nobody seemed to be having much fun.

In addition, the biggest mystery of all was earning its reputation as such, while doing an even better job of getting under Kyle's skin: she still couldn't figure out what Bethany had to do with all this. There seemed to be no connection between her and the events Kyle saw.

In spite of all this, Kyle was still feeling much better as she moved closer toward the answers she needed. She just hoped her body would hold up long enough for her to get there. All that energy flowing through her had taken its toll, turning sleeping and eating more into luxuries than necessities. All that, and she also had her private practice to worry about; still, she couldn't let go. Not now. Not when things were finally starting to come together.

Hardly a time to relax, Kyle thought. On the contrary—if anything, it was time to start getting busy.

Chapter Fifty-Nine

Sheriff's Station
Faith, New Mexico

As recommended, Cameron checked with Georgia Simpson at Peak's Bakery to see if she had spotted any unusual vehicles moving through town. As it turned out, she'd seen plenty, but nothing of any use to Cameron.

On the other side of town, Della Schumacher, the one-woman neighborhood watch program, ended up being more help to Cameron than he ever could have imagined. Still dismayed over the loss of her beloved cat, and fearful of Faith becoming a new hotbed of homicidal activity, Della decided to make it her job to keep a vigilant watch over everything within a hundred-foot radius of her house. Even more so than usual.

Along with keeping her eye on things, Della also made a point of calling Cameron several times throughout the day and updating him with what she considered to be suspicious activity. To Cameron, it sounded like a whole lot of nothing—other than her neurosis working overtime.

Before he knew it, his phone was ringing late into the night, with more reports of odd occurrences, or at least what she considered as such.

Della's self-appointed role as informant and confidante extraordinaire was an interesting departure from the uncooperative, cold attitude she'd displayed when Cameron had first encountered her. To him, both extremes were a nuisance. At best, Della's calls seemed insignificant. At worst, they were just annoying.

Except, that is, for one.

Cameron was just about to eat lunch in his office and almost regretted picking up the phone after hearing Della's grating voice on the other end.

"Got a hot one for ya," she said.

"What's up, Della?" Cameron replied, trying to curb his irritation.

She whispered into the phone as if relaying classified information. "This morning…strangers…driving…down the street…*very* suspicious…"

Cameron grabbed his pen, tightened his grip on the phone. "Say what, now?"

Her whispers became softer. "Yeah, and they ain't from around here, either…I could tell. They was prowling around like they was lookin' for something."

"Not a plain white van by any chance?"

She paused, surprised by Cameron's knowledge. Loudly now, almost shouting: "*Ay-ffirmative.*"

"Did you get a chance to see who they were?" he asked.

"Ten-four." She continued her television dialogue. "Two men. Sunglasses. Subjects were observed getting out of the vehicle."

"Happen to get a license plate number?"

"*Ay-firm.* Was able to secure a vantage point where I could ascertain that information."

"Go ahead," he said, pushing the pen against a notepad, the phone resting between his shoulder and ear.

"That would be: *Horace, Steven, Jeffrey, FOWER, THUREE, SEVEN, NYE-YEN.* I repeat, that's—"

"No need to repeat it, Della. Got it. What time was it?"

"That would be zero eight fifteen."

He tilted his wrist and checked the time. It was five minutes past noon. "See where they went?"

"Subjects observed traveling southbound," she replied matter-of-factly, "onto Jefferson."

He visualized the intersection. "They turn onto Melvin or keep going straight?"

"Kept going straight. On toward the highway."

"You said they got out of the vehicle. What were they doing?"

"Got out to prowl around," she replied.

"Where, Della? *Where* were they looking?"

"The Foley place."

There it was. A connection. "Gotta go, Della. Thanks."

"But…how 'bout…"

Cameron didn't wait to listen to the rest of what she had to say. He'd already heard everything he needed.

CHAPTER SIXTY

Fulton Street
Faith, New Mexico

Cameron sped down the road, talking to Frank on his cell phone. "We've got strangers in town."

"Strangers? What kind of strangers?"

Cameron couldn't tell if his boss was confused, annoyed, or both. "Don't know, but I'd sure like to find out. Lane Smith saw them first, around eight this morning, driving past his shop in a plain white van. Two males. Della Schumacher saw them, too."

"The whack-job that lives next to the Foley place? You sure she wasn't having one of her psychotic breaks?"

"She had the same information Lane told me, Frank."

"Well, Lane's solid. So what were they doing here?"

"Good question. Schumacher saw them snooping around the Foley place just after Lane spotted them at Judith's shop."

"Now that *is* interesting. Anybody happen to get a license number?"

"Lane tried but couldn't see it well enough. All he could tell was New Mexico plates. Schumacher, though, *she* nailed it."

"Well what do ya know? The old nag proved herself useful. Run the numbers yet?"

"Yeah. Last owner came back to Rent-n-Ride, in Albuquerque."

"Call 'em?"

"Yep. Said none of their vehicles have plates matching those numbers."

"Strange."

"Put a call in to the DMV—said it could be a dead registration, a vehicle they sold at an auction, and the new owner never completed the process."

"No coincidence, I'm sure. Where you at right now?"

"Just passed Beacham Street," Cameron said, "headed for the Foley place to see if I can figure out what they were doing there."

Cameron heard commotion in the background. "Frank? You still there?"

"Yeah. Hang on a sec. Somebody's pounding on my door," he replied, then shouted out, "I'm on the phone, for God's—"

More commotion—and voices. Cameron couldn't make them out.

"Holy shit," Frank finally said after returning to the call. "Something's going on at Felice's. We got shots fired."

At the same time, Cameron heard the radio chatter. He spun his car around in the middle of the intersection and sped in the other direction, turning on his flashing lights.

"Already got it, boss. Headed there now."

"Following right behind you," Frank said.

Chapter Sixty-One

Felice's Diner
Faith, New Mexico

The restaurant's front window was shattered, shards of glass everywhere, glistening in the hot midday sun. A few deputies stood outside, talking. They stopped to look at Cameron when he pulled up.

"What do we got?" he asked.

"A shooting," Deputy Avello replied, his voice low and solemn. He paused. "It's one of our own...Banks...he's dead."

Cameron looked at Avello, then inside, then back at him again. He'd heard what the deputy had said, but his mind seemed to reject it. The words *Banks* and *dead*—they didn't seem to fit together.

"Sir?" Avello finally said.

Cameron swung back into the minute. "Banks is...dead?"

"Yessir."

"How?"

"Another deputy did it, sir... He killed him."

Cameron was still watching all the commotion inside, but when he heard what Avello had said, quickly turned his head back toward him. "*What*? Another...*who*?"

"Ronnie Geller," Avello said. "Ronnie Geller shot and killed Shawn Banks."

"I don't get it… What in the world… *Why*?"

"He says Shawn attacked him."

"Where's Ronnie now?"

"Inside. They're talking to him out back by the kitchen."

Cameron didn't say anything else. He ran inside.

A few moments later, an engine roared and tires screeched as Frank pulled up. He got out of his car and surveyed the looks on the deputies' faces.

That was all he needed to see.

~

Beyond the time clock, beyond the signs purporting a safe working environment, Geller sat on top of a large, plastic pickle bucket with Cameron kneeling beside him. Face flushed, eyes red-rimmed, the deputy had been sweating so much that his short-cropped hair appeared soaking wet. In addition to all that, his hands were still shaking—so were his legs—and he had a distant look in his eyes.

Cameron looked up and saw Frank headed straight toward them, his pace rapid and determined. In an attempt to divert the oncoming train wreck, he turned back to Geller, placed a hand on the deputy's shoulder, then said, "Be back in just a minute."

Geller nodded, slowly, absently.

Cameron stood up and walked toward his boss.

"What the hell now?" Frank asked, eyes fixed hard on the deputy.

"Geller killed Shawn Banks." The conversation felt like an instant replay of the one Cameron had had earlier, except now *he* was the one giving the bad news.

"Geller did *what…*?" Frank shouted. "What in God's name for?"

Cameron looked over toward Geller. "He claims Shawn attacked him."

"Oh…shit." Frank said, realizing the implications. "Anybody call the state troopers yet? They gotta be here."

"On the way," Cameron said.

"I don't get it. Now we have *deputies* offing each other? What the hell's going on?"

"It's not quite that simple, Frank."

"You're damned right it's not—it's bullshit," he said, then began moving toward Geller.

Cameron grabbed his shoulder. "Just hold on a minute. Calm down. I *have* this."

Frank turned back and stared at him.

Cameron took a deep breath. "Look. He was just about to spill when you came in. He's a mess right now, Frank, a complete mess. Wasn't even saying much till I calmed him down. Now he's ready to talk. I can do this. *I'll* get what we need. But I need a moment… *alone*."

Frank shot Cameron a long, level look, measuring the words, then reluctantly, and very slowly, he nodded.

~

Geller was sitting with his face in his hands when Cameron came back to talk to him. He placed a palm on the man's shoulder, and the deputy looked up instantly, seeming not to recognize him.

"Let's go outside, Ronnie. You look like you could use the fresh air," he said, then glanced back at Frank, who was still watching their every move, "and I'm kinda feeling like I could, too."

Geller stood up and walked stiffly toward the back door. Cameron followed him.

Outside, Geller leaned against the brick wall, tilted his head back and released a drawn-out breath. As he did, Cameron looked down at the deputy's hands; they were still shaking.

"Why don't you tell me what happened, Ronnie, from the beginning," Cameron urged, gently.

Geller looked at Cameron, his expression void. Then, after a few moments, he spoke with a trembling voice. "I came in to grab some lunch. Shawn was at the counter with his back to me. Figured I'd go over and invite him to join me at a table."

Cameron nodded.

Geller took a long, shaky breath, then said, "Pretty much immediately, I realized something wasn't right. He had his face buried in his hands, like he was upset or something. I said his name a few times, but he wouldn't answer, you know? Wouldn't even look up." He paused. "I knew him and his girlfriend split up a while back, so I figured maybe it was about that."

"You thought he might still be upset," Cameron confirmed.

"Yeah. I was worried about him, and I could tell the people around him were, too—they were staring, and everyone was looking at me, like, *do something.* So I put a hand on his shoulder and asked him if there was anything I could do to help him, if he needed something, you know? But he just sat there, totally unresponsive. I thought maybe he was sick or something, like he needed medical attention, you know? I didn't know *what* was going on, but I knew I couldn't just leave him there like that. I kneeled down at his side, like this." Geller knelt next to Cameron. "Then, all of a sudden, he just explodes, knocks me, and I go flying, right onto the floor—totally unexpected—I mean, it came outta nowhere. I was stunned. I couldn't believe he did it. I know Shawn, a real nice guy, you know?"

Cameron nodded. This was starting to sound familiar.

"Knocked the wind right out of me, you know?" He stood up. "When I finally got to my feet and got my bearings, I saw him standing there, looking me right in the eye. It was the weirdest thing I've ever seen, boss. It was like I barely even recognized him."

"Why was that?"

"This is gonna sound strange." Ronnie paused, trying to find the right words. "He had this wild look in his eyes. I mean, *really crazy*...and creepy, you know?"

"Creepy? How?"

"It's hard to explain. The eyes—they were, like, dark...and flat, like there was nothin' behind 'em. Like they didn't reflect any light."

Cameron looked away from Geller, thought about it for a moment, then back at him. "*Dark*?"

"Yeah. Like they were almost black."

"Ronnie?"

"Yeah?"

"Shawn's eyes were blue."

Ronnie appeared stunned, said nothing.

"Blue," Cameron repeated. He was talking to himself as much as to his deputy.

"I...I'd never noticed before—to tell you the truth—but take my word for it, boss: they were *not* blue when I saw them. They were dark—dark as night, as tar."

Cameron felt his cheeks getting warm. "So what happened next?"

"So he was standing there. His face...he looked so...angry. No, it was worse than angry, much worse. I've never seen him like that before. *Never.* You know how Shawn is..." He stopped, shook his head, then spoke quietly. "I mean, *was*. Easygoing, always seemed so happy. But this was like, something else."

"Like what?"

Ronnie spread his fingers apart on both hands and looked down at them, then up into Cameron's eyes. "I don't know, like he wasn't even human."

Cameron swallowed hard, forced his words out. "Then what?"

"He pulls out his gun and takes aim, right at me. You shoulda seen the look on his face—I've seen that look before. I knew what it meant. He was going to kill me. I had to think quick. So I lunged at him. As I do, he squeezes off a round. It missed me by a hair, went right over my shoulder and through the front window. Before he could take another shot, I landed right on top of him and his gun fell out of his hand. I got up and reached for mine, but as I did, he reached over for his—it was laying on the floor, just a few inches from his hand. He fired off another round but couldn't get good enough aim 'cause of how he was lying there on the floor. But *I* could…and I *did*." Geller threw his hands out, palms up, pleading, tears forming in his eyes. "I *had* to do it, I had to kill him."

"He was going to kill you, Ronnie. You did the right thing."

"I *killed* him," he said, staring at the ground shaking his head. "I killed Shawn."

Cameron stepped back and locked his hands behind his back, watching Geller try to compose himself, before speaking again. "And you have no idea what got into him? What might have caused all this?"

"Sheriff," Geller said, "you know him…I know him. To tell you the truth, I don't have a clue *what* the hell happened back there. But as sure as I'm sitting here, I do know one thing."

"What's that?"

"The person I killed back there—that wasn't Shawn."

Cameron tilted his head, narrowed his eyes. "Who was it, then?"

"That," he said, "was some kind of monster."

Chapter Sixty-Two

City Morgue
Faith, New Mexico

Faith Community Hospital's morgue was the holding area for all deceased persons prior to autopsy or burial. Cameron and Frank felt an obligation to go there—one, to pay their respects to a fallen deputy, and two, to see if they could find evidence that might help explain why things went so wrong, so fast.

Shawn's body lay on a metal table with the standard white sheet covering him. Not long ago, they'd been standing over Bradley Witherspoon's corpse in much the same manner. Although the circumstances were a lot different here, it didn't change the haunting fact: both were deputies. Both were dead.

A gentle electrical hum buzzed steadily in the background, practically inaudible, though for Cameron, it seemed to blare.

"You wanna to do the honors, or shall I?" Frank finally asked with a combination of regret and disgust.

Frank's sorrow did not evade Cameron, who said nothing, then reached for the corner of the sheet, lifting it. As he did, he could barely feel his fingers or even the sheet in his hand. His body and mind were both numb.

They both looked down at Shawn's face.

Cameron reached to pull the cover back over the body.

Suddenly, Frank threw out his hand.

Caught off guard and blocked from going any farther, Cameron looked up. "What, Frank? What's going on?"

Frank said nothing. He dropped his hand and continued staring at Shawn's corpse, eyes wide and round, face frozen, and breathing heavy and loud.

Cameron noticed his boss trembling. "You're scaring me, Frank. Say something."

Slowly, Frank pointed toward the body. His voice was labored and hoarse. "The finger…look at his finger."

Cameron gazed at Frank, then at Banks' hand. As he did, his eyes widened with recognition. "Oh, no," he said, shaking his head vehemently, as if begging the truth not to exist. "*Oh…no.*"

On Banks' left finger was a gold ring, the Masonic logo imprinted on its face, and on each side, a trillion-cut black onyx.

With a chip missing from one of them.

Frank slowly raised his gaze toward Cameron. "The fragment you found on Witherspoon…the stone."

It was the exact same shape and size. Cameron couldn't speak; he could barely even breathe.

"Christ," Frank said. "*Holy…*Shawn Banks killed Bradley Witherspoon."

Chapter Sixty-Three

45687 Monument Path Way
Albuquerque, New Mexico

It was late evening, and Kyle had finally arrived home. She'd hoped to get there sooner, but one of her patients had forced a change in plans—the boy had fallen and busted his sutures wide open. Kyle had to spend the last few hours cleaning and repairing the damage.

She plopped down onto her couch and opened a can of grape juice she'd planned to drink earlier. It was warm now, but she didn't much care—it was still wet, and that was all that mattered.

Sitting motionless for a few moments, Kyle enjoyed the near silence surrounding her. The only sound she could hear was the refrigerator as it clicked on and off to the commands of an indecisive thermostat. She tilted her head back and closed her eyes. Right away, thoughts of Bethany crept into her mind, but she quickly chased them away.

She reached for the remote on the coffee table and turned on the television. After mindlessly flipping through channels, she settled on the local news. As the opening music started, Kyle realized she hadn't been keeping up on events lately. Time just hadn't permitted. *Bethany hasn't permitted*, she thought as she propped her feet up, grabbed a copy of *Cosmo*, and began flipping through the pages.

She hadn't been paying much attention, until the anchor's sharp voice prompted her to look up at the screen.

"A scare today at University Hospital," the woman said in a tone that seemed to bark rather than inform. "A man walked into the emergency room with a rifle under his arm—and anger on his mind. Casey Gold is live at the scene. She has more…Casey?"

The video wiped across the screen, revealing the somber-faced reporter holding a microphone to her chest as if it were a delicate, burning candle. Her expression seemed to mimic concern. Fast-paced music played in the background, communicating a distinct sense of urgency.

"Good evening, Dory," Gold said slowly, with a tone declaring tragedy. "Everyone got out, but the suspect remained inside. Fifty-one-year-old Ronald Matherson refused to surrender."

To Kyle, the scene didn't look much different from any other day, save for the lone police car parked out front, its blue and red lights flashing on and off in short, contained spasms. It seemed obvious the news crew had arrived much too late. A woman strolled across the screen, looking as if she hadn't a care in the world.

The reporter continued as images of a cold scene dragged on: "SWAT teams were called. The standoff went on for two hours, during which Matherson made several demands. He asked for a cold meatloaf sandwich, heavy ketchup, crust removed, a peanut butter milkshake…and for the president's resignation. He got nothing. Authorities decided to wait it out. About an hour later"—long pause—"he gave up, without incident."

Kyle moved to the kitchen, opened the fridge, and surveyed the contents. Cooking would be too much of a bother, she thought, then closed the door. An all-night Chinese diner up the street seemed her only option at this hour. Kyle felt grateful they delivered, a true blessing for her tired muscles and aching bones.

She grabbed the phone book and opened it to the restaurant section and as she did saw something out of the corner of her eye.

Something speeding across her living room.

She screamed and lurched back simultaneously.

It was gone before Kyle could look up to identify it, but she knew the figure was human, knew it was dressed all in white.

She blinked hard, then rushed into the room, heart racing—pounding—inside her chest. When she got there, Kyle instantly felt ice-cold air nipping at her skin, then a warm hand on the back of her neck. She jumped, turned around.

Nothing—or nobody—was there.

The sound on the television rose steadily, as if someone were hiking the volume with a remote.

"Six-year-old Bethany Foley, the youngest child, was also killed."

Kyle froze, eyes gaping, slack jawed, as if it were her own photograph on the screen.

The final piece of the puzzle was staring her right in the face.

Chapter Sixty-Four

45687 Monument Path Way
Albuquerque, New Mexico

Kyle had become used to seeing Bethany at the strangest times and in the most peculiar places, but never anything like this.

Before, she'd always appeared in her deceased state. Now, in the photo, she looked very much alive. Gone were the dark, sunken circles beneath shadowy eyes, as were the filthy tangles of hair framing a frightened, despondent face. *This* Bethany was a striking contrast—a beautiful, golden-haired child with soft, pink skin and stunning green eyes, as clear and bright as polished emeralds.

It created a new perspective for Kyle knowing there was another side to this lost and wandering soul. Bethany had had a life before all this. She'd been a happy, vibrant child, not the foreboding picture of despair Kyle had become so accustomed to seeing. It was almost as if she were looking at a different person.

Unfortunately, that feeling of warmth wasn't a lasting one; it dissipated quickly, as pictures of the Foley murder scene flashed across the screen. Kyle cringed as she watched file footage of officials removing body bags from the house and rolling them toward plain white vans. One of them—about a third the size of the others—was hard to miss. It was Bethany's body.

"Several days later, and authorities in Faith are still at a loss to explain why the son, eleven-year-old Ben Foley, gunned down his family, then took his own life," the news anchor continued. "Sheriff's deputies found the boy inside his bedroom closet—shot to death—an apparent suicide. The massacre is just one in a series of killings in and around the town, which, before this, was relatively crime-free. Officials in Faith remain baffled, unable to connect any of them, unable to explain why they occurred."

Bethany hadn't died in an accident. She didn't suffer from some sudden childhood illness, and she wasn't part of the World War II scenario Kyle kept seeing in her visions.

As soon as the story ended, she made a dash for the kitchen. There was no time to check her computer; time was of the essence. She pulled open a drawer, grabbed a New Mexico road map. Struggling with its unwieldy size, and spreading it out on the table, she searched for Faith.

Spotting it down toward the bottom, she used her fingers to measure the distance between Faith and Albuquerque, then compared it to the legend, trying to figure out the drive time. The town appeared to be a good two hundred miles south, about a three-hour trip if she went the speed limit, less if she drove faster.

She grabbed the telephone and started punching keys, swatting at a lock of hair that had fallen down in front of her face, as if shooing away an annoying fly.

~

Josh was sleeping when the phone rang. He reached over and felt around for it on the nightstand. Running his fingers over the receiver, he fumbled before pulling it toward him and moaning, "Hello."

"It's me," Kyle said.

"Hi, you," he replied with a groan and a yawn. "You sound funny."

"I've got it."

"Got what?" Josh asked, feeling less tired but more confused.

"I've figured it out. I know who Bethany is."

Josh swung his feet over the edge of his bed and leaned forward. "You do? Who?"

"She lived and died in Faith."

"Sounds like the title of a book."

"It's a place, right here in this state, just a few hundred miles south of here. She was murdered, Josh, along with the rest of her family. Her brother did it, shot them all to death in the middle of the night, then killed himself." She was still breathless. "I *saw* her, Josh. Caught it on the news. They showed her picture."

Josh reached for the switch on the lamp, clicked it on, squinting while allowing his eyes to adjust to the light. "So you know why she's been contacting you?"

"Yes...and no. It's about what's been going on in her town lately. There've been a bunch of murders. What it has to do with the images from World War Two—that's where I'm lost right now. Still can't make a connection. It's all from an era that happened long before she was even born."

"Weird... What now?"

There was a short pause, and then she said, "I'm going to Faith."

"I don't think I like the sound of that," he said slowly.

"I've got to, Josh," she insisted. "Don't you see? This little girl's been trying to tell me something. Now I finally know where she lived. This is huge. Everything I need is waiting for me right there. This is exactly what I've been looking for."

"Then I'm coming with you."

"No!" Kyle said sharply. "Don't. Please. I need to go by myself. It would be too obvious if both of us showed up there."

"I can't let you go alone, Sis. You know nothing about this place or what you're walking into," he pointed out. "Don't you get it? People are getting murdered. You wanna end up being one of them?"

"I'll be okay, Josh. I've gotta go. I'll be careful, I promise."

"Jeez, Kyle."

More insistent now. "I'm going, Joshua."

He said nothing for a few seconds, thinking it over, then groaned. "You're a grown woman, and about as pigheaded as they come. I can't stop you—we both know that—but I *can* make demands, and I'm going to."

Now Kyle was groaning. "Demands?"

"Yeah, demands. I'll be damned if I'm gonna stand by and let you walk head-on into this kind of danger without doing *something*."

"And what are these demands?" asked Kyle.

"You stay in touch with me. You *call* me…without fail. Understand?" He didn't wait for her to reply. "You call me before you leave here. You call me when you're halfway there, and you call me once you arrive. Got that? And after that, it's every five hours—again, without fail—and I'm warning you, Kyle, if you don't play by the rules, the rules change: this becomes *my* game."

Kyle groaned again.

"That's right. Big brother's comin' to town with both barrels loaded, and I'll be bringing my posse with me. Think I'd be conspicuous at your side? Just you wait. I'll stick out like a clown at a funeral."

Kyle didn't like his conditions or the way he was strong-arming her. But she *had* called him, and on some level, she knew she needed the safety net he was offering.

"Okay," she said, finally relenting, "if I must."

"You must. And keep your cell phone with you at all times. I want to be able to reach you. No turning it off. No letting the battery go dead. I mean it, Kyle."

"I swear. I will," she said.

"And one more thing."

"What *now*?" she snapped.

His voice softened. "Take care of yourself."

"I will, Josh, I promise."

"Love ya, Sis."

"Love ya back," she said.

Josh hung up the phone and smiled, but not for long.

He sat, thinking for a few seconds.

"Forgive me, Sis," he said as he picked up the receiver again and dialed, "but you mean way too much to me, and I'll be damned if I'm gonna let you walk through *this* fire alone."

Chapter Sixty-Five

State Route 25
Albuquerque, New Mexico

By the time Kyle had gathered her things and headed out the door, it was close to midnight. If everything went as planned, she would be in Faith before morning.

Bethany had died at the hands of her eleven-year-old brother in a bloody massacre that ended not only her life but her parents' as well. Her sense of trust was no doubt destroyed the instant she saw him aiming the gun at her. If she couldn't trust him, who *could* she? No wonder she always seemed to be running away. Kyle tried to imagine what it must have been like for the little girl to wake up and see her brother aiming the gun at her. Did she see his face? Look into his eyes? Could she feel the rage coming from him in those final moments before he pulled the trigger and ended her life?

Kyle chased the thought away with another, although it wasn't much better.

According to the news, Faith had been a peaceful town before all this. Now Kyle wondered if she was putting herself at risk of becoming one of those statistics. Josh had probably been right in his hesitation to let her go there—maybe her adrenaline rush had clouded her better judgment, causing her to jump in too fast.

No turning back now, she thought as she watched her headlights tearing holes in the darkness.

After several miles and deep in thought, Kyle realized she'd lost track of time. A sign emerged from the shadows: FAITH, NEW MEXICO: 85 MILES.

Like a double shot of espresso to the brain, she perked up, feeling wide awake again. She'd be there soon. Her nerves reactivated as anxiety charged through her body.

About a half hour later, signs of civilization began slowly emerging. On the distant horizon, tiny lights dotted the countryside, first spread wide apart, then in tighter clusters, as Faith drew nearer. Kyle felt a push of adrenaline as she exited the highway off-ramp that would lead her straight toward her destination.

She was not prepared, however, for what she saw next. If she thought her excitement was elevated before, Kyle was in for an even bigger surprise now—it was about to reach new heights.

Nesting on a grassy knoll was a church with a large sign out front; it listed service times, invited people to Friday night bingo, and announced the upcoming chili cook-off. But that wasn't what caught Kyle's attention. Beneath those words, there were more—ones that sent a chill sailing up her spine:

Empty hearts make empty souls.

Words with a haunting message.

Words that had become familiar to Kyle.

Now she knew why.

Chapter Sixty-Six

State Route 25
Ten miles outside Faith, New Mexico

Empty hearts, empty souls.

Kyle had been trying to figure out the meaning of those words ever since Bethany had first said them.

The Restoration Church stood on the edge of Faith's outer limits. Since there was only one way in and one way out, anyone wishing to enter the town needed to pass by. Bethany had planted the seed early on, knowing Kyle would recognize it when the time was right.

She descended a steep mountain grade, then traveled on to the main artery leading directly into town. Though it was still dark, Faith's charm shone through. Quaint little shops lined both sides of the street, flanked by neatly groomed tree lawns. The whole scene looked almost too perfect. *How*, she wondered, *could something so ugly have happened in a place this beautiful?*

Kyle yawned. Not sleeping all night was finally taking its toll, and she felt exhausted, desperately in need of rest. Off in the distance, a motel seemed to call her name, its flashing, neon VACANCY sign winking at her with the promise of a warm bath and clean sheets.

Chapter Sixty-Seven

Felice's Diner
Faith, New Mexico

One o'clock in the afternoon.

A late lunch for Cameron. It seemed as if he'd barely had time to breathe, let alone eat. The shocking news about Shawn Banks had sent his mind reeling, his body feeling like it was running on empty. He'd decided to drop by Felice's for a quick bite.

On his way out, Cameron watched a woman and a boy crossing in front of him; the child sneezed.

"*Mijo!*" she fussed. "Cover your mouth when you sneeze. You want to get everybody else sick?"

Everybody else sick.

Just a cold, he tried to tell himself, but then another thought quickly entered his mind. *Another murderer? Another boy waiting in the wings? Waiting to kill?*

He pushed it away. *Calm down, Cam.* But how could he? How could he be calm knowing this *thing*—whatever it was—had been taking hold of his town, sweeping through it like a deadly tornado, one that seemed to be gathering intensity with each passing minute?

Someone else coughed. Cameron swung his head in the other direction—an older man. He waited with caution for the cough to continue. It did not.

Cameron suddenly changed his course, heading straight toward Blake's Pharmacy.

"Afternoon, Sheriff," said the pharmacist, looking up from behind the counter with a smile, as Cameron entered.

He barely nodded back; he was on a mission. Bypassing several aisles, he headed for the cold and flu section. When he got there, he stopped and stared.

The flu medicines were gone. All of them.

"Blake?" Cameron said, his eyes still fixed on the one spot.

"Something wrong, Sheriff?" Blake replied, now standing beside Cameron, interest piqued.

Cameron directed his focus on the shelf again. "Been selling a lot of 'em lately?"

"I can look in the back and see if I have more. You got a case of the flu, Sheriff?"

"No, Blake," he replied. "I have something worse."

Chapter Sixty-Eight

Sheriff's Station
Faith, New Mexico

Cameron went back to his office.

All the pressure, the strain, they were playing tricks on his intellect, causing his imagination to work overtime, something he didn't need right now. If he worried about every cough, sniffle, or sneeze, he'd drive himself crazy, and that, he decided, would only drive him back instead of forward.

I need to stay on track…stay with the facts.

He thought about his two deputies, one dead, the other his killer.

Shawn Banks had managed to fly under the radar, where he'd remained throughout the other murders. Nobody saw him acting any differently, and even if they had, most would have attributed it to the breakup with his girlfriend.

Unfortunately, she wasn't able to offer much.

Shannon Westerly hadn't seen anything unusual in her ex-boyfriend's behavior prior to the breakup—at least nothing that she was willing to admit; in fact, when asked why she'd ended the relationship, her answer was simple: he bored her—both in bed and out.

Not the answer Cameron had hoped to hear. For one, he wasn't interested in his deputy's sexual prowess, or lack thereof, but most important, it led him straight into yet another dead end. He didn't need any more of those; in fact, he was sick of them.

In effect, all it proved was that Shawn's inclination toward violence had started postbreakup. That meant there was nobody around to see his personality take such a drastic turn, and that meant Cameron was stuck exactly where he'd started.

Another brick wall.

Someone pounded on the door.

Grabbing a handful of paperwork, Cameron shuffled through it, trying to appear busy, then shouted "Come in!"

Frank stuck his head in. "What's with the closed door?"

"Needed to clear my head," Cameron replied. "A few moments of solitude."

Frank entered, stared at him for a moment, thinking it over. "You look like shit."

"Thanks," Cameron said before going back to his work.

Frank settled into the chair opposite the desk, locked his fingers behind his head, and then leaned back, appraising Cameron with interest.

Cameron stopped what he was doing but did not look up for a few seconds. When he finally did, he met his boss's gaze, coupled with a shit-eating grin. Cameron folded his hands, rested them on his desktop, then returned a sarcastic smile. "Yes?"

"Just got done talking to the ME in Albuquerque."

"Did you?" Cameron replied, shuffling more papers.

"Yeah. Just finished Shawn Banks' autopsy."

Cameron didn't say anything. The words *Shawn Banks* and *autopsy* still didn't seem to fit together. They never would.

Frank held up a folder. "Got something for you right here."

Cameron looked up at him, drumming his fingers on his desktop. "If you know something, Frank, now's the time to let it out."

"I do." He paused for dramatic effect, then spoke around a widening smile. "Stomach ulcers."

"What about 'em?"

"Shawn Banks had them." Frank slapped the folder on top of what Cameron was doing. "How do you like me now?"

"I like you a lot more," Cameron said, grabbing the folder, opening it, while warming to the idea. "You mean ulcers as in *Ben Foley* ulcers?"

"I mean *just* like Ben Foley's. And something else. They were able to get a better fix on them this time because they were far more advanced."

Cameron clicked his pen several times as he glanced over the folder's contents.

"And these weren't your everyday run-of-the-mill ulcers," Frank continued. "There was a shitload of them, and very close together. The stomach lining looked like it was literally being eaten away."

"Eaten away?"

"Yeah. Perforated all to hell." Frank stopped himself, working through his own thoughts. "Say...were you ever able to find out if Ben was taking any meds that would've caused the ulcers, or if he had any medical history?"

"I did. Negative. On both counts."

Frank nodded as if agreeing with himself, then gazed out the window.

"What?" Cameron said.

"That request you made with Gavin? The one to check Banks for the flu virus? Smart move—very smart, indeed."

With everything going on, Cameron had forgotten all about it. "Yeah? And?"

Frank raised his eyebrows. "Had it."

"No shit?"

"No shit."

Cameron looked up as if watching an idea fly past him, then back at Frank. "Ryan Churchill still across the street in holding right now?"

"Yeah, sure."

His grin began to widen. "Wonder how his tummy's feeling?"

Frank nodded. "*Ulcers*."

"And if *he* does," Cameron said, "I'm willing to bet Judith had the same symptoms as well."

"If we can just find her."

Cameron stood up and walked to the window, gazing sightlessly through it. "First they come down with flu symptoms, then the stomach ulcers…and then they kill. After that—after it's all done—they have no memory of any of it."

"The *hell's* causing it?" Frank asked.

Cameron grabbed the phone, started dialing, then spoke into the receiver. "It's Dawson. I need Rainey." He paused and listened. "*Find him*. Right away… Tell him to call me. Tell him it's an emergency, that I need to send Ryan over to the hospital for tests. *ASAP*."

A knock on the door interrupted them.

Betty poked her head in. "Have a message for you," she said, handing Cameron a card.

He read it, then looked up at her, shaking his head.

"She came by while you were at lunch," Betty said with a shrug. "Says she has information that might help you figure out what all's been going on around here."

"Doctor Kyle Bancroft," he read aloud, trying to place the name. Then he looked over at Frank. "From Albuquerque?"

Frank shrugged.

Cameron flipped the card over, then read the handwriting on the back.

Call me ASAP. I think I can help.
Staying at the Graybill Motel—Room 167
Cell Phone: 505-555-3434

He picked up the telephone and dialed the number.

Chapter Sixty-Nine

Felice's Diner
Faith, New Mexico

The lunch counter at Felice's was the last place anyone had seen Shawn Banks alive. Cameron set his gaze on the exact spot where the deputy had been sitting and kept it there: a reminder of that day, he thought, doubting he'd ever be able to see it as anything else.

Just that morning, Cameron had attended Banks' funeral. Standing over the casket, he wondered how many more of these he'd have to see before long.

Moving his eyes away from the lunch counter and across the room, everything looked like business as usual. The shattered window had been replaced, the blood cleaned up, even the bullet hole in the wall—gone—filled in and covered up by a fresh coat of paint.

Nothing left, he thought, nothing except the memories, and no amount of paint, plaster, or soap could cover up those.

As expected, an upper endoscopy had revealed that Ryan Churchill, in fact, did have stomach ulcers. Solid evidence,

Cameron thought, showing a common connection among several suspects, evidence that could move him closer to the truth. Now he just needed to figure out what had caused them.

Cameron looked at the door and then his watch. He'd done it about five times, maybe even more, since first arriving. He and Bancroft were supposed to meet at four o'clock. It was four fifteen. She was late, and he was annoyed.

He checked his watch, then the door again. As he did, a tall, slender woman with strawberry-blonde hair falling just below her shoulders walked through. She wore faded blue jeans and a bright green polo shirt.

Cameron stood up to make it easier for her to find him. She smiled as she joined him and sat down.

"I apologize for being so late," she said right away, scooting her chair forward. "It's not my style at all, but a water main broke just outside my motel, of all things. Had to go up the street and check in to another place just to take a shower…*such* a mess."

He knew about the main and forgave her lateness instantly. "Not a very nice way to welcome guests into our town, now, is it?"

Kyle dismissed the comment with a wave of her hand while glancing around the restaurant. "No big deal. These things happen. I have to admit, I actually hadn't expected Faith to be this nice. It really is quite lovely."

"Funny, people always seem to say that when they come here." Cameron paused, then added, "Not sure why."

"I think it's because we tend to overlook small towns," Kyle said, smiling a thank-you to the young waitress as she placed a glass of ice water before her.

"You may be right about that," Cameron replied.

Before Kyle could say another word, a strange sensation overcame her. Waves—or something like them—moved on the air, glowing and expanding as they traveled. She began feeling disoriented and lost her sense of balance. It took a moment to realize that the powerful aura was coming from Cameron. Kyle watched wordlessly as the beam of energy expanded around him. Before long, it saturated the entire room with its white-hot glow.

Trying to regain her composure, Kyle glanced away for a moment, hoping she didn't look as dazed as she felt. Initially, Cameron had appeared gentle, quiet, and soft-spoken, but the force flowing out of him now was a study in contrasts; he was a powerhouse of continuous, blinding energy.

"It's a good life, though," she struggled to say, her voice overshadowed by uncertainty.

"I'm sorry?" Cameron asked, confused.

"Living in a small town…I mean…there's nothing like it."

Cameron gave a quick, single nod, as if suddenly catching her drift.

But Kyle couldn't stop watching the aura stirring around him. Within the powerful strokes of light was a palpable energy mixed with emotions: anguish, guilt, intense heartache. She not only saw the energy; now she could feel it, too.

"You okay?" Cameron asked.

Kyle reached for the glass of water, took a quick gulp, nodded. "Fine. Just feeling dehydrated. This heat you're having is unbearable. Think it just caught up with me, is all."

Cameron nodded back, remembering where the conversation had let off. "You grow up in one? A small town?"

Depression, deep and endless.

"I did," Kyle replied, battling to maintain her perceptual stability in the storm of raging emotions. Increasingly, she was feeling more disoriented, more dazed.

Cameron noticed. He leaned in toward her, studying her eyes, unaware that *he* was the cause of the problem.

For Kyle, this experience was different from the ones she'd had earlier. Gone was the flurry of images ticking through her mind; now there were *feelings* bombarding her, pure, raw emotion.

Agonizing misery. Self-loathing.

The sensations were becoming intolerable. Kyle threw her hands over her face and shook her head, as if trying to hide from them, but it didn't work. She looked up, rolled her eyes into the back of her head, and began falling from her chair.

Just that instant, Cameron reached across the table and grabbed both her wrists, but to his surprise, he felt a burning, stinging sensation—she was hot to the touch. Instinctively, he loosened his grip, releasing her, causing her to lean and fall—slowly at first, then more quickly—out of her chair.

Cameron raced around the table just in time to catch Kyle before she hit the floor. Other people in the restaurant saw the commotion and began to stir, realizing something was wrong.

"Call an ambulance!" Cameron shouted out, lowering Kyle gently onto her back, her limp body hugging the floor. Within seconds, her skin had gone from scorching hot to icy cold. He reached over and felt for a pulse. To his relief, she still had one, although rapidly pounding.

An anxious crowd gathered around them, whispering and wondering who this stranger was, passed out on the floor.

Several minutes later, two paramedics came rushing through the door, and Cameron felt a wave of relief as they took over, attaching tubes, checking her vital signs, and trying to get her to wake up. She was unresponsive. The medics slid her onto a scoop stretcher, pulling canvas straps across her chest and legs.

Cameron stood back, watching, worrying, but most of all, with many questions still wandering through his mind: Who was this woman? And why had she come here? Even more troubling, what had caused her to collapse onto the floor?

Within seconds she was gone, rushed off to Faith Community, with Cameron in his car following closely behind.

Chapter Seventy

Community Hospital
Faith, New Mexico

Kyle opened her eyes to find Cameron sitting motionless, just several feet away, and watching her. It only took her a few seconds to realize where she was and what had happened.

The menacing aura that had surrounded him earlier was gone now; still, she knew that even though she couldn't actually see or feel the energy, it hadn't gone far. This sort of thing often changed in form and intensity, but rarely did it ever go away completely. Kyle couldn't help but wonder where it was coming from. Even more of a concern was what had caused it.

"Feeling okay?" Cameron asked.

"I'm not sure yet," Kyle replied, her voice soft and breathy, her mind still groggy.

"Do you remember what happened?"

"No…I mean yes…well, sort of." She rubbed her eyes with the heels of her palms, then suddenly looked up. "What time is it, anyway?"

Cameron turned his wrist to look at his watch. "About seven forty-eight."

Kyle shifted her gaze out the window next to her bed. A remnant splash of ginger sunlight streaked across the western skies. Was it the settling dusk or the rising dawn? She couldn't be sure. Time had evaded her the minute she'd lost consciousness. She looked back at Cameron. "As in seven forty-eight…*at night*?"

"You got it," he replied, letting a yawn escape and feeling the long day wearing down on him. He still had no idea who this woman was, or why she'd come to meet him. Her collapse only seemed to widen the mystery.

As soon as Kyle found the clock on the wall, her expression fell.

"What's wrong?"

"Nothing." But she was thinking of her obligatory call to Josh. Kyle had been doing well keeping in touch until now. She eyed the phone on the nightstand. If she called him soon, she'd still be okay.

Cameron followed her glance with curiosity. "Got somewhere you have to be?"

She looked up at him quickly and tried to appear casual while forcing a laugh. "Do I look like I have somewhere to go?"

"We were having coffee," Cameron said, changing the subject. "Or about to, anyway."

"That part I remember."

"Then you passed out."

"That's where things got a little murky—actually, a lot murky." She rubbed the back of her head, a shadow passing over her expression.

"Took quite a fall there," Cameron said, turning his head to look out the window.

Kyle took the opportunity to size him up. *Nice looking*, she thought, *if you like the type—a blond-haired, blue-eyed Ken Doll.* She'd dated a few in her time, but nothing good ever came from any of them—always seemed to lack substance, and too self-absorbed to be able to give very much of themselves.

Cameron looked back and caught her staring. She looked away, pretending it meant nothing. *He* pretended not to notice, then said, "There's this matter about why you came here."

"Yeah. I know. I'd hoped to get to that. But I need to give you some background before I go into…"

Just then, the doctor walked into the room, changing the topic, changing the mood. "Good evening," he said, his voice brisk, while appearing preoccupied. He flipped through pages on a clipboard, sighing the whole time. "Well, Doctor, everything looks fine. You're in excellent shape. All your tests came up normal. No real explanation for why you passed out. Could be exhaustion." He glanced up. "You do appear a little dehydrated. How about sleep? Getting enough?"

"Not very much," she admitted.

Now Cameron was checking *her* out. She caught his gaze, then shot him a look that mixed curiosity with annoyance. He didn't shy away. Instead, he smiled.

"Well, there you go, then," the doctor said, as if solving some sort of medical mystery. "Anyway, I'll go ahead and let you check out tonight—no need to keep you here. I'll spare you the get-more-rest-and-drink-more-fluids speech, you being a doctor and all."

"Thank you," Kyle said, forcing a thin smile.

"I'll also suspend with the *Doctor, heal thyself* lecture as well and just remind you that you can't take care of others if you don't take care of yourself."

"Yes, yes, you're right," she said, feigning obedience. "I do need to watch myself better." *His bedside manner sucks*, Kyle thought, but she was glad he'd diagnosed her with a simple case of exhaustion, relieving her of having to account for something she couldn't explain.

The doctor scribbled a few notes on his clipboard, looked up, then attempted another polite smile before leaving the room.

"Whatever happened to small-town doctors with charming bedside manners?" Kyle asked.

"They went the same way as the eight-track tape?" Cameron suggested. "How 'bout I give you a lift?"

Kyle was sitting on the edge of her bed. She got down, slipped her jeans on under her gown, paused to think, then looked up at Cameron. "Look. I appreciate what you've done so far, coming here and all—I do—but you don't have to—"

"You're welcome," Cameron interrupted. "It would be my pleasure."

Kyle glared at him. "As I was saying, you don't have to do all this. I'm fine."

"I know that," Cameron said. "That's not why I'm here." He grinned.

"It's not?"

"Nope. Our meeting over coffee proved nothing short of a disaster. Hoping dinner might be better. I'm just making sure you don't sneak out of town without making good on it."

"Tell me you're joking." But she was smiling, too.

"Just the part about making sure you don't sneak away. But I'm dead serious about the dinner. I'm starving. I was thinking maybe Italian. We might do better with that. I like Italian. In fact, you can take me tonight, if you're feeling up to it." *I'm babbling*, he thought irrelevantly. *What's going on?*

Kyle turned away, pulled the gown over her head, exposing her bare back to him, then tossed the garment onto the bed. After pulling on her shirt, she turned around and smiled. "Okay, Italian it is, then."

Chapter Seventy-One

6623 Hunter's Run
Faith, New Mexico

If they were serious about Italian food, Cameron and Kyle were out of luck. The only place in town that served it had already shut down for the day. The closest they were going to get was the local pizza joint on Cedar and Third. Since neither had eaten all day and both were famished, they settled for pickup and dinner at Cameron's house.

A pebbly driveway led to a craftsman-styled bungalow, complete with wraparound porch and a set of short-stacked steps tumbling down the center. Almost immediately, Bentley materialized in the doorway, launching himself off the top step, and hitting the ground running, his thick club of a tail swatting the air. Kyle froze as the robust canine continued charging toward her at a rapid clip.

"Bentley, *off*!" Cameron shouted.

Immediately heeding his owner's command, the dog twisted direction just before plowing into Kyle. Once past her, Bentley turned and walked back, tail tucked between his hind legs, gazing up at Cameron with big brown eyes that seemed to beg forgiveness. While passing Kyle he licked her hand, the canine equivalent of passing the olive branch. From there, he moved over to Cameron to do the same.

"You okay?" he asked her.

"What was *that*?" Kyle asked instead.

"That would be the welcoming committee, better known as Bentley, the overfed Labrador."

"That's your welcoming committee? What's your guard dog look like?"

Cameron smiled and shrugged. "He's just excited to see you. Don't get new company around here much."

~

It was a beautiful New Mexico evening. Jasmine decorated the air with its fragrant aroma while scrub oak branches twisted in the background, creating sounds not unlike waves of rushing water. They decided to take advantage of the ambience by having dinner on the front porch.

Cameron dragged a wrought-iron garden table, with Bentley following closely behind. Upon reaching the top step, the chunky brown dog scanned the yard once, let out a big yawn, then dropped to the floor, falling asleep almost the instant his chin hit the deck.

Once again, Kyle felt Cameron's energy begin to stir as he leaned over to lay down paper plates, not nearly as powerful as before, yet much more specific: *a loss. Something treasured. Something dear.*

Kyle wondered what that was, but before she could grab hold of the thought, it escaped, almost as if being swept into the wind that blew past them.

"You okay?" Cameron asked, noticing Kyle's sudden change of expression.

"Sure…fine," Kyle replied, knowing she'd lied, and sensing that something vague had just slipped through her fingers. She did her best to act as if it hadn't mattered.

The breeze shifted, and the scent of Kyle's hair suddenly caught Cameron's attention: mint, or lavender, or maybe both; he wasn't sure. Memories swirled through his mind. Memories of Sarah. He tried to ignore them.

But not before becoming entangled in Kyle's intuitive grasp.

She's not coming back, Kyle thought, then wondered who it was and why.

An awkward silence fell between them, neither knowing what to say, but for different reasons.

Chapter Seventy-Two

6623 Hunter's Run
Faith, New Mexico

Kyle and Cameron sat on the porch swing.

Somewhere, mixed within the silent, emotional exchange of information, Kyle felt an attraction to Cameron. She knew it was neither appropriate nor timely.

Cameron, on the other hand, not only felt the connection, he wanted to act on it. But before he could, Kyle broke the mood.

She stirred. "There's something you need to know."

Cameron turned his head toward her. "Something wrong?"

Kyle smiled and closed her eyes. "Nothing's wrong."

"What, then?"

"I need to tell you why I'm here." She took a deep breath. "You know, before last night, I never even knew Faith existed."

"So how'd you find us?"

She looked at him for a few seconds, studying his face. "Actually, Faith found me."

"Not sure I follow," Cameron said.

Kyle smiled, trying to find the right words. "Have you ever heard the term *retrocognition*?"

"No," he admitted.

"*Postcognition*?"

He shook his head.

Kyle gazed up, trying to think. White, shimmering stars no larger than pinholes glistened against a sable sky. "Let me see if I can explain this: it's when people can see events from the past without ever being there."

"See them how?" Cameron asked.

"The images can come in dreams or appear almost like hallucinations—very vivid." She hesitated. "People experience an event as if they're actually there, right in the middle of it all. They can see and hear—sometimes even smell—everything. In essence, they become transported back in time, back to the event."

"I'm sorry, I don't know if I can—"

"I know what's causing all the horrible things that have been happening here."

He shook his head, his face a mask of confusion. "Are you saying that you've been seeing everything that's been going on here?"

"No." She looked down, fumbling with her fingers, then back up and into his eyes. "What I'm saying is that I've been seeing the cause."

"The cause," he repeated, even more baffled.

"Yeah, I've been getting inundated with images, but I'm having a difficult time figuring out the connection," she said. "It's not making much sense, but I know it's all coming from right here, from this town."

Cameron shook his head back and forth quickly. "Look, I don't mean any disrespect, but I work in law enforcement. We operate on tangible, physical evidence, not psychic phenomena. I need facts—facts that can hold up in a court of law."

"Of course you do. It's unconventional—I know that—but this *is* real." She stopped and smiled. "I'm a doctor. I draw my conclusions from the same well that you do. I use solid, empirical evidence to make decisions, too. I don't diagnose my patients based on strange vibrations that come to me." She hesitated. "But I don't ignore them, either. If I get a feeling about something, I may pursue it, but I never just accept it as fact without being able to prove it. That would be crazy—it would go against everything I learned in medical school."

"So what are you saying?"

"What I'm saying is that the world isn't one-dimensional. There's room for both the tangible *and* the ethereal."

Cameron considered her words. "Look, I'm not saying I don't believe you, or even that it doesn't exist. I'm just having a hard time seeing how I'd be able to use it to solve what's been happening here."

Kyle shrugged. "Law enforcement agencies have been using psychics to solve their most difficult cold cases for years. It's not something that's publicized, or even accepted among peers, but it *is* happening, and no matter how strange it may seem to some, it's hard to refute the results. Cases *are* being solved."

She was right. Cameron had heard of psychics helping to solve murders and missing-person cases, but he'd never considered whether it was a valid crime-fighting tool—not until now. "I've heard of it before, but I'm still having a tough time getting my mind around it."

Kyle had been watching his face, watching his reaction. She could tell he was struggling with the concept. "Are you aware both the US and British governments have conducted experiments using psychics? And I'm not talking centuries ago—I'm talking about as recently as the past five years. They were trying to see if they could use the psychics' remote-viewing abilities to spy on enemies."

Cameron raised his eyebrows in surprise.

"Look, I know this is a lot to accept, and I would be just as doubtful as you are right now if I were you. It's why I don't share this with people unless I see a need for it. I think what's been happening here qualifies."

"It may qualify, but—"

"Let me put it to you this way: I run a successful private medical practice. I graduated at the top of my class at the Columbia School of Medicine. I'm board-certified three times over in three different specialties. In addition, I'm on faculty at the University of New Mexico School of Medicine. Do you get where I'm going with this?"

"I think so."

"The point I'm making here is that I'm not just some crackpot who's had a break with reality. And I didn't just drive to a strange town I've never heard of with some half-baked theory I cooked up along the way. The fact is I didn't even know what was going on here—all I knew was that lives were at stake and for some reason, the answers why were coming to me." She paused and smiled. "I'm trying to help you."

Cameron had already decided the situation in Faith was far from normal and that the solution would be as well. He just hadn't realized he would have to go this far to find it. He took a deep breath.

Kyle watched him continue wrestling with his thoughts. "Look. I'm not trying to convince you of my abilities. You don't even have to believe I have them. All I'm asking is that you investigate the information I'll give you. If it materializes into something, then great; if not, no worries—it's just another lead that didn't pan out, no different from your everyday telephone tip. It doesn't matter how you find the missing pieces, as long as you find them, right?"

She was right. He'd always considered tips from the public, no matter how bizarre they sounded at times, and from people who had far less sense than Kyle seemed to have. She wasn't crazy—of that, he was sure. This was different. *She* was different.

"So what do you say?" she asked.

Cameron looked at her, appeared to be weighing all the information. "You plead your case well. It's something I would never normally even begin to consider. You're pretty persuasive."

Kyle looked away, smiled. "I've been told."

Cameron sat silently for a moment. She was so beautiful, so intelligent, not like anyone he'd ever met. How could he *not* believe her? "Okay, I'll go along, but there are some rules we need to follow. It's crucial."

"Name them."

"One, this stays between us. Not a word to anyone. If my boss gets even a whiff of what's happening here, he'll not only have my job, he'll have me committed."

This was beginning to sound familiar. It was her and Josh all over again. "Understood. What else?"

"Second, you work with me and only me. Nobody else. You don't discuss the case with anybody."

She smiled. "I think I can live with that."

He took a very deep breath. "Now let's go see if you can help me take back this town."

Kyle raised an eyebrow. "The way I see it, you just did."

Chapter Seventy-Three

6623 Hunter's Run
Faith, New Mexico

The moon was bright, the night clear. They'd decided to take a walk.

Kyle and Cameron began putting their plan in order. She would tell people that she was in town looking to buy property, that she was interested in relocating to Faith and wanted to spend some time getting to know the area. It seemed logical.

Kyle told Cameron what she'd been experiencing before coming to Faith, about the images in her mind and the strange dreams. She explained it all, every detail. Cameron agreed that none of it seemed to fit in with what was happening there.

"World War Two's so far away from what's going on right now," Cameron said.

"I know. That's been the problem all along—trying to make sense of it all." Kyle shook her head, eyes focused straight ahead. "It just doesn't seem to fit."

Cameron knew what she meant. He'd been experiencing the same thing on his end, just in different ways. "There's only one hospital in this town, always has been: Faith Community. Before that, there was nothing here."

"Even back as far as World War Two?"

"I'm pretty sure, but I can ask some of the old-timers. Lane Smith is as close to being the town historian as we'll ever get. He's a barber, but he's been here longer than anyone else. At least among the living."

Kyle hesitated for a moment. "I've told you *what* I know. What I haven't explained is *how* I know it."

"You said the information came by way of dreams and images."

"And that's true. What I haven't explained is the mode of delivery."

"Mode of delivery?"

"Yeah." She laughed. "These things don't just drop into my head all by themselves. There's usually a medium…a messenger."

"So who's the mess—"

"It's Bethany Foley."

Cameron stopped and stared straight ahead. "You get messages from dead people."

"Yeah, that's generally how it works."

"Look, we're getting into some dangerous territory here."

"I know it sounds creepy, but it's been happening all my life."

Cameron's voice began to falter. "No, you don't understand. I lost my—"

She interrupted him, intent on her own thoughts. "Listen, I never even knew who Bethany Foley was until last night. For weeks, I saw her face but had no idea why. It wasn't until I saw a news report about the Faith murders on TV that I made the connection. She's been trying to tell me something, trying to get me to come here. I don't know for sure, but I have a strong suspicion she knows what's going on, and why."

"I knew her brother Ben very well."

"Any idea why he did it?"

"If we knew that, we'd be able solve this whole mess." His tone came out sharper than he'd meant for it to.

Kyle looked injured by his reply. She walked a few steps ahead of him, wrapped her arms around herself, and did not turn back. "Look…I'm not here to cause problems, Cameron. I'm here to help you solve them."

He sighed with regret. "I realize that."

She turned back around and faced him. "You seem to forget. This isn't a vacation for me. I've turned my entire life upside down: I've left everything I have back at home, my practice, my family… my life."

She'd never said anything about having a husband or any children. "Your family?"

Her eyes showed a hint of tears. "Well, the only family I have left. My brother. We're very close. Both our parents are gone."

He felt worse now. "I'm sorry. The last thing I want to do is hurt your feelings. You have to know that."

She remained silent.

"Look. I'm trying to process all this, but it's not easy, not for someone like me."

"Someone like you?"

Cameron had almost told her about Dylan. Now the atmosphere was far too unsettled. He decided to be vague, instead. "Yeah. I've never had to rely on information like this to solve a case. It's unusual."

She stepped toward him. "I know it is, and I'm trying my best to be sensitive to that. It's why I waited to tell you about Bethany, but I couldn't keep it from you. It's information you're going to need."

"I realize that. I just need you to be patient. I'm moving as fast as I—"

"I *am* being patient, and I *do* understand. Believe me, I've faced this kind of resistance my whole life. I never chose to have these abilities. They sort of just chose me. But I need you to know that I take them very seriously."

Cameron nodded, avoiding eye contact with Kyle, as if doing so might prevent her from seeing into his past.

Little did he know, she already had.

Chapter Seventy-Four

Desert Spring Motel
Faith, New Mexico

Cameron had offered to let Kyle stay at his place, but she declined. While the invitation was appealing—the idea of another night at a motel didn't thrill her—she fought the urge, telling him she thought it would be best if she didn't. Kyle wanted to keep a clear head. Sleeping under the same roof would only serve as a distraction.

Standing in the vanity area near the bathroom, Kyle switched on the light and glanced in the mirror. She grimaced. Her face awash in a greenish-yellow glow, she wondered why the lighting in motel rooms was always so unflattering. Pulling the clip from her hair, she placed it in her mouth and gathered the strands into a fresh ponytail.

Suddenly, she noticed someone standing directly behind her, staring at her through the reflection in the mirror.

The clip fell from her mouth, dropping into the sink and making a sharp, tinny noise as it bounced against the porcelain. Kyle spun around.

No one was there.

She looked at the door; it was wide open.

Kyle ran to it, checked outside. A vehicle peeled out of the parking lot, then sped away.

Her heart was pounding against her ribs, and her stomach muscles felt tight, restricting her breathing. She shut the door, locked the deadbolt and leaned against it, eyes closed.

Somebody had been inside her room. Waiting for her. Watching her. This was no vision: this was real flesh and blood.

The notion sent an icy sensation throughout her entire body. She could handle the images in her mind; she was used to those. But an intruder in her real world—that was something she hadn't expected. The idea of someone singling her out made her feel frightened, vulnerable. Kyle moved to the window and peered out through the drapes, scanning the immediate area.

Everything was still and silent.

She reached for the phone, punched in Cameron's number. As he began to answer, she interrupted him. "Can you come and get me?"

"What's going on?"

"I'll explain when you get here."

"I'm on my way."

"Hurry," she said and hung up the phone.

~

Ten minutes later Cameron was knocking on her door. Kyle peered through the peephole, relieved to see his face on the other side. She pulled the door open, and their eyes met. The fear on Kyle's face said everything. He gazed into the room, then back at her. "Let's get out of here."

She said nothing, nodding as she walked past him and out the door.

When he turned back around, Kyle was already leaning against the hood of his car, arms wrapped around herself, and staring off at nothing.

~

Kyle sat at Cameron's kitchen table. He handed her a cup of hot green tea, which she took eagerly, wrapping her fingers around it, staring at the contents.

"Any idea who'd want to follow you?" he asked, taking a seat across from her.

"I was going to ask you the same question." She finally took a sip, looked inside her cup again and swirled the liquid.

"Can't imagine. Nobody here even knows you."

"All the more reason," she said. "Maybe they don't want me here. Maybe they don't like strangers."

"This town may take notice of strangers, but we don't chase them away."

She looked up at him. "Whoever it was—he was *inside* my room, waiting. That scares the hell out of me."

"You're staying here from now on," he said firmly.

Kyle said nothing. She couldn't shake the image from her mind; that reflection in the mirror, the way he stood there, gaping at her. So calm. So creepy.

"Did you get a chance to see his face?"

"Not really." She shifted nervously, sipped the tea, and then put the cup back on the table. Her hands were still shaking. "It was dark in that corner of the room. I couldn't see much."

"Was there anything you *could* make out about him? Anything at all?"

Kyle tried to think, then shook her head with a frown. "He slipped away so fast. By the time I got to the door, he was already taking off out of the parking lot."

"Wait a minute...you saw the vehicle?"

"Not much of it."

"How much?"

She shrugged. "Just the back end."

"He wasn't driving a white van by any chance, was he?"

Kyle looked up at him suddenly. Her face went blank.

Chapter Seventy-Five

6623 Hunter's Run
Faith, New Mexico

"This isn't the first time I've heard about them," Cameron told Kyle.

"*Them*?" she asked. "There are others?"

"Yeah. At least two."

"Who are they?"

Cameron frowned, shook his head. "I don't know much, really, other than a few people have seen them in town, too. Sounds like they're looking for something."

"Where have they been seen?"

"Judith Hedrick's shop, for one. And they were over at the Foley place, as well." He thought for a moment. "That seems to be ground zero. It's like that place is holding the secret to what's been happening here, like I keep being led back there."

"Bethany," Kyle said suddenly.

"What?"

"She's orchestrating all this, has been from the start. She's the catalyst."

"So what's the connection?"

"She piloted me here—literally—from hundreds of miles away. She's trying to tell me what's been happening." Kyle's voice softened. "So frightened."

"Who?"

"Her… The way she would come and go. The information came in tiny spurts at first. I thought she was playing games—you know, the way children do—but it wasn't that at all."

"What was it?"

"She was scared."

"Of what?"

"I don't know. It's like she's been running—running from what happened." Her voice trailed off and she looked at Cameron for a moment, then her eyes opened wide. "That's it! That's what it is! She wants to clear her brother!"

Cameron shook his head. "Can't be."

Kyle looked up at him, puzzled. "Why not?"

"Because there's no question: he definitely did it."

"Yeah, but we don't know *why*. Don't you see? She's been trying to tell me all along—the dreams, the images, *everything*. They tell the story. It's all starting to make sense!"

"So what's the story?"

"Sorry. Can't help you there. If there's one thing I've learned about Bethany, it's that you can't rush her. She controls the flow of information. She decides when and how…and only when she feels safe."

Chapter Seventy-Six

1500 Block of Gentry Street
Faith, New Mexico

"Unit one."

"This is unit one."

"Receiving a report of a domestic disturbance at 2244 Hathaway Street. Stanley Gilchrest residence. Neighbors report subject holding wife and kids hostage inside the house, threatening to..."

(Static.)

"You're breaking up. I copied, subject inside house. Ten-nine?"

"Subject is holding a rifle—I repeat—holding a rife and threatening to kill his family. You copy?"

(Pause.)

"You copy, Sheriff?"

"Holy sh..."

(Static.)

"Yes, yes...copy. Send backups to the scene, but tell them do not attempt entry into the residence—I repeat—do not attempt to enter that house until I get there. Under no circumstances...is that clear? Do you copy?"

"Copy, Sheriff, do not enter the house. Affirmative. What's your twenty?"

"Gentry and First, about three minutes away."

"Copy. Gentry and First. Three minutes away."

(Static.)

"Unit one, come in."

(Audible sigh.) *"This is unit one. What is it?"*

"Got another one."

"Another what?"

"Call…this one's on Fairhaven."

"WHAT? What's happening on Fairhaven now?"

"Assault."

"An assault?"

"Female victim. Beaten and raped in the back alley. Behind the drug store."

(Pause.)

"Sheriff? You still there?"

"The drug st…" (Brief pause.) *"What in God's name's going on?"*

"Don't know, but victim's no longer at the scene. Been transported to Faith Community."

"Continuing on to…"

(Unintelligible.)

"You're breaking up, Sheriff, can you ten-nine?"

"I said, continuing on to Gilchrest residence. Send a unit to secure the Fairhaven scene…another to the hospital—if you can find someone—I'll get there whenever I can. Do you copy?"

"Yeah, copy. Heading on to Gilchrest residence. Sending a unit to Fairhaven to secure the scene, another to the hospital."

"Affirmative. Affirmative. Anything else going on I need to know about?"

"Negative. Not yet."

"It's the 'not yet' that worries me. Over."

"Copy that, Sheriff."

CHAPTER SEVENTY-SEVEN

2244 Hathaway Street
Faith, New Mexico

Stanley Gilchrest had fled the scene by the time Cameron arrived, leaving behind a much shaken—but nevertheless alive—wife and kids.

Cameron sat in his squad car taking notes with the door open, one foot inside, the other out, and feeling as if he had a foothold on hell.

A short time later, Frank arrived, apparently roused from the comforts of home, wearing torn gray sweatpants, an Arizona State ball cap, and a yellow T-shirt with the words "In my world, you don't exist" written across the chest. Classic Frank. He walked up to the passenger window, poked his head inside and scowled. "Armageddon. Fucking Armageddon."

Cameron gazed up from his notes to make eye contact for a moment, then looked back down and continued writing. "Gilchrest's gone. Took off just before I got here."

"Anybody out looking for him?"

Cameron looked up again, this time shooting him a what-do-*you*-think sort of expression.

"Can't take anything for granted anymore," Frank said, crossing his arms and looking around at the crime scene. Then he looked in on Cameron. "What about at the hospital, the other victim?"

"Christina Hawkins," Cameron said, "Raped, beaten, stabbed…and dead. We lost her en route to the hospital."

"Never made it."

"Never stood a chance," Cameron replied. "She was in bad shape."

Frank opened the door and got in. He stared out at the scene for a moment, then at Cameron. "So tell me. How come Gilchrest didn't kill his family?"

"Oh, he tried, 'cept the neighbor, Sam Johnson, put a stop to it. Cowboy style. Ran inside firing off shots with his rifle. Stanley tried to shoot back but couldn't match the firepower." Cameron nodded toward the house. "Took off out the back door."

"*Idiot.* Who the hell told him to go play Rambo?"

"He cast himself in the role," Cameron said. "A little sooner and I probably could have gotten things under control, *and* got Stanley into custody. Now he's running around town, gun and all."

"Or someplace else," Frank said. He opened the glove box and started rifling through. "Put a call out to everywhere within a fifty-mile radius of here. Make sure they're on the lookout for him. We need to cover our bets in case he's headed out of town."

"Already took care of it."

"Good," said Frank, continuing his search of the glove compartment.

Cameron watched with bothered interest. "Something I can help you with there?"

Frank pulled out a wad of papers, tossed it onto the floor. "Antacid. I need an antacid."

A thought crossed Cameron's mind, then a shadow of apprehension seemed to follow. Frank looked up and noticed. "Don't worry…it's *not* ulcers—it's heartburn."

"Wasn't thinking about that. Was thinking about something else."

"What's that?"

"Christina Hawkins."

"What about her?"

"Not just her… How she was raped. How she was killed."

"Beat the hell out of her…right?"

"Yeah. Did that. But didn't stop there."

Frank shook his head.

Cameron looked at Frank for a good ten seconds before he spoke. "After he smashed in her face, and *after* he snapped her neck in two, *then* he went on to rape her. But just raping her—at least in a conventional manner—apparently wasn't enough…"

"I don't—"

"He used a knife…to penetrate her."

Frank shook his head, seemed to draw a blank. "*What the hell kind of sick fuck…?*"

"Don't have to tell you what that did to her insides…sure you can imagine."

Frank said nothing after that. He didn't have to.

CHAPTER SEVENTY-EIGHT

6623 Hunter's Run
Faith, New Mexico

Kyle went to bed, her mind feeling like a windmill set on high speed and spinning out of control. Faith was coming apart, seams and all.

She needed Bethany's help, and she needed it fast.

Kyle turned off the lamp beside the bed and laid her head on the pillow. In her mind, she tried to create vibrations, hoping to attract the little girl—hoping to get the information she so desperately needed.

Within minutes, sleep came.

And for the first time since this all had started, so did her dreams, at the perfect moment.

A familiar, bright, and overlit hallway, almost blinding, and a nurse moving a patient. Roughly. She pushed the gurney, racing around the corner so quickly that the patient nearly slid right off, his legs flopping to one side as they made the sharp turn. A quick shift in direction corrected the problem, sliding him the other way. He let out a sorrowful moan, but his face revealed no emotion, remaining expressionless, vacant.

The nurse gripped the metal handles with small, bony hands, barely able to reach around them. Her leathery skin drew tight over protruding knuckles and gnarled blue veins that resembled shiny fish scales.

She kept her speed, slamming the gurney into, and through, two swinging, stainless steel doors. Metal crashed against metal, producing a deafening sound. The patient reacted with a violent jerk but did nothing else. To the right of the doors hung a sign: FIFTH-FLOOR SUBJUGATION UNIT.

The nurse moved into a room filled with doctors and even more nurses—a sea of white coats and vacant expressions. Kyle recognized the scene. *Lewison*, she thought, from her earlier vision, *the one they had "parked." He's next.*

They transferred him onto a shiny metal table. One of the doctors reached above and pulled down the hinged metal arm with the domed light. Someone flicked a switch, and a giant burst of light exploded, covering the room like a neon blanket. Although the patient was looking up into the lamp, he didn't seem the least bit affected by its blinding intensity. The pupils remained dilated—and dark.

Another nurse entered, rolling in a small and flimsy metal cart. On it, lying across a blue paper towel, was a syringe filled with a brownish-colored liquid. A small, wet circle formed just below the tip of the needle where some had leaked out, expanding as it absorbed into the towel.

Almost like a choreographed dance, three nurses stepped forward. They each tightened one of three heavy leather straps across the man's chest, stomach, and legs. The one going across his stomach also bound his arms against his sides. The flesh beneath the straps ballooned along the edges, turning it bright pink; still, the patient showed no reaction, staring into the light above him, expressionless.

The nurse grabbed the syringe and held it up to the glaring light, which transformed it into a brilliant amber color. As she pushed up from the bottom, a tiny, liquefied ball began to extrude from the long slender tip. Lowering it down, eyes glued to the spit-sharp needle, she pressed the point against the skin on his arm, where it plunged, deeply, disappearing into flesh. The liquid inside the syringe slowly descended downward until gone.

At first, the man showed no outward reaction.

Then everything changed.

The patient went from impassive and lifeless to an acute state of hyperawareness. The pupils began to shrink, his eyes regaining their color, their resilience. Color returned to his face as well, and tiny beads of sweat began squeezing through his pores, growing large, then inching down his skin like raindrops sliding along a windshield.

He began to twitch.

Then, as if some external forced had grabbed hold of his body, he started jerking back and forth, rocking the table and causing the legs beneath to skip off the floor.

One of the nurses stepped back. The patient looked up, locking eyes with her, and in that instant, he suddenly stopped moving.

Then something happened, something Kyle didn't expect: a smile. A horrible one.

An orderly stepped forward, but he seemed to know better, avoiding eye contact with the subject. He raised his hands just above his head and slapped them together, forming a tight fist. Then, he threw them down onto the patient's chest with a force so powerful it produced a deep, hollow thump that reverberated throughout the room.

The patient let out an intense, gut-wrenching howl that resonated.

The orderly looked over at the doctor, who nodded back at him with a restrained, approving smile. He smiled back.

Through all this, Kyle stood in the corner of the room watching everything unfold. Then, suddenly, she felt her head move to the right at a speed that did not feel natural, as if being directed toward a specific spot, to an open doorway.

Bethany appeared on the other side. She walked through it and right up to Kyle. The little girl stood for a few moments, staring, saying nothing, her expression vacant and dreary.

Without warning, the little girl opened her mouth, and a thick, muddy sludge poured out, splattering as it hit the floor, then sailing up through the air. It was the same color Kyle had seen swirling in the small child's eyes—that putrid, greenish color. It looked like mud, and the smell was thick and foul. The sludge continued to pour from Bethany's mouth, and Kyle could feel it oozing around her feet, warm and wet.

"What?" she pleaded with the girl, disgusted by the thick, slimy mess now crawling between her bare toes. "What is it? Tell me! *Please tell me*!"

Bethany stared up toward the ceiling.

Kyle looked up too, then back at the girl, shaking her head quickly, confused by the gesture.

Bethany revealed a hint of a smile, then nodded and said, "Look up."

The girl turned around and began walking away.

"Look up?" Kyle shouted out to her. "Look up where?" Kyle had, but all she'd seen was the broad, empty ceiling.

Bethany turned around. "Today is the last day. The deadline is now."

"I don't understand!" Kyle shouted back, although it sounded more like a plea for help.

Bethany turned back around and kept walking. When she got to the doorway, she went through it, disappearing upon reaching the other side.

Kyle didn't know why, but she had a strong feeling this was the last time she would ever see Bethany Foley.

Chapter Seventy-Nine

6623 Hunter's Run
Faith, New Mexico

The next morning, the first thing Kyle did was reach for her notepad. The dream had jolted her awake in the middle of the night, and she'd spent at least an hour taking notes, describing as many details as she could recall. Bethany had come through for her with the information; now all she had to do was figure out what it meant.

Fifth-floor subjugation unit. She thought about the words, ran the definition through her mind: it meant to bring under control, to make submissive.

She looked up and stared at the wall. *Submissive? Control?* Was that what this was all about? Some sort of mind control? She remembered the groans she'd heard coming from behind locked doors. Had she been wandering through some kind of human storage facility for those trapped inside themselves, people in some sort of vegetative, nonresponsive state?

She remembered the orderly, how he'd slammed his fist down so hard onto the patient's chest. The sound it made was horrific. The subject responded to it with a harsh moan, but only after getting the injection. Was it some kind of test to measure the patient's responsiveness?

And what about that shot? He'd reacted violently to it, even began to shake and writhe. It was as if he'd started coming back to life, going from unresponsive and catatonic to awake and explosive. He'd frightened the nurse just by smiling at her, and for a brief moment, it appeared that *he* had turned the tables, making *her* the submissive one. Even while bound by the heavy leather straps, he was still able to strike fear in her.

It was the smile: that menacing, eerie smile.

A switch went on in Kyle's head. She remembered her earlier dreams, about the violence, the blood. That syringe with the brown liquid. Something in it must have been powerful enough to alter the patient's mental state. She'd seen it before, once during that dreadful blood match, and again, when all the patients got loose, killing each other, as well as the medical staff. They all had that same intense look in their eyes.

The deadline is now.

Bethany's words still echoed in Kyle's head as she threw on her clothes and rushed toward the living room. Cameron was already gone. On the table was a note:

Gone into town. Back in a bit. Make yourself comfortable.
—Cam

She spotted Bentley lying on his side on the kitchen floor, legs splayed, snoring, his barrel chest rising and falling with each labored breath. He opened his eyes to glance up at Kyle, smacked his lips, and within seconds was fast asleep again. Her presence was no longer a cause for alarm, but it didn't elicit much excitement, either. She decided she'd live with that.

Kyle grabbed her car keys and moved outside—although she wasn't sure why—then glanced around, taking in a whiff of fresh morning air, trying to decide what to do next.

Then the words came back to her—the ones that had come straight from Bethany's mouth, her parting message.

Look up.

Kyle did but again saw nothing. Look up where?

On pure impulse, she jumped into the car and drove toward town. As she did, something began to happen: the closer she got, the stronger the vibrations became. Kyle's mind felt like a homing device aimed at its intended target, her grip on the steering wheel becoming so tight her knuckles were turning white. Sweat formed on her forehead, and the nervous apprehension felt like it was chipping away at her. She turned onto Main Street, then to Oakdale. One more block and she'd be in the center of town. That was where she needed to go; she had no idea why, but something was drawing her there, pulling her in like a giant magnet. Something awaited her, something important.

Kyle turned the corner and instantly knew that she'd arrived. She stopped the car, got out, then moved to the middle of the intersection. Her frame of mind had shifted; she could feel it. In a trancelike daze and blocking oncoming traffic, she hardly cared. A few horns blew while other people shouted—still, she didn't budge, standing steady, immovable. Then she looked up, just as Bethany had told her to do.

And she saw it.

That was it. *That* was where she needed to go.

CHAPTER EIGHTY

Old Highway 10
Faith, New Mexico

Every road seemed to lead back to the Foleys' house—yet each time Cameron went there, it was like driving right into a brick wall.

Or banging his head against one.

Now, after everything that had happened within the past twenty-four hours, he was more convinced than ever that the answers he needed were still hiding there.

Kyle, too, had seemed to feel that the Foleys were at the heart of the mystery. It all came back to that family, and still, nobody could figure out why.

It was time to begin listening to his heart instead of his mind. It was time, Cameron decided, to go back to that house.

~

Cameron had barely put his car in park when he saw curtains yank open in Della Schumacher's second-story window. Within a few moments, she was at his side. Lately, she'd fancied herself an integral part of the investigation. Cameron fancied her a nuisance.

"Had the place staked out all day, Sheriff," she said, trying to keep pace with him as he walked toward the Foley house. "Subjects haven't returned since their original visit, but not to worry. I'm still surveilling. Gonna keep a 5150 on the perimeter."

"5150's the code for someone who's mentally ill," Cameron said, hands on his hips while staring up at the house.

She jabbed the heel of her hand into her forehead as if she'd known it all along. "Of course. What in the world was I thinking?"

There's no telling, Cameron thought, then said, "Della, when those two men came poking around at the Foley place, where exactly did they go?"

Della placed two lanky fingers beneath her chin and fluttered them back and forth, as if it were helping her think. She stared down at the ground a few seconds longer, then back up at Cameron. After all that, she replied, "Everywhere."

"More specifically?" Cameron asked.

She pursed her lips. "Well…they didn't go inside the place… that much I know. Mostly stood over there for a real long time." She pointed toward the rear of the house, where an open field lay. Beyond that was a small creek flanked by an old well pump and plenty of dry scrub brush. The area appeared as far removed from all the action as one could get.

Follow the trail, Cam, he told himself. *Look beyond the obvious*. His eyes refocused, fixed on the area as he moved toward it.

"They was up to no good. I can tell when someone's up to no good," Della shouted out to him, then appeared crestfallen when he didn't respond.

Cameron remained intent as he continued moving forward. He was on to something.

The well's pump clicked, startling him. He drew his attention to it, then at the vacant house, then back at it again. He knelt down to get a closer look. Immediately, as if being hit by a thought, he turned his head and gazed at the creek, no more than a hundred feet or so away. He stood straight up, looking at the waterway as if it had taken on a whole new meaning. *Water,* he thought, *water that feeds right here.*

He moved forward again. Reaching an area with heavy brush, he let his gaze drop down toward the ground. Everywhere around him, mustard weed poked up through the ground, making it difficult to see beneath it.

But someone had been through there. He could see spots where the weeds looked flattened. *Foot traffic*, Cameron thought.

The tracks kept going, and Cameron kept following. They ended at the creek bed. He took a deep breath; it felt like the first that he'd taken since he'd started walking. Cameron knelt down and gazed upstream as far as he could see. The river fed the creek. The junction was even farther away. He looked at his reflection in the water as if it might somehow give him the answer he needed.

And it did.

All this time, that answer had been right in front of him—or, actually, right below him. He turned around to find Della standing several hundred feet away and looking perplexed.

"Sheriff, what's going on?" she hollered.

Cameron answered her with silence and then ran directly toward his car. When he got there, he pulled open the door, jumped inside, then sped off, leaving behind a thick cloud of dust.

Chapter Eighty-One

Sentry Peak
Faith, New Mexico

The unpaved, road twisted and turned for what seemed like miles. As she navigated her way through a sea of potholes, Kyle's body jerked from side to side. Nobody had maintained the road for quite some time—that seemed obvious; not that there was any need. Nothing seemed worthy of the miserable trip, certainly not the equally miserable building perched high atop its staggering peak.

Her thoughts abruptly jumped to Cameron. Kyle had left in such a hurry that she'd forgotten to tell him where she was going. If anything happened, nobody would even know where to find her. She grabbed the cell phone lying on the passenger seat. No signal—that didn't surprise her much; she wasn't exactly in an area where there would be any.

After rounding the final corner, Kyle slammed the brakes and looked on with astonishment at the massive towering structure standing before her. Had she not known better, she almost could have sworn it was staring right back. Seeing it up close for the first time, she couldn't decide which was bigger, the actual size or the essence of evil that seemed to surround it.

The place was in shambles, its brick walls crumbling in spots. Kyle zeroed in on the entrance, where she found two stone gargoyles snarling back at her. Just above them, three angels hovered, scorn spilling from their eyes like raging waterfalls polluted by evil. Two gun turrets sat anchored on each side of the building, ascending beyond the rooftops and leaning toward the heavens—they appeared awkward, out of place.

Ugly as all that looked, it was the least of Kyle's concerns. More troubling was the razor wire and electrical fencing—rows and rows of it—hugging the entire structure. The tangled mess was several layers deep and just as high, with a message that was abundantly clear: *stay away.*

But she couldn't, not after coming this far, not when she knew how much was at stake. Kyle stared out her window and for the first time realized it wasn't the building she saw anymore—it was defeat, as big and as real as the fence itself standing before her.

There are only two reasons to guard a secret, she thought. *It's either precious…or it's dirty.*

Kyle had a feeling she knew which this one was. She also knew she needed to figure out how to get inside. Driving on, she leaned forward and gazed up through her windshield. Slowly creeping along the fence line, she circled the complex on a road that seemed to go on forever, looking for an answer.

Then she saw one.

A gate was propped wide open. She stopped the car and studied it, almost questioning her own eyes. While happy to discover the breach, she also felt wariness tug at her insides. Gates didn't just unlock themselves, especially ones in a place as well fortified as this.

Someone else is here, she thought, and with that, fear hit her mid-gut, worse than a hammer, worse than anything she'd ever felt. Kyle knew she needed to get inside, regardless of the cost, regardless of what awaited her there, and regardless, even, of the risk to her own life. She checked her useless cell phone again, then tossed it back onto the seat before getting out of the car and approaching the open gate.

As Kyle moved closer, she felt an odd sensation—cold vibrations pushing through her body, gathering intensity with each step she took until finally reaching almost intolerable levels.

Then she felt something else, something that made her jump: a sensation near the base of her spine, a warm hand—Kyle was sure of it—pushing hard, as if urging her forward past the intricate array of zigzagging steel, and closer toward the entryway.

Toward the core.

The vibrations and the feeling on her back suddenly stopped, and suddenly Kyle saw a massive group of broad, colossal steps leading straight up toward the building. *Higher and higher*, she thought as she began scaling them. *I keep going higher and higher.*

Fear and exhaustion met her at the top, and something else, too—those two hideous gargoyles, with a greeting she could have well done without. The close proximity did them no favor—they were even uglier than she'd first thought.

She had to get inside but first needed to get past the enormous mahogany doors in front of her. Wrapping her hands around one of the large brass handles, she pulled, struggled, then finally managed to get the door open wide enough to slip through.

Once she did, Kyle knew exactly where she was.

Chapter Eighty-Two

Sentry Peak
Faith, New Mexico

Walking through the front doors was like stepping between the deepest folds of her subconscious. All of Kyle's dreams, all the images—everything—they were coming to life right before her eyes. It was like seeing a movie after reading the book; it all matched.

She was standing in the middle of that hospital, the one to which Bethany kept leading her through visions and dreams. Only now, she was there. *Really there.*

Kyle turned a corner and found a stairwell leading up. When she reached the second floor, she gazed down a long, empty hallway and recognized it as the same one from her dreams, one of many with locked doors and agonizing screams. The steel gurneys were still there as well, scattered about, although now nowhere near as slick and shiny as she'd remembered them. It seemed there was only one thing still missing from this picture, perhaps the most important one of all: the people. Without them and their painful moans, the place was strangely quiet.

Studying the hallways, Kyle could see how the whole layout fit together. They all seemed to lead back to one place, the nerve center, a round, raised platform surrounded by thick, steel mesh and yet another layer of dusty glass. Kyle had no trouble pulling open the door that led inside. Although it was made of sturdy steel with a series of locking mechanisms, in their present condition, they were barely functional.

Inside, she studied the instrument panels running along the outer walls and their array of green and red buttons, along with a few chairs pushed up against them. For Kyle, the whole setup looked rudimentary, certainly by today's standards, but for that era, it was probably state of the art.

Then she looked out through the glass. *An observation area*, she thought as she studied the four hallways converging toward her like giant octopus arms. *A lookout.*

The third and fourth floors appeared identical to the second: four curved hallways leading back to another glass-and-steel-protected observation booth.

The fifth floor, however, was different—very different. At its core was the infamous Subjugation Unit, and judging by her dreams, it was where all the horrors lay as well.

She walked inside.

Much as in her visions, the operating room seemed to be the unit's focal point. Kyle studied her surroundings, then shivered.

Beyond that, she noticed another room, one she hadn't seen before in her visions. Curious, she headed toward it, then inside.

Only about twenty by twenty feet, it was barely a room, more like an enclosure. The walls were thick, solid concrete, but oddly lacked any sort of ceiling. Along them, every few feet, were thick leather cuffs with steel buckles—worn from use—dangling by the ends of short metal chains. *Torture devices of some kind*, Kyle thought; there was no mistaking that. Looking them over, she estimated that even a tall person would still hang several feet off the ground once hooked up to the barbaric devices, thanks to the help of metal steps with locking wheels parked beside each station. Kyle walked along the walls, studying them, while at the same time feeling a hybrid of disgust and horror: layer over layer of age-old bloodstains covered the cold concrete, much like thin sloppy coats of red paint.

Subjugation indeed, she thought. *Now I know how.*

But she still didn't know why.

Kyle wondered what happened to the patients after they were robbed of their minds. *Where did they go after being subjugated?*

This was no hospital; this was a concentration camp, one designed with only one goal in mind: to break the human spirit, destroy the soul.

And by the looks of things, they'd done their job well. This place, this hell on earth, posed as some sort of medical facility, but in reality, it did the exact opposite of everything she'd learned that medicine was supposed to do.

Kyle began feeling queasy again. She didn't just want to leave the unit; she wanted to leave the building. Where she once felt exhilaration over finding her answers, she now felt nothing but revulsion. It was all far worse than anything she could have imagined—more, even, than in her dreams and visions.

Ugly outside, even uglier inside, she thought. *Nothing about this place is good.*

She backed away, eyes still fixed on the bloodstained walls, then heard a loud screeching noise beneath her foot. Startled, she stepped sideways and looked down, but hardly felt prepared for what she saw.

A rat scurried away, and in its mouth was what appeared to be a bone fragment.

She screamed.

Kyle couldn't take another minute of it. She ran out of the room, back into the hallway.

Fast as her feet could carry her, she headed into the stairwell, pulled the door closed behind her, then leaned against it, drawing a steadying breath. After that, she hurried back down the steps, toward the main floor.

But when she got there, something else caught her attention—something that told her she was wasn't going anywhere; at least, not yet.

It was a sign, and it pointed directly toward the basement: AUTHORIZED PERSONNEL ONLY.

The last thing she wanted to do was explore any more of this godforsaken place; but she still hadn't found all her answers, and the sign told her she just might.

Musty darkness met her at the bottom of the stairway. Flicking on her key chain light, Kyle moved cautiously into the room, smelling something as she moved forward. It was the same strange odor that came from the brown liquid in her dream, only now it seemed much more powerful. Overwhelmed by the fumes and feeling dizzy, Kyle threw her hand over her nose as she moved on, trying to take shallow breaths, but that didn't seem to help. With each step, the odor became more potent. When she reached the end of the room, she came to another door with yet another sign…and another warning: NO UNAUTHORIZED PERSONNEL BEYOND THIS POINT.

A series of rusted but still-functioning dead bolts covered the door. Kyle turned each of them, then grabbed a large, metal latch and pulled it down. The door began to crack open, and as it did, the odor became even stronger and more volatile. Kyle walked into and down a narrow hallway. While she could smell a lot, she could see very little. Her key chain light was quickly losing power. Soon it would be out, leaving her in complete darkness.

Trying to compensate for the lack of power and time, Kyle increased her speed, trying to reach the end of the hall before her only source of light dwindled down to nothing. Then she came upon another door and pulled it open. Surprisingly, as she did, the odor seemed to lessen. It took her a moment to realize why: she was outside again.

Kyle looked around, only to discover she was standing in the middle of a giant stockyard, surrounded by more razor wire and chain-link fencing.

Steel barrels—rows and rows of them—were lined up and stacked tall. Beneath them, a thick, dark liquid oozed out, leaching into the soil, which sopped it up like a hungry sponge.

Kyle looked out past the fencing. No more than twenty feet away, a small creek ran alongside the yard.

And then something hard and heavy struck her in the back of her head.

~

The two men grabbed Kyle's arms and legs, then dragged her down a long tunnel, her body swinging violently back and forth, knocking hard against the narrow walls.

Moving toward the first floor, they carried her up the steps, leaving a trail of blood along the way. When they reached the lobby, they dropped her onto the floor. More blood oozed from her head, then spread out onto the filthy linoleum beneath her.

She was near death. They knew they could leave her there and she would probably bleed out and die within a matter of minutes; still, they couldn't take any chances in the event she somehow managed to survive. They needed her gone. *Fast.*

One of the men pulled an automatic pistol from his coat. Jabbing the barrel end into her mouth and aiming it upward, he locked his finger into the trigger.

The gunfire erupted, echoing throughout the room.

Chapter Eighty-Three

Sentry Peak
Faith, New Mexico

The man holding the gun in Kyle's mouth let go of it before he could fire, dropping it onto the floor as a bullet hit him squarely in the chest.

His partner looked up to find Cameron standing there, holding his weapon straight out, now aiming directly at him. The man moved his hands as if raising them up in surrender but stopped at his belt, fumbling for something. Cameron fired another shot, hitting him between the eyes, forcing him backward and slamming him onto the ground.

Cameron rushed over to Kyle, knelt beside her, and reached down for her wrist, trying to feel for a pulse.

But there was nothing. She was already gone.

He tore off his shirt, wrapping it around her head, trying to stem the flow of blood, then began administering CPR, but she wasn't responding. There was no sign of breathing, no detectable pulse. Not knowing if it made any difference, he continued administering CPR anyway—he wasn't willing to give up hope.

There was nothing. She was unresponsive. She had passed.

He dropped his head onto her chest, listening, hoping and praying he'd missed her pulse.

Again, nothing.

Cameron felt his own pulse race as his heart sank. Yet another life he couldn't save—another death he might have prevented, had he only moved quicker.

And worst of all, someone for whom he'd begun to care deeply.

CHAPTER EIGHTY-FOUR

Sentry Peak
Faith, New Mexico

Kneeling over Kyle, Cameron thought he heard something behind him. He looked up and around but saw that nobody was there. Then he realized the sound was coming from beneath him. He looked down; it was Kyle, and she was breathing shallow breaths, which suddenly turned into one giant gasp for air.

Cameron reached down quickly and brushed the hair away from her face. "Kyle! Can you hear me?"

She didn't respond, but he could see she was still breathing, and for him, that was all that mattered. Without thinking twice, he gathered her in his arms and carried her outside. After laying her across the backseat of his car, he jumped inside and sped off, traveling down the hill as fast as he could manage.

~

Community Hospital
Faith, New Mexico

It took Kyle several hours to wake up, and when she did, Cameron was standing beside her, looking down, smiling.

She gazed up with surprise, feeling groggy and bleary-eyed.

As things came into focus, she noticed someone standing directly behind him. It was Josh. He, too, was smiling.

Cameron reached over and placed his hand over hers, not letting his eyes leave her.

"Okay?" he asked.

"Yeah." Kyle blinked hard a few times, then nodded weakly. "Except it seems like I keep ending up in this damned hospital."

Cameron laughed. "What better place for a doctor to be?"

"Uh-uh. I'm on the wrong side of the bed." She grimaced with pain and reached up to touch the back of her head. "Ouch."

"Got a pretty good whack there. You remember what happened?" Cameron asked.

Her voice was frail. "Not very much, but I'm guessing this dent on my head was the result."

"He saved your life, is what happened," Josh interrupted.

"I should have known you'd come to the rescue," she said, smiling. "White horse and all."

"No white horse. Just a white Taurus, courtesy of the good people of Faith."

Kyle attempted a laugh, and then winced again with pain.

"Question," said Cameron. "How is it you managed to leave out the fact your brother's a cop? Seems kind of relevant."

Kyle looked to her brother and winked. "Oh yeah. I did leave that out, didn't I?"

"Yeah, kinda did."

"I thought it would be better to keep him out of the picture."

"Out of the picture?" Josh protested.

Kyle ignored him, keeping her gaze on Cameron. "I just thought it would make things more complicated. I was going to tell you…eventually."

"Eventually?" Josh said. "How eventually?"

She glanced over at her brother. "After this whole mess got cleared up."

"You missed a call—" Josh started to say.

"Yeah, about that…" She reached around to feel the wound on the back of her head again. "I would have…'cept I kinda got into a bit of a bind—it would have been difficult to call you while my head was being bashed in."

Josh shrugged. "Okay. I'll give you that. Wouldn't have mattered anyhow, I suppose. I was already on my way about the time your head was hitting the floor."

"You…*what*?"

Josh smiled. "Had you tailed."

"*Tailed*?" she repeated the word, almost as if she didn't know what it meant.

"I promised I wouldn't come with you," Josh said as he walked over to the bed. He leaned over and kissed his sister's forehead. "And I kept that promise. But nobody ever said I couldn't send someone on my behalf."

Kyle gazed up at Cameron, incredulously.

Cameron put his hands up in surrender and said, "I knew nothing about it."

"Hired one of my off-duty pals. He called me when he saw you heading up the hill." Josh stopped to give her a reprimanding expression. "By the way, you shoulda known better. What on *earth* were you thinking?"

"I was thinking that I had to do what I had to do. Just like you would've. Besides, your *pal* didn't do a very good job protecting me."

"Didn't need to. Appears you had someone else watching out for you." Josh smiled at Cameron.

Cameron fought his own smile and lost, looking down at the floor bashfully.

Kyle gazed up at him and said, "I don't think I've ever seen that."

"What?" Cameron asked.

"You...I've never seen you smile like that. You almost look like a different person."

Cameron shrugged. How many times had he heard that? But this time, it seemed different—*felt* different. "Guess I never had any reason to, until now."

Kyle shook her head, almost looking disappointed. "You had reason to, you just never knew it."

Cameron said nothing.

She frowned. "That pain—it runs so deep—it's so intense. You've been carrying it around on your shoulders for so long now. When are you going to let it go?"

Cameron looked as if he'd just seen a ghost. He stared at Kyle with a blank expression. "How do you know about...?"

Kyle reached up and held his hand. "Because I felt it."

CHAPTER EIGHTY-FIVE

FAITH BEACON

MURDERS LINKED TO SECRET WWII PROJECT
Experts Say Toxic Waste Leaked into Soil for Years

By Raymond Acevedo

In a bizarre turn of events, a toxic spill is being linked to a string of sadistic homicides in and around town during the past few weeks.

Hazardous materials crews are working around the clock to stabilize what could turn out to be the worst toxic spill in the state's history. Officials say it might be months, maybe even a year, before Faith's water supply is again safe enough to drink. Truckloads of bottled water are being shipped into town in order to meet high demands.

In all, ten people died, two of them Faith sheriff's deputies, as well as the daughter of State Senator Connie Champion.

Twenty-year-old Felicity Champion's body was discovered more than a week ago lying in a drainage ditch along Old Highway 10. Authorities believe longtime Faith resident and business owner Judith Hedrick was the killer.

Hedrick's body was discovered just two days ago on a bank along the Foundry River between Lower Faith and High River Valley.

Assistant Sheriff Cameron Dawson says Hedrick committed suicide by jumping off the Stanton Street Bridge, which crosses the river.

The reason is not yet known.

World War II Experiments the Key

Dawson says the murders were an indirect result of top-secret clinical trials conducted by the US government more than fifty years ago. The experiments were carried out in a building located at the top of Sentry Peak, overlooking Faith.

The property was purchased in the 1940s from Louis Wicker, son of real estate tycoon Franklin Wicker, who built the structure.

It is unknown for what purpose.

The US military then converted the multistory building into a makeshift hospital, where they conducted their secret experiments.

A serum called beta dioxide alphapeptium, or BDA, lies at the center of the controversy. Scientists developed the drug to use on troops during World War II. The substance, administered by hypodermic needle, was developed with hopes of making US soldiers more aggressive during combat.

Researchers tried to refine the drug to make it more manageable, but their efforts failed. Some subjects had no reaction at all to it, while others went violently out of control.

In March of 1947, the government shut down the project after the experiment went awry. A violent outbreak pitting patients against staff ended in a riot, with eleven staff members killed, many others trampled and beaten. Seven patients also died during the melee. Officials decided the project was too risky to continue.

After that, the building was left abandoned and vacant.

Officials cordoned off the structure, surrounding it with razor wire and electrical fencing to keep out intruders.

Soil Contamination

After shutting down the project, the government disposed of the volatile chemicals, pouring them into metal drums, then storing them in an outdoor stockyard connected to the building. Through the years, the acidic material ate through the containers, seeped into the ground, and eventually found its way into the nearby Foundry River, which runs adjacent to the building. That river feeds into an aquifer supplying well water to many local residents.

Authorities reason that's how the substance infiltrated the town's water supply.

Bizarre, Cruel, and Inhumane Testing Methods

Files from the experiments, also stored inside the building and now being made public, reveal the secret experiments involved a battery of sadistic and inhumane practices.

When patients were not under the influence of BDA, they were held in vegetative states with the help of a sedative called atronium citrite, or ATC, also being developed by the government.

While sedated, the patients were stowed away in containment units located on the first through fourth floors and kept there until needed for experimentation.

Besides putting the subjects into a catatonic state, the sedative also produced distinct and unusual side effects. Patients were often heard making a peculiar, high-pitched, almost continuous hum that fluctuated in volume and intensity. Often they would lose control of bladder functioning as well.

BDA also had its share of side effects, many of them even more troubling.

Besides making patients violent, flu-like symptoms prior to the actual onset were common, as were severe ulcerations of the stomach lining. For reasons unknown, the drug also caused an odd condition, later dubbed *tar eye*, where the pupils dilated to a size so large that the entire eye took on a blackened appearance. Others went into a full-blown self-destructive state, turning on themselves, tearing away at their own skin, hair, and in some cases body parts such as fingers, toes, earlobes, and even genitalia.

Although the main effects of the serum were quite volatile, they were also short-lived, only lasting approximately one hour, and once the drug wore off, subjects had no memory of their actions. Scientists engineered it that way to avoid future cases of what we now know to be posttraumatic stress syndrome.

The clinical trials always resulted in death for the victims. Subjects were given the serum, then put through a series of highly unconventional tests. A part of the Sentry Peak facility, called the Subjugation Unit, was essentially a torture chamber. Patients were strapped naked to concrete walls while others, under the drug's influence, beat them to death. Other times, the subjects were confined to so-called fighting cells, where they were allowed to beat one another to death.

Researchers claimed to be doing all this in an effort to study the drug's efficacy and develop lower, more manageable strength levels. However, for reasons unknown, they never did.

False Pretense

The government recruited subjects for the experiments by way of the enlisted service. Those facing disciplinary actions, such as courts-martial, were given the opportunity to sign up for the trials as an alternate form of punishment.

Once the victims died, their families were advised they were killed in the line of duty.

Authorities say they do not yet know how many people died during the experiments, but it could number into the thousands. They are in the process of sifting through an inordinate number of records so that families can be informed of how their loved ones actually died during the war.

Odd Happenings

The murders weren't the only things visiting Faith. Several local residents reported seeing a pair of strangers roaming around town. The two men, seen on several occasions, were described as wearing dark sunglasses and driving a white, older model van.

According to Dawson, the men, later identified as Samuel Swenson and Scott Faraday, were from Spesartine & Agrough, the pharmaceutical corporation subcontracted by the government to help develop the two serums. Fearing bad publicity, the company sent the men to investigate. Had the trials been a success, they stood to make millions of dollars. Among other things, Spesartine & Agrough currently manufactures Sezdal, one of the nation's top-selling antianxiety medications.

But authorities later learned the two were planning to do more than that. According to Dawson, they were caught trying to start a fire in the facility to destroy the chemicals and cover up the spill. Sheriff's deputies interrupted that process only minutes before it was to occur. The two suspects were shot to death after a confrontation with law enforcement.

The CEO of the pharmaceutical company, Samuel Agrough, grandson of cofounder Phillip Agrough, is under investigation and could face charges of obstructing justice, as well as conspiracy to commit arson.

Authorities don't yet know if anyone will face prosecution for conducting the actual trials, as they took place many years ago, and all the key players have probably long since passed away; however, Senator Champion says a congressional investigation will follow, and anyone who played a role in the experiments will be prosecuted to the full extent of the law.

The names of any existing and living murder suspects are being withheld for their protection, but they are not likely to face prosecution.

Proving that the substance affected the suspects, however, may be a challenge. In an attempt to keep the serum's components a secret, scientists designed the chemicals to dissipate quickly into the bloodstream. By the time the subjects became violent, the compound was already on its way to being undetectable, leaving no traces of ever having been present.

More than likely, experts will have to map out the path the toxin traveled by way of the Foundry River and use that to draw conclusions about who was poisoned.

Chapter Eighty-Six

Desert Spring Motel
Faith, New Mexico

As long as the monster on the hill remained, it would always serve as a constant reminder of the darkest period in Faith's and the country's history, when virtue took a holiday and depravity a front row seat.

The government opted to tear the place down rather than sell it. Besides having no use for the building, the administration wanted nothing more than to disassociate itself from it. Putting it out of sight would also put it out of mind.

Faith, it seemed, had gained international infamy, even becoming something of a tourist attraction. More and more, local residents saw unfamiliar faces popping up around town. It was hard not to feel like they were living under a microscope.

Cameron and Kyle had uncovered a dirty secret, one buried not only beneath the ground but beneath an elaborate legacy of lies and deception, a secret that refused to remain hidden. Ten people had lost their lives, and an entire town its sense of cohesion and well-being. Cleanup crews would purge the ground and nearby river of the poisons that for years had defiled them, but nothing would ever wash away the pain and loss left in people's hearts.

~

Kyle stood in her motel room folding clothes. It was time to go home.

She'd left the door open, hoping to allow the sunlight to brighten up the otherwise dreary space and hadn't even heard Cameron when he walked in.

"Hey," he said, half greeting her, half wanting to avoid startling her.

She spun around and flashed a warm, welcoming smile.

"Good morning," she said, then paused to look at her watch. "Or should I say good afternoon?"

"Say good afternoon," Cameron replied with a grin.

He looked like a shy little boy with a crush. Kyle laughed, and he gazed at her quizzically.

"What?"

"Your smiles," she replied, "they're so fleeting."

"I guess that's because my happiness always seems to be that way, too."

Kyle resumed her folding, shaking her head with a frown. "You're awful hard on yourself."

Those words struck a familiar note, not unlike the ones he'd heard so many years ago from the first love of his life. He wanted to give himself a break—he needed one—he just didn't know how.

"I'll work on it," Cameron finally said, forcing an unconvincing smile and an even less convincing lie.

Somehow, she wasn't sure she believed him, anyway.

He paused for a moment to think, then said, "It's funny, you know."

"What is?"

"This whole thing. I mean…not funny funny, but interesting… how people's paths cross, what brings them together—" He stopped himself, and a pained expression suddenly materialized on his face. "I'll miss you."

Kyle felt a lump forming in her throat. She'd been thinking the same thing but was afraid to tell him. There still seemed to be so much left unsaid between them. "I wish there were an easier way for us to do this. I don't want to say good-bye, but I have to."

"I know…" he said. But he didn't. "Will you come back?"

"I don't know." Kyle could see the loneliness in his eyes. Even worse, she could feel it.

"Why not?" Cameron replied, half asking, half challenging her.

She placed a folded shirt inside her suitcase and turned around, only to find his eyes meeting hers. "Please don't make this any harder. You don't know how much I want to stay."

Cameron caught her hands and held on to them, as if never intending to let them go. "Then stay. Don't go. Stay here with me."

Kyle sighed. She felt exhausted, as much emotionally as physically. "I have a private practice back at home, Cameron. My only family life is there."

"That's logical. It makes perfect sense." He put his hand over his heart. "But right here, that's where you lose me."

"Maybe someday," she said, turning around and hastily moving more shirts into her suitcase.

"Maybe…" Cameron repeated the words as if trying to make sense of them, while at the same time sounding defeated. Then he tried to lighten the conversation. "Well, at least you got all your questions answered."

Kyle started zipping her suitcase. Suddenly she stopped, looking up at the wall, thinking. "As far as this town goes, yes, but there will be new mysteries to uncover… There always are."

"What kinds of mysteries?"

Kyle laughed and shook her head. "Who knows? It never stops. I'm constantly being bombarded with information."

"Must be annoying as hell."

She continued to pull the zipper but struggled. Cameron noticed and stepped forward to help. For a brief moment, they were skin to skin, and she felt a strong urge to move into his arms and close her eyes. Instead, she pulled away, as if the action in some way would minimize the emotion.

"It can be, sometimes," she said with an awkward smile. "Other times it's not. I guess I've just become used to it by now."

"Well, at least this one is solved. Case closed."

"I suppose…"

Cameron noticed her apprehension. "Is there something more I should know? Something relevant here?"

"I'm not sure. Can't tell whether it belongs here or somewhere else."

"It could be your next assignment: *earth calling Kyle*," he joked, forcing a smile.

Kyle looked down as if deliberating over something, then up at Cameron. Her expression was very serious. "There's a strong image that's been with me. I have no idea why. But it doesn't seem to be relevant to anything that's been happening here."

"What is it?"

"A child."

"Another one? Who is she?"

"Not a she—it's a *he*, and he's been hanging in the background ever since I came here. That's why I think he may have some kind of connection to this town," Kyle said, her tone distant. She paused, then added, "I'm just not sure how."

Cameron felt his heart strike hard. He was afraid to ask but did anyway. "What does he look like?"

"He's six or seven, maybe? Blond. Very blond, in fact—a real towhead." Kyle laughed. "A beautiful child. Big blue eyes and—"

"Like mine?" he asked impatiently while gazing up at her.

She looked into his eyes, and a flash of recognition crossed her face. "Yeah, actually…a lot like yours."

Cameron looked away. He focused his attention on a picture on the opposite wall. Generic motel art.

Kyle sensed his discomfort. "What's wrong, Cameron?"

He turned around and took a deep breath.

Kyle noticed tears forming in his eyes. She tilted her head, watching him, concerned.

"I know who he is."

Chapter Eighty-Seven

Desert Spring Motel
Faith, New Mexico

"Your son?" Kyle asked, still stunned. "I didn't know..."

It made sense now, the anguish, the guilt, the deep sorrow—feelings that had been eating away at him all these years. Kyle herself had felt them when they'd first met, so strongly, in fact, they'd landed her in the hospital.

Like Bethany, Cameron's son had not yet crossed over, was still trapped between two worlds. Kyle wondered what unfinished business the boy had that had kept him here so long. She had a feeling it involved the tall, blond-haired, blue-eyed man standing in front of her.

"I knew the minute you began describing him that it was Dylan." He turned and sat down on the bed.

Kyle took a seat beside him and placed a gentle hand on his shoulder. He could smell her perfume; the aroma wrapped itself around him like a hug. It felt comforting.

For a few moments they sat, saying nothing. Kyle had always figured she was drawn to Faith for one purpose: to help solve the mystery taking over the town. Yet, there had been another reason for coming here, one she had not realized until now.

"What does he want?" Kyle asked suddenly. "Why do you suppose he stays?"

"Does there have to be a reason?"

Kyle turned to face him. "The deceased usually cross over to the other side right away, but some are left behind."

"You're saying my son is one of them?"

"Yeah. I think so…just like Bethany, who needed to exonerate her brother, your son also has something he needs to take care of before he can leave this world."

"What is it?"

"I don't know." She stood up and walked across the room, facing a corner, her back toward him. "You could talk to him and find out."

The blood drained instantly from Cameron's face. After all these years—contact with the son he lost, the one he missed so terribly, and who occupied his mind every single moment. How could it be?

Kyle turned around to look at him. "You don't have to be here, but I do need to do it. He needs my help so he can cross over. I know how painful this must be."

Cameron met her eyes. "I want to be here. I *need* to be here."

Kyle nodded.

"When can we do it?" he asked.

"Right now, if that's okay."

He fell silent. His heart felt like a boulder sinking in a river of despair. He hadn't expected that.

Kyle realized she'd just thrown him a curve. She spoke gently. "Sorry. I didn't mean to catch you off guard."

"How will you get him here?"

Kyle looked at him for a moment, then smiled softly. "He's already here, Cam."

His eyes filled with tears, brimming over and rolling down his cheeks. Then another. He looked toward the other wall and brushed them away, as if denying their existence.

Kyle walked quickly back to the bed and wrapped her arms around him, holding him tight. She could hear his quiet, aching sobs.

Then she began to cry, too.

CHAPTER EIGHTY-EIGHT

Desert Spring Motel
Faith, New Mexico

Cameron broke from her embrace, wiped away a final tear, and looked into Kyle's eyes, his voice becoming firmer. "Let's do this."

She studied his face for a few seconds, then stood up, focusing her attention toward the corner of the room. Dylan had been standing there the whole time. Cameron turned to see what she was looking at but saw nothing. It didn't seem to matter. He knew. Her eyes told the story.

Kyle walked toward the boy and knelt down so she could be at eye level with him. She smiled warmly, and the child smiled back, his expression seeming older than his years. Kyle wasn't surprised: children who died often seemed to receive the wisdom they'd missed because of a premature death. With Dylan, however, it seemed more pronounced than usual.

"Hello, Dylan. My name is Kyle," she said in a voice appropriate for a child.

The boy nodded as if showing his approval. Cameron watched the exchange from across the room. He couldn't see Dylan but felt his son's presence through Kyle.

Kyle appeared to be listening to the boy, and her hands seemed to be holding his. It looked so strange to Cameron, and the immediacy overwhelmed him.

She remained focused on Dylan while she spoke. "He wants you to know that he misses you."

"I miss you, too." Cameron forced the words out, sobbing and speaking through fresh new tears. His voice dropped to a whisper. "I miss you more than you could ever know."

Kyle wiped a tear from her cheek, still looking into Dylan's bright blue eyes, as if he were the only person in the room. "He says he knows that. He's always known that."

Overwhelmed, Cameron was speechless.

Kyle sniffled, then smiled, and Cameron leaned forward with interest. "He wants to know if you remember the time when you drove all the way to soccer practice before realizing you'd left him behind at home."

Cameron laughed through his tears. "I was so nervous about coaching the team. I don't know where my head was that day."

"He says he and his mom looked all over the house for you. They couldn't figure out where you went."

Cameron smiled, shaking his head in a way that seemed reminiscent. "Dylan loved to tell that story."

Kyle looked back at Cameron for the first time since she'd started talking to Dylan. She smiled and winked at him. "Looks like he still does."

Cameron's eyes filled with tears, and his voice caught, barely a whisper. "God, I miss him."

Kyle watched Cameron for a moment, smiling sadly, then turned her attention back to Dylan. "He says that's what he loved about you most—your laughter. He loved when you laughed."

Cameron realized that part of him no longer existed. It had gone away when Dylan had.

"He says you don't do that anymore. Laugh, that is. He wants to know why."

Cameron, still choked up, said, "I don't know. Nothing seems funny anymore, I guess."

"He wants you to laugh again the way you used to do back when he was still around. He misses seeing and hearing you laugh…and smile. Says you always made him feel better about things when you smiled. Like everything would be okay, even when it wasn't."

The words hit him like a punch to the gut. When Dylan was still alive, laughing and smiling seemed so natural, so effortless. He had reason to then—every single day was filled with so much joy. Now they were full of nothing but sadness…and loss.

Kyle perked up and smiled.

Cameron looked over at her, curious. "What?"

Kyle hesitated for a moment. "He says he likes me. He thinks you should marry me, that he won't mind."

"Tell him I'm working on it."

Kyle shot him a look, then turned back to the boy. Her face became serious. She listened to Dylan, then shook her head sadly, looking down at the ground, trying to gather the right words. Kyle turned to Cameron. "This is important." She took a deep breath. "He wants you to know his death was not your fault. That he doesn't blame you, and you shouldn't blame yourself."

Cameron winced. He turned his head away and squeezed his eyes shut: the answer he'd always hoped for but never expected to get.

Kyle held her hand up toward Cameron, still focused on Dylan. There was more. Cameron watched and waited as if his next breath depended on it. Kyle listened while nodding her head. She turned toward Cameron, paused, then spoke very softly. "He says it's time."

"Time for what?"

"It's time to start living again. He's no longer alive, but you still are. He wants you to stop acting like you died that day. Life is precious…and short. You don't realize that until you no longer have it. One life lost is enough. Stop throwing yours away. Take advantage of what you still have. Embrace it."

His son was right, but the truth had never hurt so much. It cut like a knife through the tough outer skin he'd always pretended to have.

"He wants you to move on and live out the rest of your life. With happiness." She stopped, as if being interrupted, listened some more, then nodded her head, eyes closed, as if with sadness. "Do you remember that night you almost killed yourself?"

Cameron's head shot up in surprise. He tensed, not knowing what to say. Then shame replaced the emotion. He gazed at the floor, embarrassed. "I'll never forget it."

Kyle kept her eyes trained on Dylan, concentrating on what he was saying. "Remember when you felt something wrapping tight around your shoulders? Something warm?"

"Yes," he said, shocked.

She turned to Cameron and smiled. "That was him, Cam—it was Dylan. He says he hugged you. It was his way of begging you not to do it. And you listened. He thanks you for listening to him."

Cameron was still and silent. He remembered that night as if it had happened only a few minutes ago. That moment changed everything, although he never understood why. He'd made the decisive choice to go on living.

Kyle looked at Cameron for several seconds before she spoke, as if knowing that what she was about to say would hurt. She spoke softly. "He says that if you don't live your life, his will have meant nothing."

Cameron dropped his chin to his chest and closed his eyes, saying nothing for a long time.

Kyle stood up and came over to him. "He's leaving now, Cam. He's said what he needed to tell you. He's ready to pass through to the other side."

Cameron looked up quickly, his voice panicked. "Wait! Tell him not to go…not yet!"

Kyle looked over at Dylan and nodded. She turned toward Cameron, waiting for him to speak.

"Tell him…tell him thank you. Thanks for…for everything…for giving me the best years of my life." He spoke through tears. "And that I love him…I love you, Son!"

"I love you too, Daddy."

Cameron looked around the room, startled. The voice was not Kyle's; it was, without mistake, Dylan's: familiar, filling the air like an echo, then fading as quickly as it had come.

A flash of light exploded in the corner of the room, then dissipated, with his son standing in the middle of it. Dylan looked exactly as Cameron remembered him: soft yellow hair, blue eyes, cheeks the color of peaches, and a smile that seemed like it would never end. Cameron gazed at his son, for once feeling a sense of deep inner peace. He wanted the moment to last forever but knew it could not. Finally, he whispered, "I'll always love you, Son."

The vision shimmered and then faded away.

Kyle smiled sadly, reaching for his hand. "He's gone, Cameron."

He was. Gone. And that was something Cameron could finally live with and no longer feel any guilt about. His son would find happiness. So would he.

They embraced.

He pulled away and looked into her eyes. "Thank you, too. Thank you so much…for everything."

Kyle shook her head. How could she take credit for a moment so beautiful? She realized this was good-bye for them too, that she might never see him again. She knew she'd fallen in love with him. Unfortunately, however, life dealt the cards, and life did not see the two of them sharing theirs together.

She reached for his hands and squeezed them. "Good-bye, Cameron."

He just smiled.

Kyle didn't know that when Cameron decided he wanted something badly enough, he never took no for an answer. He'd already lost two people who had meant the most to him. He wasn't about to lose this one, too.

He wanted her—more than he could remember wanting anything else. She'd never had the chance to see that part of him—there had been too many other things happening at the time—but she would, just as Sarah once had.

Kyle may not have known it, but this was not the last she would see of Cameron Dawson.

He would make sure of that.

Andrew E. Kaufman's newest novel,
The Lion, the Lamb, the Hunted
(Available now)

Glenview Psychiatric Hospital looked like it could drive people insane if they weren't already. Chain link and razor wire surrounded the perimeter, and beyond that, ivy snaked its way up dirty redbrick walls. I let my gaze follow it to a bar-covered window where an elderly woman looked down on me, her face as white as the long, stringy hair that framed it. She nodded with a vacant, fish-eyed expression, then flashed a menacing, toothless grin, sending chills up my spine. I turned my attention away quickly, headed for the front door.

Glenview had once been a private facility, but the state had taken it over several years before. From the looks of things, they hadn't done much to improve it. I moved down a dimly lit, claustrophobic hallway so narrow that I doubted two people could walk it side by side. The asylum-green walls were cracked and chipped, the floors covered in nondescript, skid-marked tile. The overall theme: dismal and cold.

I came to the gatekeeper for this palace of darkness: a receptionist behind a Plexiglas partition blurred with fingerprints, grime, and other slimy things I was afraid to think about. Her expression told me she was sick of her job. Couldn't say I blamed her. Then I heard static and a speaker going live.

"Can I help you," she said. It sounded more like a statement than a question.

I leaned in toward a metal-covered hole in the glass. "Patrick Bannister, for Dr. Faraday."

No verbal response, just a loud buzzer and a simultaneous click as the lock disengaged; I pulled the door open and found her waiting on the other side behind a service counter.

After signing in with my ID, I handed over my cell phone. Then a security guard arrived to escort me through a sally port that looked more like a cave. Smelled like one, too. Next stop, a service elevator: high stink-factor there as well, like a nasty old gym locker.

As I stepped off onto the fifth floor, I fell into sensory overload. The stench was so wicked and fierce that it burned through my sinuses—excrement, sweat, and cleaning agents all blended into one nasty funk that kicked my gag reflex into action. Then came the sounds: a woman's hysterical laughter echoing down the hall, clearly not inspired by anything funny, along with lots of cursing and other peculiar, vaguely human cries I could hardly identify. As we moved past the metal-grated security doors, patients peered at me with flat, vacant expressions, creepy smiles, and wild eyes that made my skin crawl.

Finally, we came to a port in the storm: the nursing station. The guard nodded to the woman behind the counter, she nodded back, and he left me there. In her early fifties, she was a striking brunette, one of those women whose looks seem to improve with age: high cheekbones, dark-lashed, pale blue eyes, and a pair of legs that could give a twenty-year-old a run for her money. The nametag said she was Aurora Penfield, Nursing Supervisor.

"Patrick Bannister," I said, "for Dr. Faraday."

In a dutiful, mechanical manner, she reached for the telephone and punched a few buttons, giving me the once-over while waiting for an answer.

I smiled.

She didn't.

Then I felt a tug on my leg. Startled, I looked down into a pair of dark, cavernous eyes staring up at me: a woman squatting on the floor, probably in her sixties but with a distinctly childlike quality. Tangled, grizzled hair surrounded a hopeless, miserable face. She barked at me, then snarled, baring her teeth.

"Gretchen!" Penfield said, leaning over the counter, her tone cross and unwavering. "Move away *immediately*!"

The woman looked at Penfield, looked at me, then frowned. I spotted a yellowish puddle forming between her feet. Two orderlies stepped quickly toward us; they each grabbed an arm and pulled her up, then guided her away.

Nurse Ratched went back to her work as if nothing had happened and said, "Doctor's on his way. Please take a seat."

I did.

A few moments later, a side door opened and Dr. Faraday appeared. He was somewhere in his sixties, tall and slender, with a thick head of silvery hair and wire-rimmed glasses that missed the fashion curve by a good twenty years. His face registered zero on the expression scale, as blank as the wall behind him. We shook hands; his were rough skinned and ice cold.

He led me down a corridor and past a door with a glass observation window. Inside, a patient sat in the corner, hands under his gown, giving himself pleasure. He made direct eye contact with me and started jerking himself with more enthusiasm and fervor. Then he stopped, and a shit-eating grin slowly spread across his face. I looked away, feeling my nausea return for a second round.

When we reached Faraday's office, he took a seat behind his desk, and I sat across from him. "Jean Kingsley," he said, removing his glasses and rubbing his eyes. "Haven't heard that name in years."

"I'm doing a story about her son's kidnapping and murder."

He put his glasses back on, looked down at some paperwork. "I've reviewed her records. What exactly would you like to know?"

"We can start with the basics, her condition, how many times she was admitted, and for how long."

He puffed his cheeks full of air, then let it out slowly. "Mrs. Kingsley was a very sick woman. She suffered a series of breakdowns—three, to be exact—rather significant ones. She was admitted here after each of them. The duration increased with each visit, as did the severity of her condition."

"How long was her last stay?"

He rubbed his chin, glanced up at the clock. "About a month."

I made a few notes. "Any indication why she killed herself? I mean, other than the obvious. Anything unusual happen that day?"

"Not at all. Mrs. Kingsley was dealing with enormous guilt over her son's murder. She blamed herself. As time went on, her memories and perceptions about the kidnapping seemed to become more distorted, as did her impression of reality as a whole."

"Distorted in what way?"

"Her recollection about what actually happened, the circumstances leading to it—none of it made any sense, and most of it seemed to lack truth. After a while, it started sounding like she was talking about someone else's life rather than her own. She was a different person."

"What kinds of things did she say?"

He gazed down at his notes, threw his hands up, shaking his head. "I honestly wouldn't know where to begin. Purely illogical thinking."

I leaned forward to glance at his notes. "Can I have a look?"

He dropped his arms down to shield them and stared at me as if I'd asked the unthinkable. "Absolutely not."

"But Mrs. Kingsley's no longer alive, and her husband gave me permission."

"That's not the point, Mr. Bannister. It's at my discretion whether or not to release them, and I choose not to."

I paused and shot him a long, curious gaze. He broke eye contact by picking up the phone, hastily punching a few buttons, and then said, "Ms. Penfield, please come to my office immediately."

"Dr. Faraday, you should understand my intentions here. I'm not trying to—"

"I understand your intentions just fine. You have a job to do. So do I."

Penfield walked in, spared me a quick glance, then gave the doctor her attention. He said, "Please put these records back where they belong."

She nodded, moved toward his desk.

I tried again. "Doctor, I don't want to put Mrs. Kingsley or this hospital in a bad light. I just want to tell her story so people can understand the hell she went through. Not seeing those records would be missing the biggest part."

Penfield looked at me with an expression that was hard to read. I couldn't tell whether it was animosity or…well, I just couldn't tell.

The doctor said, "The answer is still no, Mr. Bannister. The records are confidential. End of discussion."

Penfield grabbed the last of the papers, closed the folder. "Will there be anything else, Doctor?"

Faraday shook his head, and she threw me another quick glance before going on her way.

He said, "Now, where were we?"

I nodded toward the door. "We were discussing those records you just had whisked out of here."

"Look." He exhaled his frustration, shook his head. "I'm sorry if it came out wrong. It's not that I'm afraid you'll put us in a bad light or anything like that."

"Then what is it? Because quite honestly, I'm a little confused about what just happened here."

He gave me a lingering stare, then said, "Let me put it to you this way. Some things are better left alone. Trust me, this is one of them."

"I'm not following you."

"What I'm saying is that the picture you'd see of Mrs. Kingsley would not be a flattering one. And it wouldn't serve any purpose other than to make her look bad."

"Doctor, with all due respect, good or bad, it's reality, and it's my job to write about it, not hide it."

He shook his head and pursed his lips.

I tried another option. "Look, if you won't let me see the records, can you at least tell me more about what happened while she was here?"

He seemed to be evaluating my words and then with reluctance in his voice said, "With each visit, she became more disturbed, more agitated…and more lost in her own mind. We couldn't help her. No one could. Things were becoming extremely tense. And unpleasant."

"Unpleasant how?"

"We were concerned about the safety of others."

"Why?"

He hesitated and then, "There were threats."

"What kind?"

"Death threats. To the staff and other patients—actually, to anyone who came within shouting distance of Mrs. Kingsley. Quite honestly, she frightened people. We'd made the decision to move her to the maximum-security unit, and her husband was in the process of committing her. Permanently."

"Do you know what brought this on?"

He pressed his hands together, looked down at them for a moment, then back up at me. "When I said Mrs. Kingsley was a different person, I meant it."

I narrowed my eyes, shook my head.

"She was experiencing what we call a major depression with psychotic features."

"Which means…?"

"She was severely delusional, seeing and hearing things that didn't exist, and…" He let out a labored sigh. "She began assuming an identity other than her own."

"What identity?"

"She called herself Bill Williams."

"She thought she was a man?"

He nodded.

I glanced down at my notes, raked my fingers through my hair, looked back up at him. "Was she in this state all the time?"

"No. She'd slip in and out."

"When did it start?"

"Toward the end of her last stay."

"So, close to the time she died," I confirmed.

"Yes."

"And who was this Bill Williams?"

"Nobody, I'm sure. But in her mind, she *was* him. Her vocal tone became deeper. Her mannerisms, even her facial expressions...all convincingly masculine. It was a startling transformation."

I leaned forward. "Did she give any details about him? Who he was?"

"Just that he was a murderer."

"She took on the role of a killer..."

"Yes, and according to her, one of the most dangerous killers of our time, maybe ever."

"What did he do?"

"Question should be, what didn't he do? She reported that he began murdering when he was nine years old. Lured his best friend into a shed behind his house, then beat him to death with a claw hammer to the point where the child's face was unrecognizable."

I shuddered.

"She talked about it frequently—as Bill Williams, that is. She...I mean, *he*...took great delight in the feeling in his hands when the hammer made powerful impact with flesh and bone... the release, the euphoric pleasure."

I shook my head, the shock rendering me speechless.

"And it doesn't end there. He just kept going. Several years later after his mother remarried, he climbed into their bed while she and the stepfather were asleep and began spooning the husband.

Then he shoved the man's face into his pillow...and a kitchen knife up his rectum. The mother woke in the middle of the night drenched in blood. Bill had wrapped the man's arms around her, then went off to his room and peacefully back to sleep."

"Good *Lord*," I said. "All this created from her mind?"

"I'm afraid so. A very disturbed mind, I remind you, one that had lost contact with any form of reality."

"Did this Bill—or Mrs. Kingsley—talk about anything else?"

"Plenty. In her final days, she spent a good part of her time bragging about the murders he'd committed."

"What did she say?"

"Horrible things. Gruesome things. Some of the most disturbing I've ever heard—and trust me, I've experienced a lot here."

"Details?"

"I've actually tried to forget them...but with a few, I've had a hard time doing that."

"You can't tell me?"

"I'd rather not."

I drew in some air, blew it out quickly. "Can you tell me why she'd dream up someone so horrible, let alone want to assume his identity? Who was this guy?"

Dr. Faraday gazed out the window and shook his head very slowly. A tree branch shifted in the wind and threw an odd shadow across his face.

I waited for his response...

Acknowledgments

I didn't write this book alone.

Well, I did, but in a way, I didn't. I say that because throughout this process I had the support and love of so many people who, through their encouragement, helped light my way, even during my darkest moments of uncertainty. Were it not for them, I'm not so sure this book would have ended up being what it is. They inspired me to keep writing through those difficult times—the ones when I faced a blank screen and a nasty case of writer's block, those lonely *moments of truth*, filled with self-doubt or a general lack of confidence. There isn't enough room on this page, or in this book, even, to name all of them, or for that matter, to thank them. But truth be known, this novel is a product of their love and support.

To Jeannette Angell Cezanne, my editor extraordinaire and good friend, who is in fact truly extraordinary. She whipped me into shape when I deserved it, encouraged me when I needed it, and praised me on the occasions I warranted it. Through it all, she made sure not a single word was wasted and even managed to teach me a thing or two about writing along the way.

On the technical side, I'd like to thank Dr. Matthew Leone, professor of criminal justice at University of Nevada, Reno, for lending his broad and extensive knowledge so that I could accurately portray the crimes and investigative aspects of this book. In addition to doing that, he also read the entire manuscript and gave me his input. To Steven B. Takami, FBI special agent, retired, for lending his investigative and critical eye to the project so I could portray his fictitious counterparts in an accurate and respectful manner. To Dr. Craig Nelson, San Diego County deputy medical examiner, for allowing me to view one of his autopsies so that I could depict the important work he does. During that process, he not only carefully explained everything he was doing but also handed me each organ as he removed it so I could fully describe them in my book. Kind of gross, I know, but nevertheless one of those important and necessary experiences for a writer. As if all that weren't enough, once it was all over (and he probably figured he was through with me), he never seemed to grow tired of my numerous and almost daily questions, even providing me with literature I needed to help make the dialogue in those chapters sound authentic. That kind of cooperation and attitude is what every author hopes for but doesn't often get; for this, I am extremely grateful. He is a true professional in every sense of the word. Also from the San Diego County Medical Examiner's Office, Rick Poggemeyer, for putting up with my persistent and very likely annoying requests to view an autopsy, and for then making it happen. To Tim Stepetic, associate director for administrative services, New Mexico Office of the Medical Investigator, who conversed with me on a regular basis and answered all my questions so that I could accurately represent the people in his office and the fine work they do. To Kyle Myer, hydraulic engineer, Fort Collins, Colorado, for sharing his knowledge about water: how it works, where it goes, and what it can (and can't) do. I had no idea how complex it could be. Who knew? To Toni Ensminger, my medical consultant, who has been happy to answer my frequent and tedious medical questions about the flu virus and various other medical ailments so that I could get things just right. To my many test readers who took the time to read the manuscript during its various draft stages and then give me their (honest) opinions about it. Their input was invaluable.

To the Rickrodes, my second family: Deanna, who has been, without a doubt, my number-one fan (not in a Stephen King sort of way; in a good way). Not a second passed during this process that she didn't believe I could do this—not only that, but do it well. As if that weren't enough, she also kept me well stocked with chocolate so I could keep the midnight oil burning. What more could one ask for in a friend? To Kay and Paul, who took care of me during the difficult times in ways I know I'll never be able to repay.

To my father, Donald Kaufman, who has always been there to hold the net beneath me for as long as I can remember, who has never once faltered in that respect, and who continues to do so without fail. Even as a writer, I have trouble finding the words to thank him.

And finally, to my mother, who lost her courageous battle with cancer and never got the chance to read this novel. It is to her I dedicate this work with great love.

About the Author

Andrew E. Kaufman lives in Southern California, along with his Labrador retrievers, two horses, and a very bossy Jack Russell terrier who thinks she owns the place.

His debut novel, *While* the *Savage Sleeps*, a forensic paranormal thriller, broke out on four of Amazon's bestsellers lists, taking the #1 spot on two of them and third place on the much-coveted Movers and Shakers list. It also dominated six of their top-Rated lists. His next novel, *The Lion, the Lamb, the Hunted* was on Amazon's Top 100 for more than one hundred days becoming their seventh bestselling title out of more than one million e-books available nationwide and number one in its genre. Andrew was also a writer for *Chicken Soup for the Soul: The Cancer Book* (Simon & Schuster/2009), where he chronicled his battle with the disease.

His newest novel, *Darkness* and *Shadows*, is due out in 2013.
After receiving his journalism and political science degrees at San Diego State University, Andrew began his writing career as an Emmy-nominated writer/producer, working at the CBS affiliate in San Diego, then in Los Angeles. For more than ten years,

he produced special series and covered many nationally known cases, including the O.J. Simpson Trial.

For more on Andrew and his work, please visit his website at: http://www.andrewekaufman.com